The Advocate's Justice
Teresa Burrell

Copyright

Dedication

To JP, for all your years of inspiration and love and for never giving up on me.

Acknowledgments

A special thanks to the following people for always being available to answer my questions
and providing me with the information I needed to write this book.

Apollo Madrigal
Michael McCormick
Dean Settle
Dené Servantes
JP

Thank you, **Denise Bowman**, for suggesting the "J" word for The Advocate's Justice.

Thanks to my team for making my writing life so much easier.

Assistant: **Robin Thomas**
Cover Designer: **Madeline Settle**
Editor: **L.J. Sellers**

And, of course, my fabulous beta readers:

Beth Sisel Agejew
Linda Athridge-Langille
Vickie Barrier
Meli White Cardullo
Gena 'Fortner' Jeselnik
Janie Greene-Livingston
Crystal Kamada
Sheila Krueger
Lily Qualls Morales

Rodger Peabody
Colleen Scott
Sandy Thompson
Brad Williams
Denise Zendel

Also by Teresa Burrell

THE ADVOCATE SERIES

THE ADVOCATE (Book 1)
THE ADVOCATE'S BETRAYAL (Book 2)
THE ADVOCATE'S CONVICTION (Book 3)
THE ADVOCATE'S DILEMMA (Book 4)
THE ADVOCATE'S EX PARTE (Book5)
THE ADVOCATE'S FELONY (Book 6)
THE ADVOCATE'S GEOCACHE (Book 7)
THE ADVOCATE'S HOMICIDES (Book 8)
THE ADVOCATE'S ILLUSION (Book 9)
THE ADVOCATE'S JUSTICE (Book 10)
THE ADVOCATE'S KILLER (Book 11)
THE ADVOCATE'S LABYRINTH (Book 12)
THE ADVOCATE'S MEMORY (Book 13)
THE ADVOCATE'S NIGHTMARE (Book 14)
THE ADVOCATE'S OATH (Book 15)

THE TUPER MYSTERY SERIES

THE ADVOCATE'S FELONY
(Book 6 of The Advocate Series)

MASON'S MISSING (Book 1)
FINDING FRANKIE (Book 2)
RECOVERING RITA (Book 3)
LIBERATING LANA (Book 4)

CO-AUTHORED STANDALONE

NO CONSENT
(Co-authored with L.J. Sellers)

Chapter 1

JP Torn, a San Diego private investigator, opened his eyes and picked up his cell phone to see the time. It was nearly midnight, so why was his doorbell ringing? Louie, his beagle, jumped off the bed and ran to the front door, making a muffled bark as he darted across the living room floor. His bark grew louder as he approached the door.

JP slipped on his jeans, took his gun from the nightstand, and followed Louie. He flipped on the porch light and looked through the window curtain. All he could see was a female who stood less than five feet tall. She looked like a child. He cautiously opened the door, his gun at his side, and glanced around. He saw no one else. On the lawn, a few feet away, lay an old bike. Louie barked again. JP reached down, placed a hand on the dog's head, and he became silent.

"Are you Johnny Torn?" the young girl asked. She sounded like a grownup, but her apprehensive face was that of a child. Her light-brown hair was partially covered by a beanie. Her brown eyes looked desperate from behind tiny red glasses.

"Yes, but most people call me JP. Who are you?"

"My name is Morgan. My brother was arrested, and I need your help."

"Are you alone?"

"Yes. Can you help me?" She shivered.

"Come inside where it's warm and we'll talk."

As Morgan walked in, JP glanced around outside once more. He closed the door behind her and locked it, still unsure if this was some kind of setup, but he couldn't leave this child outside in the cool night air. He led her to the kitchen and flipped on the electric tea kettle his girlfriend, Sabre, had left there for him. JP loved children, but he hadn't been around many and was never sure how to handle them. He wished Sabre were there now. She would know what to say and do.

"Would you like some hot tea?" JP asked, as Morgan sat down on a barstool.

"No, thanks. I just need your help." She rubbed her hands together, as though they were cold.

"How do you think I can help you?"

"I need you to get my brother out of jail, or juvie, or wherever he is."

"When was he arrested?"

"A couple of hours ago. It took me a while to get here. I had trouble finding your house in the dark."

"You rode your bike here?"

"Yes."

"From where?"

"It was only a few miles. At least it would've been, if I hadn't gotten lost," Morgan said.

"How old is your brother?" Before she could answer, JP asked, "How old are you?"

"I'm ten. My brother's fifteen."

Only ten? She seemed so mature. "Tell me what happened leading up to the arrest," JP said.

Morgan told her story, seemingly choosing her words carefully. "The cops came and knocked on the door. I answered it, and they asked for my brother. I retrieved him from his room, and they put handcuffs on him and said he was under arrest. I ran out back and got my mom and my grandma. They came inside and started bellowing at the cops, but the cops wouldn't stop. They showed my mom a document, and then they went through the house looking for stuff. They really tore it apart."

JP was surprised by her use of *retrieved* and *document*; those were words an adult would use, but in the syntax of a child. It sounded odd. "Do you know what they arrested your brother for?"

Morgan gulped. She looked away and then back at JP. He waited. The only noise in the room was the tea kettle boiling. Finally, she said, "Murder."

The electric pot shut itself off. JP walked over, picked it up, and poured hot water into two cups with peach-flavored tea bags. He brought them to the counter and put one down in front of Morgan. "If you don't want to drink it, just hold the cup. It'll warm your hands."

She reached for the cup, wrapping her hands around it.

"Do you know who they think your brother killed?"

"His name was Bullet. That's not his actual name, but everyone called him that. He was my grandma's boyfriend. We all live with her, and Bullet used to live there too. But he left a few days ago. Conner didn't kill him. I know that."

"And how do you know?"

"I just know."

"Do you know who killed him?"

She shook her head. "I just know Conner wouldn't do it," Morgan said, with teary eyes.

"Did the cops take anything from the search?"

"They took Conner's phone, his tablet, some of his shoes, and a gun."

"A gun? Whose was it?"

"I don't know. I never saw it before. They took it from Conner's closet. You've got to help my brother," she pleaded. "Can you?"

"I don't know. Maybe. But first, tell me, why did you come *here*?"

"My dad told me to come here if something like this occurred."

Again, with the adult words. "Did your dad expect Conner to be arrested?"

"No," she spurted. "Just anything strange that might happen. He said if there was ever any trouble we couldn't handle that we should find you. So when the cops left, I told my mom I was going to bed, then I snuck out and came here looking for you."

"Where is your father?"

"He's in prison. In Donavan. Before he left, he gave me your address and phone number. But I don't have a phone, and they took Conner's, so I had to come here. Daddy said if anything went wrong that I should find Uncle Johnny. That's you."

Oh no. "What is your father's name?"

"Gene Torn."

"My *brother* Gene?"

Chapter 2

"We need to get you home to your mother," JP said. "I'm sure she's worried."

"She's partying. She doesn't even know I'm gone."

"What do you mean?"

"She already has some guys over, and they're drinking a lot. She won't even notice I'm not there. Can't we just go see my brother?"

"Maybe your mom is at the station with your brother."

Morgan gave a funny little laugh. "I don't think so."

"But you said she was upset and yelling at the cops when they took Conner."

"Yeah, but then she went back to her party in the backyard."

JP knew he couldn't keep this little girl at his house without her mother's permission, niece or no niece, and he wasn't even certain she was telling the truth.

"Wait here," he said. JP walked into the bedroom, put on his cowboy boots, and grabbed a t-shirt, pulling it over his head as he returned. "Let's go."

"Where are we going?"

"To your house to see what's going on, then we'll decide what to do." JP grabbed his black Stetson, and they headed for the door.

Morgan looked up at JP's hat, and then down at his boots. "My dad wears a hat and boots too, but yours are shinier."

The girl was silent most of the way, except when she was giving directions. As they approached her home, they could hear the music blaring. JP parked behind the other four cars in front of the house. When he shut off the engine, Morgan began to fidget.

"Please don't make me stay here without my brother," she pleaded. Her eyes were wet, and a single tear rolled down her cheek. "Please, please."

JP thought for a second. "Is there somewhere we can stand and see what's going on in the backyard without being seen?"

"Yeah, right over there." She pointed to her left. "There's a tree stump on the other side of that car."

They walked around the cars in the driveway, and Morgan stepped onto the stump.

"Do you see your mother?"

"Oh yeah."

JP could see a few heads on the other side of the yard, but he needed a better view. Morgan hopped down and JP stepped up. He saw three men and two women milling around, all with beer bottles in their hands. Two men were smoking. Then he spotted a couple sitting on a block wall off to the left.

"Which one is your mother?"

"The one on the wall with the naked guy."

They walked back to the car. JP took out his phone and made a few calls to find out what he could about Conner. The information was slim. He started the engine and drove away.

"Did you find Conner?" Morgan asked.

"They have him at juvenile hall, but they haven't finished booking him yet."

Her face lit up. "Can we see him?"

"Not tonight, Munchkin."

Morgan's shoulders drooped and the smile left her face, but she didn't say anything.

"I'm sorry," JP added. "First thing in the morning, I'll find out everything I can."

They drove in silence for a few minutes until Morgan asked, "Are you going to take me back home?"

"Do you want to go home?"

"No."

"Your mom's gonna realize you're not there pretty soon, and she'll be worried. She'll probably call the cops."

The girl snickered. "Trust me. She won't call the cops. She hates cops. Besides, she won't even know I'm gone until she wakes up tomorrow afternoon."

"Is there somewhere else I can take you? Another relative or a friend maybe?"

"We don't have any relatives here, except you."

"Friends?"

"Not where I can stay. But I'm not going to live at *that* house without my brother," she said with conviction. "If you take me back, I'll just leave again."

JP was afraid to find out why, and he didn't want to interrogate her. He just knew taking her home with him was not a good idea. He wasn't even sure she was family. For all he knew, this was his brother Gene's idea of a sick joke.

Morgan interrupted his thoughts. "Why don't you take me to your house? If you don't want me in your way, just give me a blanket and I'll sleep outside."

JP gulped. "I have a better idea." He picked up his cell phone and called Sabre.

Chapter 3

Attorney Sabre Brown was awake and waiting for JP and Morgan when they arrived. She had known JP for years. Her best friend, Bob Clark, was JP's friend as well. JP was Bob's private investigator. Soon after JP and Sabre met, JP started investigating for her as well. After much soul searching and many mishaps, they eventually started dating and had been together for almost a year now. Sabre was reminiscing about their time together when she was interrupted by the doorbell.

"Sorry to bother you so late," JP said.

Sabre brushed her hand through the air in a dismissive gesture. "This must be Morgan."

"Yes," JP said. "Morgan, this is Sabre."

"Hello, ma'am." The girl studied Sabre's face. "You're very pretty."

"Thank you," Sabre said. She didn't feel particularly pretty in her sweats, and she hadn't brushed her hair. She reached up and ran her hand through it. The light brown strands still had some soft curl and fell softly to her shoulders. "Come in and sit down for a minute," Sabre said. "Can I get either of you anything?"

"No, thanks," Morgan said.

JP shook his head.

"I called my friend, Maxine Quinn, at the Department of Social Services and told her what was going on," Sabre said, as they sat down. "She notified the authorities in case a call comes in from Morgan's mother. Morgan can stay here tonight, and we'll sort this out tomorrow."

"Uncle Johnny said you're an attorney. Does that mean you can help my brother?" Morgan asked.

"I'm certainly going to try. I'll go see him first thing in the morning."

"I best be going." JP stood up and looked at the sweet little girl. "You're going to be okay. Sabre will take good care of you tonight, and we'll deal with everything else tomorrow."

"Do you think Conner's okay?" Her soft voice searched for hope.

"He'll be okay tonight. Don't you worry, Munchkin." JP smiled and nodded. "Goodnight."

"Goodnight, Uncle Johnny," the girl responded.

"Yeah, goodnight, *Johnny*," Sabre said with a smirk.

After JP left, they got up off the sofa, and Sabre noticed the girl was shorter than she had seemed at first. When Morgan spoke, she sounded so grown up, but she was only four-ten, about six inches shorter than Sabre. They walked upstairs to the guest room. The queen-size bed was covered with an assortment of aqua-and-coral pillows. In the middle sat a soft, cuddly, stuffed bear.

"Wow," Morgan said. "It's all so pretty. And the bed is so big."

"I'll get all this out of your way." Sabre removed the pillows and put them on a bench under the window. Morgan reached for the stuffed toy.

"Can the bear sleep with me?"

"Of course. He makes a great companion. He's nice and cuddly." Sabre pointed to the door to her right. "That's the bathroom. I put out a toothbrush and toothpaste for you, and there are clean towels. On the dresser are a pair of my pajamas, which are probably too big for you, but you're welcome to wear them. I also left you a t-shirt you can sleep in, if you'd rather."

Morgan laid the bear on the bed, picked up the pajamas and t-shirt, and went into the bathroom. Sabre turned down the bedding and waited for the girl to return. Morgan came out wearing the pajama top, with the sleeves covering her hands.

"The bottoms wouldn't stay up," she said.

"I was afraid of that."

"But the shirt is long enough for a nightgown."

Sabre rolled up Morgan's sleeves. "There, that ought to work."

Morgan reluctantly got into bed and covered up, and Sabre walked to the door.

"Do you want it open or closed?" Sabre asked.

"Open."

"I have a nightlight in the bathroom, and I'll leave that door open in case you have to get up in the night. Okay?"

"Okay."

"Can I get you anything else?" Sabre asked.

"Uh...."

"What is it?"

"Sometimes Conner would sit with me until I fell asleep."

Sabre was so tired she just wanted to get to bed, but she couldn't leave the poor girl like this. She shut off the overhead light, but the room was still illuminated by the light from the hallway. Sabre walked back to Morgan's bed and sat down.

"Conner sounds like a good big brother."

"He is." Morgan gulped. "What's going to happen tomorrow?"

"I'll go see Conner first thing in the morning and try to figure out what's going on. If he wants my help, I'll do everything I can for him."

"Will they let him come home?"

"Not tomorrow for sure. They'll have a court hearing in a few days, and then we'll know more. But these are very serious charges. So, JP will probably have to investigate, and we'll have a lot of court hearings, maybe even a trial. It could take a while."

"But he's innocent, so they'll let him go, right?"

"I hope so, but I have to learn more about what happened."

The girl's eyes widened and her jaw clenched.

"Morgan, do you know what happened?"

She shook her head and her face tightened, likely with pain. "I know Bullet was a real bad man."

"What did he do that was bad?"

"He was always hitting my grandma. And sometimes he hit my mom too."

"Did he ever hit you or Conner?"

"No. He yelled at us a lot, but we stayed away from him as much as we could. Conner always told me to stick close to him."

"It seems that Conner protected you."

"He's the best." She paused. "Most of the time anyway. He teases me a lot though."

"I have a brother like that too, but he always had my back when I was young. He still does. Big brothers are pretty special. Once when we were little...." Sabre stopped, smiling to herself.

Morgan had closed her eyes and drifted off to sleep.

Sabre left the hallway light on and went to bed, wondering how she was going to help Morgan and Conner.

Chapter 4

Sabre and JP drove Morgan to Polinsky, where the social worker, Maxine Quinn, was waiting for them. Morgan had a sober look as they walked inside the building.

"Are you afraid?" Sabre asked.

"A little."

"This is a nice place, and you may have to stay here for a few days, but it's all going to be okay. And don't forget, your Uncle Johnny and I will help you."

Morgan latched onto Sabre's arm, and they walked into the interview room where Maxine greeted them. After introductions, Maxine said, "Hello, Morgan. You sure are a beautiful young lady."

"Thank you, ma'am." The girl's expression didn't change, and she held onto Sabre even after they sat down on the sofa.

"Morgan, I need to ask you some questions," Maxine said. "Are you okay with that?"

"Yes."

"Sabre said you didn't want to go home. Can you tell me why?"

"Because my brother isn't there."

"You realize you can't be with your brother right now, right?"

"Yes, but I'm afraid to be at home when he's not there."

"What's going on at your house that makes you afraid?"

"There are too many creepy men there, and my brother keeps them away from me."

Maxine spoke softly. "Can you tell me why you think those men are creepy?"

"Sometimes they're"—she hesitated—"they're naked."

"Have any of them ever touched you inappropriately?"

"They try to hug me and stuff, but Conner hides me from them." The girl started to cry. "I don't want to go home if Conner isn't there with me."

"You're going to stay here for a few days until we can investigate," Maxine said. "But I have to ask you some questions, and you need to tell me everything you can about what goes on in your home."

"Okay." Morgan sniffled.

"Who is living there now?"

"Me, my grandma, my mom, and Conner."

"None of the men you talked about are living there?"

"They stay over, sometimes for two or three days, but they don't live with us."

"Has anyone else lived with you?" The social worker took notes as she talked.

"Bullet lived there for a long time."

"Who's Bullet?"

"He was my grandma's boyfriend, but he went camping and didn't come back." The girl paused. "The cops said my brother killed him, but I know he didn't."

"Anyone else ever live there?"

"My dad when he's not in prison."

"What's your dad's name?"

"Gene Torn."

"When did he last live with you?"

"He left about a week ago. I liked it when he was there because no one dared mess with us. Everyone was afraid of him."

"Were you afraid of him?"

Morgan scrunched up her face and smiled. "No. He wasn't scary to me. He's good to me, and he's always fun."

Sabre watched JP's face as Morgan spoke about his brother. JP's face was tense, but he gave a slight sigh of relief when Morgan said Gene was good to her.

"How long did your dad live with you before he went to prison?"

"He was only there a few weeks this last time. Before that, he was home for about a year. When I was five, we all lived in Texas together for a couple of years."

"Morgan, have you ever seen any drugs in your house?"

"My mom smokes marijuana for medicinal purposes," the girl said seriously. "I think some of the guys do drugs, but I'm not around them much, so I'm not sure. They all drink a lot, and then my mom and grandma both act pretty crazy."

"What do you mean by crazy?"

"Grandma starts singing, and she can't sing. It sounds horrible. She always sings "Your Cheating Heart," and she thinks she sounds good, but it's just awful."

"And your mom?"

The girl sighed. "She has sex parties."

Sabre winced, even though she'd heard worse.

"Have you seen the sex parties?" Maxine kept her tone neutral.

"Only once. When they start, we always go to our room."

"You said 'our room.' Who do you share a room with?"

"My brother. I used to sleep with my mom, but then she started having men in her bed, so I started sleeping on the sofa. But then one night a guy tried to sleep with me on the sofa. My brother got real mad. Conner took me into his room and gave me his bed, then he slept on the floor."

"Does Conner still sleep on the floor?"

"When my dad came home last time, he got me my own bed, so we each have a bed now. He told me not to sleep in

Mom's room anymore or on the sofa. And he told Conner to make sure of it."

Maxine took a deep breath. "Morgan, I need you to tell me about the sex party you saw. How long ago was it?"

"Maybe a year."

"About how many people were there?"

"Six or eight." The girl paused for a minute. "I think there was three guys and four girls. My mom was one of them."

"Where did the party take place?"

"It started in the backyard, but then they all came inside. I think it was getting cold. I was watching TV when they came in. They were all naked. My mom yelled at me to go to bed."

"Where was your brother?"

"I don't know, but he wasn't home. He came in a little while later. The next day he put a deadbolt lock on my door so I could lock it when he wasn't there."

"Have you seen any other sex parties at your house?" Maxine asked.

"No, because I always go to my room when guys come over, but I know they have them because I can hear them."

The interview continued for another ten minutes, but little else was revealed. Morgan started to fidget, so Maxine stopped the questioning. "I think we've had enough for today. You've been very brave, Morgan."

The girl's eyes opened wide. "You're not taking me home, are you?"

"No," Maxine said. "We need to do more investigation. In the meantime, you'll stay here at Polinsky. It's a very nice place, and you'll be with kids your age."

Morgan looked at Sabre. "Can't I go home with you? I won't be any trouble. I'll fix my bed and I can do the dishes. I can even help you cook."

Sabre ached for the girl. "Morgan, it's not about that. Maxine needs to investigate and decide if she should take this to court."

Morgan seemed to stop listening and turned to JP, plead-ing, "What about you, Uncle Johnny? Daddy said you would help me. Please help me. Take me home with you."

JP's anguish was visible. "We're going to step outside so I can ask the social worker some questions. Do you mind waiting here for a few minutes?"

Morgan smiled up at him. "Okay, but you need to step up to the plate here, Uncle Johnny."

JP gently mussed her hair. "I can see you learned a few things from your father."

Once outside the room, Sabre asked JP, "You're thinking about taking her, aren't you?"

"I'm givin' it some thought."

"Are you sure you want to do this?"

"You heard her; I have to step up to the plate." He smiled. "I need to do this."

"Then I'll help you any way I can."

"I was counting on that." JP lowered his head and looked at Sabre sheepishly out of the top of his eyes. He turned to Maxine. "Can you evaluate my home?"

"First we have to see what all is going on in that home and determine whether to file a petition."

"If no dependency case is filed," Sabre said, "maybe Mor-gan's mom will agree to let her stay with JP until Conner's case is adjudicated."

"From what I've heard so far, it's likely a dependency case will be filed." Maxine nodded. "But I'll ask her mother to let her stay with her uncle until it's all sorted out."

"And if she doesn't agree?" JP cut in.

"We'll do it anyway, assuming a petition is filed and your home checks out. I'll assign a social worker to start the investigation on the case immediately."

"Can we take Morgan to see her brother this afternoon?" JP asked.

"There's no visitation on Saturday," Sabre said. "I think on Sundays it's from nine to ten a.m."

"Can we take her tomorrow morning?" JP asked Maxine.

"I don't see why not," Maxine said. "I'll call you in an hour or so, and we can make those arrangements. We can also coordinate a time to evaluate your home, JP. Are your guns all locked up?"

"Tight as the rusted lug nuts on a '55 Ford."

Chapter 5

JP and Sabre waited in the interview room at juvenile hall for Conner Torn to be brought in. They used this room for the prisoners to speak to their attorneys. There were three small spaces partitioned with solid walls, each about six by eight feet. The tiny rooms were divided by a four-foot wall, topped with plexiglass that extended to the ceiling.

The deputy brought Conner in through the back door and handcuffed one of his wrists to the bench. The teenager looked young and innocent as he stared through the thick plexiglass between them. JP felt a pang of guilt and sadness as he remembered Gene as a young boy. Conner looked so much like him.

"Hello, Conner," JP said. "I'm JP Torn. Your sister came to me last night and asked for my help."

"You're my Uncle Johnny?" His voice even resembled Gene's.

"It appears so. Did your father tell you about me?"

"He talked about you some, mostly stories about when you were kids. He said you were a pain in the ass, but that you would most likely help if I was ever in trouble. I guess Morgan thought this was considered *trouble*."

"I'd say so." JP nodded toward Sabre. "This is my friend, Sabre Brown. She's an attorney, and we both want to help if you're open to that. I know you don't know me—"

"You don't know me either," Conner said, interrupting. "How do you know I didn't kill that guy?"

"Did you?" JP asked.

"No."

"Do you know who did?"

"No." Conner spoke calmly and deliberately, looking JP directly in the eye. "Don't know that either."

"You're facing some very serious charges, Conner. We'd like to help you," Sabre offered. "Would you let us do that?"

"Sure," Conner said. "Can you get me out of here so I can take care of my sister? She's not safe in that house."

"I'll try to get you out, but it's not likely the judge will order your release," Sabre said. "Morgan is safe for now. She stayed with me last night, and Child Protective Services is involved. She'll be at Polinsky Receiving Home for the next few days."

"Can I see her?"

"We'll bring her here tomorrow during visiting hours. She really wants to see you too, but there's a lot going on right now."

"Like what?"

"Like where she's going to live. Like getting you the best defense."

"Can she stay with you?"

"I'm not related and I'm gone all day. It just won't work."

Conner's eyes pleaded with JP. "You're her uncle. She can stay with you then."

"We're working on that," JP said. "But for now, let's concentrate on you. You can't do much for her in here, so let's see what we can do to get you out."

"Okay."

"Why don't we start by you telling us what you do know. When was the last time you saw Bullet?" JP was eager to investigate.

"He was at the house." Conner looked down at the floor, then back up. "He and Grandma had a terrible fight. He punched her in the face. It knocked her back, and she hit her head against a cabinet and fell to the floor."

"You were in the room?"

"I heard the racket in the kitchen and ran in there. But when I tried to help Grandma, Bullet reached for me, and Grandma told me to run."

"Did you?"

"Yes, because I saw Morgan standing in the doorway, and I was afraid she'd get hurt. So I grabbed her up and went to my room. I locked the door behind us."

"Did he come after you?"

"He started to, but I told him I would tell my dad."

"Was your dad there?"

"No." The boy hesitated. "He left a couple of days before, but he told Bullet if he ever laid a hand on me or Morgan, he'd kill him."

"Did you believe your dad when he said that?" JP asked.

"Maybe. He would've worked him over pretty good, I know that. But Bullet must've believed him because he stopped. He was really afraid of my dad."

"What happened next?"

"A little while later, I heard the front door slam and Bullet's motorcycle drive away. We went to the kitchen, and Grandma was washing blood off her face in the kitchen sink. She was bruised, her eye was turning black, and she had a cut on her cheek."

"Did she go to the doctor?" Sabre asked.

The boy frowned. "She never went when he beat her up."

"What did you do then?" JP asked.

"I begged Grandma to call the police, but she wouldn't. She told me Bullet had gone camping." Conner shifted in his seat.

"Did you ever see him again after that?"

"No. He never came back."

"Who else was at the house that day?"

"A couple of Bullet's friends, Derek, my mom, and—" The boy paused. "Just my mom."

"Conner, are you sure no one else was there?"

He shook his head. "No one else."

"Who's Derek?" JP asked.

"A friend of my dad's."

"When did your dad come back after that?"

"He didn't." Conner shrugged. "He went back to prison."

"Before Bullet disappeared?"

Conner caught JP's eye and held his gaze, reminding him even more of Gene. "Yes," the boy said, "a couple of days before."

"Do you think Morgan may know something that'll help?"

"No," Conner said quickly. "She doesn't need to be involved."

"Is there anything else you can tell us?"

He shook his head. "So, what happens now?"

Sabre handled the question. "We'll go into court on Monday and enter a plea of *not guilty*. Then we'll set another hearing to give us time to do some investigating." Sabre's information about the case was limited, but she had researched what she could. "According to the police, the gun was found in your closet with your fingerprints on it. At least one person heard you threaten to kill Bullet, and you can't account for your whereabouts at the time of death. We'll be talking to you about each of these things as we move forward, and JP will investigate. Depending on what we find, we'll likely have a trial. In the meantime, don't talk to anyone about this. If someone questions you, tell them to call me."

Conner nodded, but didn't comment.

"Are you doing okay in the Hall?" Sabre asked.

"So far. I keep to myself and don't talk much to anyone. I try to stay out of the way as much as I can."

~~~

After Conner left, JP turned to Sabre. "There's little doubt that he's Gene's son. He looks like him. Same eyes, same mouth. Conner is lankier, but his hair is the same color and wavy like Gene's. He looks enough like my brother that I could've picked him out of a crowd."

"Do you think he's telling the truth?" Sabre asked.

"Partly, but he's hiding something."

"What makes you say that?"

"He even has the same *tell* that Gene had as a kid. He just hasn't mastered it. Gene was very good at it."

"What do you mean?"

"Whenever we'd get caught doing something wrong, I always had a hard time lying about it. Not Gene. He would look at Dad, or whoever it was, straight in the eye and lie like crazy. Gene always said people were more apt to believe you if you looked at them. He tried to teach me how to do it, but I couldn't. I expect he's done the same with Conner."

"It's true. Most people have a hard time looking at you when they lie. So, how did you deal with it?"

"I just told the truth."

Chapter 6

Morgan fidgeted in her chair. Her face was solemn as she, JP, and Sabre waited for Conner to come into the room.

"This place is kind of ugly," Morgan said, looking around the stark room. It was starting to get noisy from the visitors waiting to see their loved ones.

"It's not the cheeriest place on earth," Sabre said. "Are you afraid?"

"I'm okay, but there are a lot of sad-looking people here."

Within five minutes, a guard brought Conner into the room. When Morgan saw him, her face lit up. Her eyes widened and she gave him a big smile. Then tears started to roll down her cheeks.

"Don't cry, Morgie," Conner said. "It's all gonna be okay." His face tightened as he held back tears.

"I just want you to come home."

"Me too," Conner said. He cleared his throat. "But for now, you need to be brave. Is Unc...uh...Johnny taking care of you?" He glanced at JP and back at Morgan.

"You can call me Uncle Johnny if you want to, or JP if you prefer. Whatever works for you."

Conner nodded.

"Yes," Morgan said. "They're both taking care of me, but I'm staying at Polinsky for now."

"What is Polinsky?" Conner asked.

"It's a facility where children can stay when it's not safe at home," Sabre said. "At least until the Department of Social Services can find a home for them or send them back to their own home.

"She can't go home without me there," Conner snapped. "It's not safe for her."

"I get that," Sabre said. "We're doing everything we can."

"Uncle Johnny will let me stay with him if the social worker says it's okay."

Conner turned toward JP and looked at him like a concerned parent. "You better keep her safe," he said.

"I will." JP nodded.

"Have you seen Mom?" Conner asked Morgan.

"No. She's probably still sleeping or partying. She'll notice I'm gone pretty soon."

"Lori Leon, a social worker, went there yesterday and spoke with your mom," Sabre said. "Your mom knows where you both are now. I'm sure she'll be in contact soon."

Morgan shrugged. "Yeah, the weekend is almost over."

"I'll keep you posted as much as I can on what's going on outside," Sabre added.

"Morgie, what's it like at Polinsky?"

Sabre was impressed with Conner's change of subject and his overall maturity. She hoped it wouldn't work against him in his defense. The court would have to determine whether Conner would be tried as a juvenile or an adult. Maturity and sophistication were always factors in that decision.

Morgan glanced around the room. "Polinsky is a whole lot better than here," she said, making a face.

"It's not so bad. The food's okay, and I'm not going to be here that long. Don't you worry."

"But they said you killed Bullet. I know you didn't do it. I want to tell them that, but nobody has asked me."

Conner raised his voice. "I know what they're saying, Morgie. You need to stay out of it. They don't want to hear from a little kid who thinks her brother is innocent. Do you hear what I'm saying? Dad wouldn't want you getting involved either."

"I understand."

They chatted for a little longer with Morgan asking questions about juvenile hall—if they had internet or television, or if they went outside at all. Everyone laughed when she asked if they had a swimming pool.

"It's not exactly a country club, Morgie."

"I know, but you like to swim, and I was just hoping."

Sabre looked at the clock on the wall. "I'm afraid it's time to go, but I'll see that Morgan gets back to visit you soon."

"Thanks," Conner said. "I love you, Morgonster."

"Don't call me that," she said with little conviction. "I love you too." Morgan choked back tears as she stood up with Sabre.

JP remained seated. "I'll meet you outside. I just want a minute with Conner."

When Sabre and Morgan were gone, JP said, "Conner, I know you don't know me, or Sabre for that matter, but we're here to help. The only way we can do that is if you are straight with us. We need to know everything."

"I told you what happened. I swear I didn't kill him."

"I don't think you did kill Bullet, but you're holding something back. Chances are I'm going to find out what that is, one way or another. And if I can find it, so can the police. It'll be a whole lot better if Sabre knows it before the cops do—so you might want to think about that."

Chapter 7

The next day, Sabre and JP waited for Conner in the interview room at juvenile court prior to his detention hearing. Sabre re-read the police report. She summarized it for JP. "The report says the body of Carroll Hall was found near Cuyamaca Rancho State Park, just off Highway 79."

"His name was Carroll?" JP said.

"Yup. That's his name."

"That's tough for a guy on the streets. No wonder he went by Bullet."

"He was shot in the chest, and he had a broken nose and lots of bruises."

"So, he was beat up and shot?"

"Looks that way."

"Is there a coroner's report?"

"Not yet."

A deputy sheriff Sabre didn't recognize brought Conner in through the back door to the interview room, handcuffed him to the chair, and left without saying a word.

"Are you doing okay?" JP asked.

"Yeah," Conner said. "It's even worse in there than Dad said though."

"Have you talked to your father?"

"Not since I've been locked up."

"Have you talked to him since he left?"

"Just once. He called me a couple of days after he left and said he was back in Donovan."

"Did he call from the prison phone?" JP wondered about his brother's actual location.

"He was using someone's cell. He did that a lot."

"And you haven't spoken to him since?"

"No, but he always preached about staying out of juvie, or jail, or prison, because it wasn't exciting like the tough guys pretend once they're on the outside."

"Good advice," JP said. "Did he talk much about prison?"

"Not really. Sometimes I'd ask him questions, but he wouldn't tell me much. He said it was better if I never knew what it was like inside. Then he'd give me his stay-out-of-trouble speech. I never thought I'd be here. One minute I'm breaking my pole-vaulting record, and the next I'm eating dinner with a bunch of gangbangers."

No one said anything for a second. Sabre broke the silence. "It appears Bullet was beat up as well as shot. Do you know anything about that?"

"No," Conner said quickly, then looked straight at Sabre, "He was fine when he left. Grandma was the one who got beat up."

"You didn't touch him?"

"No."

Sabre reviewed the police report with Conner, which, other than details about Bullet and his corpse, offered little more than what he had already told them. He gave the same details he had provided earlier. Bullet had a fight with his grandma, packed up his camping gear, and took off. No one had seen him since. Conner's grandmother and mother gave the same account of the events.

"Okay. Do you have any questions about what will happen in court this morning?"

He shrugged. "Not really."

After a few more questions of her own, Sabre rang the buzzer for Conner to be picked up. Two deputy sheriffs came in the back door of the interview room. One took Conner back to a holding cell to wait for the detention hearing. The other, a friend named Mike McCormick, said, "I saw the inmate's last name is Torn. Is he a relative?"

"He's my nephew," JP said. "Keep an eye on him, will you?"

"Of course. He's been great so far. Very compliant."

"I'm more worried about him holding his own with the other kids in the Hall. He's on C Unit, and I don't think he's very streetwise."

"I'll do what I can when he's here in court, but other than that, I have little control," Mike said. "But I have a friend who is a correctional officer in the Hall. I'll ask him to help out. He's a good guy."

"I'd appreciate that. Thanks."

~~~

Sabre and Conner were seated at the counsel table after waiting for nearly half an hour for the detention hearing to commence. Conner fidgeted in his seat. Sabre reminded him to try to sit still if he could. Judge Gerald Feldman took the bench. He was in his fifties, with a receding hairline and a horseshoe pattern of dark hair sprinkled with gray on the back of his bald head and a salt-and-pepper goatee. After the clerk called the case, the attorneys introduced themselves for the record. The judge looked at the petition, then said to Conner, "The address for your father is listed as *unknown*. Do you know his whereabouts?"

"He's in Donovan," Conner said.

The deputy district attorney, Marge Benson, stood up, reaching a height of about five feet four inches tall. Her short, boy-like haircut and her drab brown suit added to her plain-Jane look. "Your Honor, we've checked the prison system. According to their records, Gene Torn is not in Donovan or any other California state prison. It's possible he's incarcerated in some other state, but so far, we haven't found him."

Sabre saw the frustration on JP's face and wondered what was going through his mind. She glanced at her client. Conner shared the same expression. Neither said anything, nor did they so much as twitch. She suddenly saw the family resemblance.

"Are you certain you don't know where your father is?" Judge Feldman asked Conner again.

"No, sir, I don't."

Conner pled not guilty to the petition, and a 707 hearing was set to determine if he should be tried as a minor or an adult. Since juveniles did not have a right to bail, Sabre asked to speak regarding the detention of her client.

"Your Honor, Conner has never been in any kind of trouble. He has no criminal record, gets good grades in school, and has a good attendance record. He's on the school wrestling team, has recently started pole vaulting on the track team, and has been working with a disabled children's sports program. Keeping this minor in a juvenile facility would only be detrimental to him, Your Honor."

"Neither of his parents are present in court," the judge said. "Where would you suggest we detain him, Ms. Brown?"

"His uncle, John Torn, is ready and willing to take him into his home. Mr. Torn is a respected member of this community. He served in the United States Marine Corps for two years, and in the San Diego Sheriff's Department for almost twenty years, until he was injured in the line of duty." Sabre knew JP's history well and was proud to tell it. "Mr. Torn was also the youngest sheriff to ever make detective in San Diego. He has worked the last ten years as a private investigator, primarily for juvenile court attorneys. He understands the system and his obligation to see that the child is present for all court hearings."

The Deputy DA, still on her feet, argued against the detention. "This minor is charged with a capital offense that appears to be pre-meditated. I'm sure Mr. Torn means well, but it's my understanding that up until a few days ago, he didn't even know he had a nephew. How could he possibly know what Conner may or may not do?"

"That is true, Your Honor," Sabre said. "However, we would not object to the court placing Conner under house arrest with an ankle bracelet. Mr. Torn is perfectly capable of providing a safe, disciplined home for his nephew. The Department of Social Services is evaluating his home right now for detention of Conner's sister with him. The two siblings are very close, and it would be a healthy environment and added incentive for both children to thrive." Sabre stopped as she realized she was making an argument that better fit in Dependency Court than in Delinquency.

Benson didn't waste any time pointing out to the court that their job was to protect the community.

"The minor will remain in juvenile hall until the 707 hearing, at which time, we will revisit the matter of detention," the judge ordered. "This hearing is adjourned."

Chapter 8

"You don't happen to be on detentions this morning, do you?" Sabre asked Bob as they walked into juvenile court together. Bob had been her best friend for years. They'd met in juvenile court when they were both rookies. They had worked closely on a very difficult case and soon discovered they made a great team. Sabre and JP socialized occasionally with Bob and his wife, Marilee, but mostly, she and Bob saw each other at court and had lunch at Pho's, a local Vietnamese restaurant, nearly every day of the workweek.

"No, why?"

"JP's niece is on calendar this morning. I want the minor's attorney to be someone reasonable. JP doesn't want a bunch of strangers coming into his home. It's bad enough the social workers are there. You know how private he is, and some of these attorneys can be real pains. There's no way the court will appoint me; there's too big a conflict. But they might appoint you."

"Most of the attorneys here have used JP at one time or another for investigations," Bob pointed out. "Nearly everyone has some type of conflict."

"Except those who don't do any investigation for their cases, and we sure don't want one of them representing Morgan."

"What courtroom is it in?"

"I don't know," Sabre said. "I haven't seen the petitions yet. They should be out by now. Let's find out."

They entered the cramped attorney lounge, which was an old broom closet that had been converted to give the attorneys some privacy. Sabre sorted through the petitions and found the one for Morgan Torn. "It looks like we're in Department Four, Judge Chino. The Public Defender has already conflicted off the case because they represented Gene Torn in the past. That leaves the panel attorneys who are on detentions today, Richard Wagner and Terry Chucas. I'm sure they'll work with us."

Bob read the petition and started through the report. "Whoa! Did you see this? I want to represent the mother. Did you know she was having sex parties?"

Sabre grabbed the petition from him. "Yes, I know she has sex parties, and I'm sure you'd love to challenge the issues in court. But JP and I need you to help Morgan."

"You know I will, Sobs, if the court lets me." Sobs was Bob's nickname for her—based on her full name being Sabre Orin Brown, making her initials S.O.B. He loved to tease her about her name. "I'll take care of this, honey. Don't worry."

~~~

Bob left with a copy of the petition and found Wagner and Chucas, who both agreed to take the parents on the case and let Bob have the minor. He then spoke to Dave Casey, the assistant county counsel.

"I'm asking to be appointed on this case for the minor, Morgan Torn, who is the niece of my friend, JP Torn."

"The private eye?"

"Yes."

"I know him," Dave said. "Good guy."

"JP has done investigations for a lot of attorneys here on juvenile cases so most everyone knows him. If that's the standard, it'll be very difficult to find anyone who can take this case. Admittedly, I know him better than most, but since he's not a party in this case, I don't see an issue. The Department is recommending detention with JP, so he will be involved. Barring any unforeseen concerns from their clients, the parents' attorneys are willing to waive any conflict issues, so that leaves you."

"I don't see it as an issue. I'll put it on the record."

"Thanks," Bob said, and left the courtroom. He sought out Sabre and told her it was all set.

"Thanks, honey," Sabre said. "You'll like Morgan. She's a sweet girl in spite of all she's been through."

"Do you know if Wagner talked to his client yet?" Bob asked.

"He's with her now." Sabre pushed her hair back. "The social worker said Morgan's mom wasn't going to fight temporary detention with JP, but she denied the allegations in the petition, so Wagner will likely set it for a jurisdictional trial."

"It's probably easier to have sex parties with the kids out of the house."

"Having them there didn't seem to stop her," Sabre said flippantly.

"Attorney Sabre Brown to Department One," a voice called over the loud speaker.

"I have to go. I'll be back after this hearing. I should be done before you are."

~~~

Sabre's hearing took longer than she expected, and when she returned, Bob was just exiting the courtroom.

"Is it over?" Sabre asked.

"The judge detained Morgan with JP. He can pick her up any time."

"Anything else happen that I should know about?"

"Wagner was appointed for the mother," Bob said. "And the jurisdictional hearing was set for a week from Tuesday. Chucas wasn't appointed for the father because no one knows Gene Torn's whereabouts."

"Morgan's mother didn't know either?" Sabre was skeptical.

"She thought he was in Donovan just like everyone else."

"JP's already started looking for him," Sabre said. "That father needs to be here for both of his children."

"It doesn't sound like a high priority for him. How is JP taking it?"

"He's angry at his brother, but that's old news. They've had a strained relationship for a very long time."

"I know what it's like to have a sibling who's a pain in the ass. I have several."

"I guess I've been lucky in that department." Sabre had warm feelings for her brother.

"Can you have lunch?" Bob asked.

"I would, but I better go with JP to pick up Morgan. He's a little nervous about this whole thing. A few days ago, he didn't even know he was an uncle. Now he's going to be in a parental role."

"He can handle it."

"*I* know he can. I'm just not sure *he* knows he can."

Sabre called JP and told him the news, then agreed to meet him at his house so they could go together to Polinsky. Before she left the courthouse, she stopped by the attorney lounge and picked up reports from her mailbox. One was a supplement to the police report on the Conner Torn case with photos of the evidence they had obtained, plus the ballistics report. She made a copy for JP and left.

~~~

Sabre and JP waited in the lobby at Polinsky for Morgan to be brought out. Sabre took the new report out of her bag and handed it to JP. "This came in today. Hopefully, it'll be of some help in your investigation."

JP flipped through the pages without reading thoroughly. When he got to the third page, which contained the evidence photos, he stopped. "What the hell?" JP reared up.

"What's the matter?" Sabre asked.

"I've got to go."

"Where?"

"To find that asinine brother of mine."

"You can't leave. We have to take Morgan home, and I don't have a car here."

JP ran a hand through his hair as he paced back and forth.

Sabre reached up and gently touched the side of his face. She could feel the tension. "We'll take Morgan to your house, get her settled, and figure out what to do next. I don't have court this afternoon, so I can help out."

JP took a deep breath and blew it out. "You're right." They both sat back down.

"What did you see in the report that got you so riled?" Sabre asked.

"The gun. I recognized it. It once belonged to my *dear* father." The sarcasm was unmistakable.

Chapter 9

JP watched Louie greet Morgan with happy licks when they came in the house. She pushed him away from her face, dropped her things, and gave the dog a big hug. "I think he likes me. Last time he scared me a little."

"He was just being protective," JP said, smiling at Morgan. He wondered how his brother had created such a precious child. "Now he knows you're part of the family."

She looked up at him and gave a slight nod. "Thanks for stepping up, Uncle Johnny."

He reached down and toussled her hair. "Come on, Munchkin; let's have a look at your new room. It's not as pretty as the one at Sabre's, but it's comfortable."

JP, Sabre, and Morgan walked down the hallway. The room had a queen size bed with a plain blue comforter, a simple oak dresser, and no pictures on the wall. Morgan looked around at the sparsely furnished room.

"I've never had my own room before," she said. "It's perfect."

"I thought maybe you and I could go shopping this afternoon and find some things to decorate with," Sabre said. "I would've done it before you got here, but there wasn't much time, and I thought it would be fun if you picked them out yourself."

Morgan grinned from ear to ear, then her face went solemn as she glanced at both of them. "Do you have another room for Conner when he gets out of juvie?"

"I'm afraid it's going to be a while before he can come home," Sabre said.

"But yes, I have another room we can fix up," JP said. "It's sort of my office, but I do most of my work in the living room anyway."

Sabre smiled at him.

JP couldn't believe he was going to be a parent.

"Take your time and put your things away," Sabre said. "We'll be in the other room when you're done."

JP and Sabre left, but the dog stayed with Morgan.

"So, what are you going to do?" Sabre asked.

"I need to find Gene. There's way more to this story than anyone is saying. Something went down when we were kids that changed all of our lives forever. I can't stand by and watch that happen to Conner."

"What was it?" Sabre asked.

"I was eight years old, and I woke up in the middle of the night. Gene was getting dressed...." JP stopped talking when Morgan walked into the room. "We'll talk about this later."

"Right. Do you know where you're going to start?"

"Yes, I'll go see Conner. That's if you're sure you're okay with the shopping thing."

"Can I go?" Morgan asked.

"Not this time, Munchkin. I'm sorry, but it's not visiting hours. They let me in because I'm working on his case."

Morgan sighed. "Okay. Tell him I miss him."

"I will."

Sabre reached out her hand for Morgan. "Let's go get some lunch and then go shopping. I'm starving." Morgan clasped Sabre's hand in hers, and they walked out together.

The sight made JP happy. But only for a moment. He had work to do. He HeHe sat down and studied the police report, this time reading every word, looking for clues that would help him find his brother and figure out what the family was hiding. He called and made an appointment to see Conner.

There was a state inspection going on at the Hall, and they asked that he come in later. Since the visit wouldn't take place for another two hours, he returned to the report and took some notes, making a list of every person mentioned and their addresses. His plan was to interrogate everyone he could until he got the information he needed, starting with Morgan's grandmother.

JP got in his truck and drove to see her without calling first. He found he usually got more honest answers when he didn't give someone time to anticipate and prepare for what he might ask.

The drive took less than five minutes. He couldn't believe his brother lived so close to him, yet he'd had no idea he was there. Even though they weren't on the best terms, it angered him that Gene hadn't let him know.

JP parked at the curb and started toward the front door, then decided he would have a quick look in the backyard first. From what he could see, no one was out there.

JP knocked, but no one answered. He knocked again. This time, a forty-something sleepy woman in a bathrobe opened the door. Her bleached-blonde, ratted hair had not been combed and stuck out in spots, strands hanging over her eyes. She pushed the mess back and shaded her face from the sun.

"Damn, that's bright," she said. "What do you want?"

"Ma'am, I'm JP Torn, Gene's brother."

"Holy, moly! I never thought I'd see the day." She stared at him for several seconds. "You ain't bad looking, almost as good as your brother. Course he's a little worse for wear." Another slight pause. "You takin' good care of my baby girl?"

"She's moving in with me today, ma'am. I assure you I'll take good care of her. And we're doing everything we can to help Conner."

"I'm Roxanne, your sister-in-law. You can call me Roxy, everyone does, except my mother. She refuses to call me anything but Roxanne. She says if she wanted my name to be Roxy, she would have named me that."

"Roxy it is."

She took a step backward into her living room. "Come on in. I'll make us some coffee."

"None for me, thanks." JP followed her into the kitchen, past three empty beer cans sitting on an end table. The kitchen had a dirty skillet on the stove, a blender with an inch of liquid at the bottom, and numerous red solo cups and empty beer cans strewn about the counter.

"It looks like you had a party here last night," JP said nonchalantly.

"Just had a few friends over." Roxy told JP to sit, started a pot of coffee, then walked back to the small table. "Your brother says you're a real jackass, but that you'll do right by those kids. Is that true?"

"I've been called a jackass before, but he's right, I'll do my best for your children. Have you spoken to Gene lately?"

"Not since he left a week ago, but he's had plenty to say about you over the years."

JP wasn't sure how he felt about Gene thinking and talking about him all those years. When they were young boys and their father had been arrested, it caused a rift between them, and they had fought constantly for years. Over time, he and Gene seemed to build a mutual hate for one another. Their mother had tried to smooth things over, but JP always felt like she favored Gene over him. His brother had left home when he was seventeen, and JP had only seen him twice after that. The visits were within a week of each other and took place in Norco Rehabilitation Center where Gene did his first stint in prison. When their mother passed away, JP returned to Texas for the funeral, but Gene was in prison at the time so they didn't see one another.

"Do you have any idea where Gene is now?" JP asked.

"No." She made a short, breathy hissing sound, showing her anger or frustration. "I thought he was in prison like everyone else did. Who the hell knows? Probably off with some cheap hussy somewhere. He comes home when he wants and leaves when he wants. He don't come home for me anymore, except maybe to get laid. I know he only comes to see his kids."

JP didn't know what to make of all that, and he certainly didn't know how to respond. "I'm here to investigate Conner's case. I work for his attorney, Sabre Brown. Anything you can tell me might help us find who really killed Bullet?"

"You don't think Conner did it?" Roxy asked.

"He says he didn't. Do you have reason to think otherwise?"

"Conner don't lie much, but I don't really know what happened." She paused. "They won't do much to him, will they? I mean, him bein' just a kid and all."

"They can try him as an adult and he could get life."

"Really? Well, that can't happen."

"But it can," JP said. "When was the last time you saw Bullet?"

"I seen him the night before he left. We had a little party, nothin' big, mind you. Me and Gene went to bed early."

"I thought Gene had already left."

"That's right. I forgot. Gene was gone. I went to bed by myself that night. I had a migraine. That's what it was." She stood up and checked the coffee pot. It was still filling up.

"Are you sure?"

"Of course, I'm sure. I just got a little confused there for a minute."

"Was anyone naked at the party?" JP asked.

"Now, why would you ask that?" Roxy tried to sound indignant.

"I'm not judging you. I don't care what you do in the privacy of your home. I'm just trying to get the full picture."

"It wasn't that kind of party. We never had those when Gene was around."

"But Gene wasn't there, right?"

"No, he wasn't, but he had just left. I didn't know where he was." She paused. "Still don't."

Roxy took two mugs out of the cupboard, removed the coffee pot, and stuck one mug under to catch the drip. She poured coffee into the other cup, then put the pot back after removing the partially filled cup. She poured in some half-and-half and added two heaping teaspoons of sugar.

"Sure you don't want some coffee?"

"No, thank you," JP said. "So, you saw Bullet at the party, but not the next day?"

"That's right. I was sleeping when he left. Mom says Bullet and her had a fight, and he got mad and left. That's about all I know."

"Is your mother here? I'd like to talk to her."

"I think she's in her room. Wait here. I'll get her. I need to get dressed anyway. I have an appointment this afternoon."

"Does Gene have any friends he might be staying with?"

"Just Derek, but Derek told me he hasn't seen Gene either." Roxy started to walk away. "I'll get Mom."

JP sat in the kitchen, waiting for Conner's grandmother, hoping she'd be more forthcoming than the rest. He was certain Conner, Morgan, and now Roxy were all holding something back, and he was pretty sure his brother was the crux of it all.

Chapter 10

When Muriel Joy Roberts walked into the kitchen, JP was surprised by her appearance. He wasn't sure what he expected, but it wasn't this. She stood about five-five, with short brunette hair that framed a perfectly oval face. When she smiled, she had a twinkle in her eye. But upon further examination, there appeared to be a soft sadness behind the twinkle. Muriel wore a skirt and tailored blouse over her trim body and didn't fit his typical grandmother image. He remembered from the report—where he'd learned her full name—that she was only fifty-eight, not that much older than he was. JP wondered what she was doing with a guy like Bullet.

"Roxanne said you wanted to speak to me," Muriel said in a slight British accent, using proper English, unlike the way her daughter spoke.

"If you don't mind. I'm trying to help your grandson out of this mess he's in."

"I really appreciate that. Conner is a good boy, and he doesn't belong in jail even if he killed that man. Bullet was a terrible person who didn't deserve to live."

"Do you think Conner killed him?"

"I'm just saying whoever did should receive a medal, not a prison sentence."

"Correct me if I'm wrong, ma'am, but wasn't he your boyfriend?"

"He was at one time, but I tried to kick him out long ago. He just wouldn't leave. He'd get mad and beat me up if I said too much to him."

"Why didn't you call the cops?"

She sighed and sat down across from JP. "I was afraid of what he'd do to the kids."

"Did he threaten to hurt them?"

"All the time. He told me he would kidnap Morgan, and I'd never know where she was or what he did to her." She stared at the wall for a second. "What's going to happen to Conner?"

"We're going to figure out who killed Bullet and get your grandson out of there. At least, that's our plan."

"What if you don't? He's so young and such a good boy." She paused. "But he's only fifteen, so he won't go to prison, right?"

"If he's tried as an adult, and convicted, he will."

"But he's just a kid."

"That's why we have to find the killer. So, if you could answer a few questions, it sure would help me."

"Of course. What do you want to know?" She fidgeted with a loose thread on her blouse.

"Can you tell me what happened leading up to Bullet leaving?"

"He woke up grumpy and started slamming things around. I tried to stay out of his way, but he kept following me around the house. I went into the kitchen because he wanted me to make him some eggs and bacon. I made an egg scramble, but there was no bacon." She looked pained. "When I gave him the eggs, he started yelling at me about not having any bacon. I walked away and poured him a cup of coffee. Just as I started toward him again, he threw his food at me, plate and all."

"Did it hit you?"

"I ducked, but it hit my arm. I spilled most of the coffee. I reacted and threw the coffee cup at him. He flew out of his chair and started punching me. He knocked me against the cupboard, and I fell to the floor. That's when Conner came in and starting yelling at Bullet."

"Did Conner try to stop him?"

"He grabbed the wooden pepper shaker and started toward Bullet. I yelled at Conner to get out, and Bullet lurched for him. Conner darted, and Bullet missed him. That's when I saw Morgan standing in the doorway, so I yelled at them both to run. Conner dropped the shaker, grabbed Morgan, and ran out."

"So Conner never touched Bullet? Or vice versa?"

"No."

"What happened after that?"

"Bullet left, but not before he kicked me a few times." Muriel twirled the loose thread around her finger.

"He left the house or the kitchen?"

"The kitchen. I heard him slamming doors, but I didn't want to get near him until he cooled down. I got up and washed my face in the kitchen sink. My nose was bleeding pretty badly. I got some kitchen towels, wrapped one in ice, and sat down with my head leaned back, trying to stop the bleeding. I was still sitting there when Bullet came back in. I remember cowering. He started laughing, called me names, then picked up his cigarettes and lighter and left."

"Did he say anything about where he was going?"

"He just said he'd be back.'"

"You told the social worker and the cops Bullet went camping. Did he tell you that?"

"No, but I looked out the window and he had camping gear tied onto his Harley. Why else would he take it?"

"What do you know about the gun the cops found in Conner's room?"

Muriel twitched. "Nothing." A pause. "I don't know anything about it."

"Did you ever see it?"

"No."

"Did you know the gun was there?"

"No."

"Were you surprised they found a gun?"

"Yes."

This was getting him nowhere. "And Conner never said anything about the gun?"

"No." The thread Muriel was twisting broke loose, and it seemed to surprise her.

"Where do you think the gun came from?"

"I have no idea."

"Did you ever see Gene with a gun?"

She shook her head.

"Did Gene ever mention a gun?"

She shook her head again, then sighed.

JP was pretty certain he wasn't getting any more information on that subject. "Who was at the party the night before Bullet left?"

"What party?"

"Roxy said you had a party the night before. Who was there?"

"Oh that. It was just a few friends. It wasn't really a party."

"Okay. Who was there?"

"Roxanne, Judd, Derek, Andy, and me."

"And Bullet?"

"Yes, of course."

"Do you know the guys' last names?"

"Judd's last name is Soper. I don't know the others. Judd and Andy were Bullet's buddies. Those three went way back. They were real tight. When one showed up, so did the other. Derek was a friend of Gene's." She looked pensive. "I think Derek's last name was Boom, no Bloome. That's it, Bloome."

"Any idea how to find any of them?"

"Not really."

"Where were the kids?"

"They were here, but they usually stayed in their room when there was anything going on."

"Was it a sex party?"

Muriel looked surprised. "Why would you ask that?"

"Because I know they've been going on in this house and the kids have been exposed to them."

"That's Roxanne's thing, not mine. I've talked to her about it, and I've tried to keep the kids away from it, but she won't stop."

"This is your house, right?"

Muriel looked down at her feet. "Roxanne has had a rough life, most of which is my fault."

"I'm sorry," JP said. "I'm not judging, but it may be time to put out the fire and call in the dogs."

Chapter 11

"Hey, Sobs," Bob called to Sabre. He caught up with her as she reached the end of the hallway. "Come into Department Three with me. I have a case where the public defender is conflicting off. Judge Chino will appoint you if you're in there."

"What's the case?"

"The children were removed from my client, the mother, for failure to protect her girls."

"That's pretty vague. What did she do, or *not* do?"

"Come with me. I'll catch you up."

Sabre was concerned because Bob was being vague. She hoped it wasn't something gruesome. She turned and walked back with Bob.

"Her boyfriend was drugging her kids," Bob said. "Then taking nude photos and selling them online."

"That's sick. Has the boyfriend been arrested?"

"No."

"Is he still with the mother?"

"He disappeared."

"Is the mother using drugs?"

"No evidence of that."

They stopped in front of Department Three. "So, what are you not telling me? Why can't the mother protect the kids?"

"It's not her first encounter with social services."

"What was the last one for?"

"Same thing."

Sabre shook her head and walked into the courtroom with Bob.

Judge Chino was on the bench. "Are you ready, Mr. Clark?" he asked.

"Yes, Your Honor."

"Ms. Brown, the PD has a conflict on this case. Are you available for appointment for the minors?"

"Yes, Your Honor. I'll just need a few minutes to look at the petition and the reports."

"Will five minutes be enough?"

"It should be, Your Honor."

The public defender handed Sabre a copy of the petitions and the two-page report. "It's all yours. Have fun." He smiled and walked out.

Sabre noted there were three petitions for the Standish family, one for each child, all girls: Riley, seven; Ella, five, and Avery, four. Each petition read the same:

The child has suffered, or there is substantial risk that the child will suffer, serious physical or emotional harm as a result of the failure or inability of his or her parent or legal guardian to supervise or protect the child adequately.

COUNT 1: On or about June 7, the mother's live-in boyfriend took nude photos of the child. The photos were placed on the internet on a child porn site, causing the child to be at substantial risk of serious physical and emotional harm, and said child's mother has failed and been unable to protect said child and said child is in need of the protection of the Juvenile Court.

Sabre scanned the details. She already hated this case. There was no way to ever get the photos down, so they were bound to haunt these girls all their lives. She couldn't imagine how it would be to go through life knowing that perverts were getting off on your childhood photos.

As she read the report, Sabre turned to Bob. "It says the father's whereabouts are unknown. Does the mother know where he is?"

"No. He left her shortly after the third girl was born to go 'find himself.' She thinks he found himself with a young waitress from Denny's. The mother hasn't heard from him since."

"How did your client manage to find not one, but two sick guys who wanted to take nude photos of her kids?"

"Just unlucky, I guess."

"Or she's sending out some kind of vibe that attracts them." Sabre read further. "It looks like she's getting them from a dating website."

"I know several people who have used online dating. It must be tough sorting through the crazies." Bob gave a small smile. "I have a good friend who found his wife that way, but he had some wild stories to tell before he met her."

"The problem is those photos will be on the internet forever," Sabre said.

"Unless some computer genius comes up with a way to wipe them out."

"That's not likely. The cops shut down these sites all the time and remove what they can. But the perverts copy the photos and use them and pass them on to their buddies. They could be anywhere in the world on thousands of sites and individual hard drives that no one can trace." Sabre sighed. "And this guy, they don't even know who he is. They have no way of figuring out where the photos went unless they can find him."

The bailiff walked over to Sabre and Bob. "Are you two ready?"

"Yes," they said in unison.

"You know I'm going to have to argue return to my client," Bob said, as they walked up to the counsel table.

"And I'll ask for supervised visits. I need to find out what's going on before she can have those kids alone."

"I know that."

"And I plan to ask that the paternal aunt's home be evaluated for possible detention."

"I know that too," Bob said. "I've already told the mother that Heidi, her sister-in-law, was the most likely place for the girls."

"Does she object?"

"She doesn't like *that woman*. I surmised as much when she kept calling her *that woman* instead of by her name. The mother wants the girls kept together, but I'm not sure she wants it enough to have them detained with Heidi."

Bob left the courtroom to speak with his client. He returned in a few minutes with Laura Standish, and they took a seat at the counsel table. Everything went as expected. The judge ordered supervised visits for the mother, a home evaluation on Heidi with discretion to detain with Sabre's approval, and for the social worker to look for other possible placements with relatives.

When the judge finished his orders, Sabre noticed that Laura was staring into space. All of a sudden, her legs and arms started jerking. Sabre poked Bob and nodded toward Laura. "Look."

Bob jumped up and stood behind his client. "Help me get her to the floor." Sabre took one side and Bob the other, and they lowered the shaking woman while the bailiff grabbed the chairs and pulled them out of the way.

"Stand back," Bob commanded. "Let her breathe."

By then, several marshals had entered the room. "Paramedics are on the way," one said. Bob and Sabre stepped aside and let the officials take over.

"I didn't see anything in the report about Laura having seizures," Sabre said. "Did you know?"

"She never said anything. Maybe this was her first."

"I was shocked when it happened, but you jumped right in, as if you knew what you were doing."

"You learn some things when you grow up with a doctor for a father. Besides, I had an uncle who had seizures. The best you can do is make sure they don't hit anything when they're flailing around."

"Good to know."

"We can't do anything more here," Bob said. "Let's go eat."

Chapter 12

The Standish girls—Riley, Ella, and Avery—were still in Polinsky Receiving Home when Sabre went to visit them. Their social worker was trying to find an appropriate family member or a foster home that could take all three together. Sabre always tried to keep siblings together when she could. She had asked for, and received, a court order that DSS make a reasonable effort to do so.

Riley was brought into the interview room first. She had blonde hair, blue eyes, and seemed younger than her seven years. She must have favored her father because she didn't resemble her mother. Sabre felt her face redden when she thought about the sicko taking photos of this little girl.

After getting to know her a little and trying to make her comfortable, Sabre had to ask some tough questions. "Do you know who Bill Nesbitt is?"

"He's my mom's boyfriend." The girl said the words slowly.

"Did he ever take photos of you?"

"Yes, we played model. He would let me use my mom's makeup. Mom didn't know we were using her makeup or I would've been in trouble."

"Did he put the makeup on you?"

"Mostly I did it myself. But sometimes he'd say I took too long, and then he'd do it."

"What kind of makeup?"

"Eye shadow, eye liner, and lipstick. Oh, and mascara. One time he put false eyelashes on me. Those weren't my mom's. I don't know where he got those."

"What did you do after the makeup session?"

"Bill would be the photographer, and I would model. He'd take some pictures, and then we'd have a tea party and he'd take some more."

"Did he have you do anything unusual or anything you didn't like when he took the photos?"

"He would have me lay on the bed hugging my teddy bear, or on my knees, saying my prayers. Stuff like that."

"And what would you be wearing?"

Riley started to rock back and forth, tugging at her hair. "Different stuff."

"Like what?"

"My pajamas, or my regular school clothes. Sometimes he would have special clothes for me. One time, he had me put on a plaid skirt and white blouse." She tugged at her hair again.

"What else?" Sabre asked.

"I would always get real tired after the tea party, and he made me take my clothes off before I could lay down."

"How many of these modeling games did you play?"

"We played three times, but I told Bill I didn't want to do it anymore."

"What did he say?"

"He said it was okay for now." She paused. "I think he started playing them with Ella after that."

"Did he take more pictures after you took your clothes off?"

"I don't know. I would fall asleep, but when I'd wake up, I'd be dressed again."

"Riley, has anyone talked to you about *bad touching*?"

"Yes, the nurse at school."

"Did Bill ever touch you inappropriately?"

The girl shook her head. "No."

Sabre wondered if Bill had done things other than snap photos when Riley was asleep. She didn't know which was worse, the pedophiles or the mercenaries who benefited from their sickness, but both made her stomach queasy.

"Did you ever tell your mother what Bill was doing?"

"Bill told me not to tell her anything or I would get in a lot of trouble for using her makeup."

"Riley, do you know what a seizure is?"

"Yes. My mom has them sometimes. Not very often though, and we know what to do."

"What do you do?"

"Ella writes down the time from the digital clock. There's one in every room so Ella can do it. I clear sharp objects and things away from her so Mom doesn't get hurt. Ella watches the time, and if it goes more than three minutes, she calls 9-1-1."

"Wow. You *do* know what to do."

"It doesn't happen very often, but we have seizure drills sometimes. We've practiced more than we've had to actually do it."

"How many times has your mom had a seizure when you were there?"

"Only twice. I worry about her being alone." Riley looked at Sabre with moist eyes. "Will we be able to go home soon?"

"I don't know yet. The courts can be kind of slow, and we need to make sure you girls are safe."

"It's my mom who's not safe living alone."

Sabre's heart pounded with empathy, and her voice cracked as she started to speak. She cleared her throat. "How well do you know your Aunt Heidi?"

"She takes us places sometimes, and she always brings us gifts on our birthday and Christmas. She would probably come more, but Mom doesn't like her."

"Why do you say that?"

"Mom says stuff all the time to her friends about how 'that woman' thinks she's better than everybody else. That's what she says, but I know she's talking about Aunt Heidi. She's kinda rich, I think. She has a big house with a swimming pool. Sometimes she takes us there to play."

Sabre sent Riley back to her room, and a worker brought Ella and then Avery in to see her.

Ella, with copper-colored hair and green eyes, looked more like her mother but with an angelic face. She told a story similar to Riley's, but with less detail. Four-year-old Avery just said Bill took lots of pictures, gave her candy, and had tea parties with her.

After the girls returned to their rooms, Sabre called the social worker and said, "I think these girls may have been drugged before the nude photos were taken."

Chapter 13

Between the internet and his deputy friend, JP was able to gather quite a bit of information about Judd Soper. The man had an extensive criminal record, but he'd never done any hard time. Several drunk-and-disorderly arrests, unpaid parking tickets, and a vandalism charge when he was nineteen were all part of his record, but he had no violent crimes. Soper's friend, Andy Rankin, was often present during the incidents and was a *known associate* in Soper's criminal record. Rankin had even been arrested on the same vandalism charge with Soper nearly thirty years ago.

When JP researched Rankin, he discovered the associate had a violent past. Rankin had served time in a state prison in Lancaster, California for aggravated assault and assault on a police officer when he was twenty-three. Rankin had been raising a ruckus in a bar, and when the police came he punched one of them. Eight years later, he was charged with domestic violence and served a year in county jail. He clearly had anger management problems. JP didn't know if Rankin was the same *Andy* who was at the party that night, but it seemed likely. He had mugshots, but he would have to have them identified.

JP was writing down the last known addresses for both men when Sabre and Morgan returned with packages in both arms. Morgan was grinning from ear to ear.

"Did you have a good time?" JP asked.

"It was so much fun," Morgan said. "Sabre bought all kinds of really neat stuff for my new room. And she bought me some new clothes and shoes—two new pairs of shoes. I've never had two at the same time."

"Sabre does like to shoe shop."

"Let's put these things in your room and unload the rest from the car," Sabre said.

"There's more?" JP asked.

"Oh yeah, there's more. She was having so much fun, I couldn't stop."

"I'll get the rest," JP said. "Why don't you help her set up her room."

JP made three trips to the car, then helped the girls hang pictures of unicorns and fairies on the walls. When they were done, Morgan stood back and looked around the room.

She sighed. "It's all so p...." She couldn't seem to come up with the correct word.

"Pretty?" Sabre asked.

"Pink?" JP guessed.

"Perfect," Morgan said. "Thank you."

Sabre and JP both smiled at her.

"Now, all I need is my brother here. What are you going to do about that, Uncle Johnny?"

JP suddenly realized how much he liked it when she called him "Uncle Johnny." He wondered how Gene had raised such a remarkable child. "I was working on that when you came in. Maybe you can help me."

"Sure. I'd be elated."

Elated? "You sure use some big words for such a little girl. Where do you learn them?"

"I look them up in the dictionary. I find a word I like, and then I use it for a few days. I call it my word of the *day,* even though I don't do one every day. But after a few days, I have it down pretty well. Sometimes I misuse it, and someone tells me, then I have to look it up again and make sure.

Sometimes, they're wrong, and sometimes I didn't quite get the connotation of the word."

"Was *connotation* one of the words you learned?"

"Yeah, I like that one. It's a good word. My dad gave me that word. He's the one who got me started doing this. He said I needed to have a better vocabulary than him so when I spoke, adults would listen. I don't think adults listened to him when he was a kid."

An uncomfortable guilt landed in the pit of his stomach as JP flashed back to their childhood. "You're right, Morgan. Adults didn't listen to Gene when he was a kid." *And I didn't either,* he thought. "You ready to help me with Conner's case?"

"Yes." Morgan nodded sternly.

"I'm going to ask you a few things, but if anything makes you uncomfortable, you let me know."

"I'll do anything to help"—she paused—"to assist my brother. That's today's word: assist."

"I would be pleased if you *assisted* me with this case," JP said. "I need to know who's been in your house the past few months. Let's start with the party the night before Bullet left. Do you remember who was there?"

Morgan looked pensive. "Mom, Grandma, Judd, Andy, and Bullet. Oh, and Derek."

"Tell me what happened the day Bullet left your house."

"I went to the kitchen and saw Grandma and Bullet fighting. The next thing I knew, Conner grabbed me and took me to my room. He left, and I waited for the fighting to stop, then I went back to the kitchen. Everyone was gone except my mom."

"What was she doing?"

"Sleeping."

"When did Conner come home?"

"In the afternoon."

"Did anyone else come back that day?"

"Grandma was back just before dark, and the rest didn't come back."

"Did any of them come back any time before Conner was arrested?"

"I don't think so."

"Do you know Andy's last name?"

"No."

"Can you describe him?"

"He's a big guy, tall and muscular, and his left arm is covered with tats. He has long brown hair that he wears in a ponytail most of the time."

JP waited for the man's image to load on his monitor. "Dang, this piece of junk is getting slower every day." When he finally had the photo, JP showed it to Morgan. "Does that look like the same guy?"

"That's him."

JP also showed her a picture of Judd Soper, even though he was pretty certain he had the right guy.

Morgan confirmed it. "I just remembered, you asked if anyone came back after the party. Soper came one day and talked to my grandma."

"Thank you," JP said. "Do you remember if anyone else came to your house after Bullet was shot?"

"Emily, Conner's girlfriend, was there a couple of times."

JP checked his notes. "What can you tell me about Derek?"

"He's a friend of my dad's. He looks a little scary when you first see him, but he's pretty nice. He only comes around when my dad's there. He never goes to mom's sex parties, but she doesn't have them when my dad's there. I like it a lot better when my dad's home. I miss him."

JP wasn't sure what to say. He was so angry at Gene for putting his kids in this terrible position, but he was also starting to think Gene really cared about them in his own twisted way.

"Do you know Derek's last name?"

Morgan thought for a second, then shook her head. "I don't think I've ever heard it."

"That's okay."

"But I know where he lives if that would help." She smirked.

"Do you know the address?"

"No, but I know how to get there. I've been to his house a couple of times. Daddy told me if I couldn't get you to do anything, I should go to Derek. It's kind of a rough neighborhood, so he didn't want me to go there unless you *refused to cooperate*." Morgan chose her words carefully. "I don't think he was real sure you would."

Her diplomacy made him smile. "Your father and I haven't always seen eye to eye on everything over the years, but I promise I will always be here for you and Conner." JP hesitated. "And for Gene, if he needs me." JP wished he'd been there sooner and chastised himself for being so stubborn and not making a greater effort to know his brother. He hadn't seen much of his younger brother, Troy, lately either. He decided to remedy that soon.

"You ready?" JP asked.

"For what?" Morgan looked surprised.

"To take me to Derek's house."

"Let's go."

"Do you think that's a good idea?" Sabre asked.

"Why don't you go with us? I just want Morgan to show me where he lives, then I'll go back later." He turned to Morgan and then to Sabre. "You both okay with that?"

They both agreed.

The girl stared at him for a few seconds, then asked, "Did you protect my dad when you were young?"

JP thought about the many times Gene had gotten into fights so JP didn't have to. Then his mind went back to when he was eight years old. It was the middle of the night. A gunshot blasted, and he heard the little boy inside him scream.

He saw Gene holding a gun and their father struggling with him, and then the dead body lying in front of them. He bit his lip and forced a half smile. "He's my older brother," JP said. "Mostly, he protected me."

Chapter 14

They left the neighborhood where Derek lived and stopped to get something for dinner. Sabre chose Popeye's Chicken because she knew JP and Morgan both liked it. JP chose the meat, all thighs and legs, and Morgan picked the sides, mashed potatoes and coleslaw.

"Do you want gravy?" Sabre asked.

"I don't really like their gravy," Morgan said. "Can I just put butter on the potatoes?"

"Of course," Sabre said.

"No gravy for me either," JP said.

"No gravy it is."

They drove back to the house, and Morgan helped as they set up the food. When they started to eat, Morgan stopped talking. Sabre noticed she was staring at her plate and picking at her food.

"Morgan, are you okay?"

She looked up and said, "Conner likes the gravy. Do you think they give him gravy with Popeye's chicken in juvie?"

Sabre held back a smile. "I don't think they have Popeye's in the Hall, but I'm sure he's getting decent food and plenty of it."

"Conner really likes to eat...to consume food."

"Was *consume* one of your new words?" JP asked.

"From a couple of weeks ago. It's a good word."

When they finished eating, Morgan wanted to help with cleanup. Afterward, they all sat down on the sofa to watch television, but Morgan kept falling asleep.

Sabre touched her gently on the shoulder. "I think it's time for bed. You start back to school tomorrow, and you need to get your rest."

Morgan stood. "Why am I going to my old school when there's a school practically across the street?"

"Since there are only a couple of weeks left, we thought it would be better if you finished up there. We also thought you might like to see your friends. I guess we should've consulted you."

"*Consulted* is a good word. I had that one a couple of months ago." Morgan smiled. "It's okay, because I do want to see my friends, but I don't think I'll tell them what's going on."

Sabre took her hand and looked into her sad eyes. "You don't need to tell them anything if you don't want to."

Morgan reached for Sabre and hugged her. "I'm glad you're here." Then the girl hugged JP. "I'm glad you're here too, Uncle Johnny." Morgan nodded toward Sabre. "You've done pretty well for yourself."

JP grinned. "You sound just like your father. Get to bed. We'll tuck you in shortly."

When Morgan left, JP asked, "Can you stay tonight and help me get her off to school in the morning?"

Sabre looked at him and smiled. "I couldn't *not* stay after that."

~~~

The next morning after Sabre took Morgan to school, JP drove back to the house Morgan claimed to be Derek's. When he'd questioned her certainty, she'd been adamant it was the correct house. She remembered the giant stone turtle near the front entrance.

JP passed the turtle, walked up the two steps that led to the front door, and rang the bell. He was about to ring it again when the door opened. A muscular man with a pocked face answered the door. He had shark-like eyes and a full head of brown-and-gray hair brushed straight back. He appeared to be in his late forties or early fifties and in great physical shape.

"I'm looking for Derek. Is that you?" JP asked.

"That depends," the man said. "Who are you?"

"I'm JP Torn. Gene's brother."

The man looked him over. "You must be the pain-in-the-ass cop."

"I'm not a cop any longer. I'm retired. I'm in the private sector now, but I'm sure I'm the one Gene calls the pain-in-the-ass." JP paused. "Are you Derek?"

The man nodded, and without comment, stepped back into the living room and motioned for JP to follow. Derek sat down in a large, brown armchair. "Sit."

JP eased into a similar chair with a round, rickety table between them.

"What do you need?" Derek asked.

"Conner's been charged with murder." JP didn't see any signs of surprise on Derek's face. "But you already knew that, didn't you?"

"I heard it."

"May I ask how you know?"

"You can ask, but I ain't tellin' you."

"Fair enough. Do you want to help Conner?"

"Any way I can."

"Tell me what you know about Bullet's death."

"I don't know much. I wasn't there when he left."

"But you were there the night before, right? During the party?" JP accidently touched the table next to him. It creaked. He withdrew his hand.

"It wasn't a real *party* party."

"You mean a sex party?"

"Yeah. Roxy don't have those when Gene's there."

"Was Gene there?"

"He had already left, but she didn't know when he was coming back. She usually waits until he's in jail or she's sure he's out of state or something before she gets going good."

"If Gene was gone, why were you still there?"

"Gene left the day before, but I was sick. My gut was hurting so bad, I couldn't walk. I stayed until I felt good enough to drive." Derek looked straight at JP. "Roxy is a crazy bitch. She'll do anyone or anything. I don't hang out when Gene's not around. We've been friends way too long for me to tap that."

So far, Derek had given the same account as the others about the night before Bullet left. JP wasn't satisfied. "Did you spend the night?"

"Yes. I was feeling a little better when I woke up."

"Did you see Bullet that morning?"

"Yes, he was asleep on the floor."

"I understand he beat up Muriel. Did you see that?"

"No, I left as soon as I woke up."

JP stood and walked toward the door. Derek reluctantly got up and followed. JP turned to him. "Have you seen Gene since then?"

"I don't make prison visits."

"He's not in prison."

"I heard he was back in Donovan. That ain't true?"

JP didn't believe him, but he was pretty sure he wouldn't get an honest answer. "Just in case you do hear from Gene, will you ask him to call me?" JP gave Derek his card. "Conner needs his help."

JP thanked the big man and left. He called Ron as soon as he got to his truck. Ron Brown was Sabre's unemployed, older brother. Ron and Sabre were very close, and JP wanted to help, so he put Ron to work whenever he could. Ron was a good guy who'd had a few bad breaks. JP knew this wasn't the kind of work Ron was looking for—or he would have encouraged him to get more training—but it brought in a few bucks until Ron could find something better. Sabre's brother had always been a photography buff and had recently taken it up again.

Ron picked up the call on the first ring.

"Can you do some surveillance for me?" JP asked.

"When?" Ron sounded eager.

"Preferably right now."

"I can be right there. Just give me an address."

~~~

JP waited in his truck, which he'd parked far enough away from the house that he wouldn't be seen. His vantage point didn't allow him to see much except whether someone left Derek's house. He was checking his messages when Ron opened the passenger door and climbed in.

"You got here quick."

"I wasn't far away," Ron said. "What am I watching here?"

JP pointed out the house. "The guy who lives there is Derek Bloome." JP handed Ron a photo and gave him a general description. "I need to know everyone who comes and goes from the house. Did you bring your camera?"

"Always."

"I need you to watch until or unless Derek leaves. Follow him if you can, but don't get too close. Call me if anything unusual happens."

"What do you mean by *unusual*?"

"You'll know it when you see it." JP smiled. "I don't know; just be careful. This guy is no slouch, and neither are his friends." JP handed Ron another photo. "If you see this guy, call me immediately. He's about five-ten, well built, with sandy blond hair. Do not approach him. Just call me. Understand?"

Ron looked at the photo, then back at JP. "What's his story? Anything I should know?"

"He's my older brother, Gene, but trust me, he's not as nice as I am." JP briefly summarized the case; and again warned Ron about getting too close. "Use that zoom lens. Gene may appear charming, but he has horns holdin' up his halo."

Chapter 15

Ron found a spot across the street that gave him a good vantage point. He could see the front door of the house, the garage, and the driveway where a Chevy Colorado truck was parked. He guessed that if Derek left, he'd likely go toward the freeway and would be going in the same direction that Ron faced.

Derek proved him right when, about twenty minutes later, he came out through his garage, got in his truck, and backed out of the driveway. The big man drove about six blocks, then made a right turn onto Sandrock Road. About a half-mile later, he pulled into the first entrance of a 7-11 parking lot. Ron drove past him, then entered at the lot's far end. He cruised to the other side of the store, turned around, and pulled into a parking spot. Ron left his car running. Three minutes later, Derek came out, opened a new pack of cigarettes, and lit up before he got into his truck and pulled away.

Derek's next stop was an In-N-Out Burger, where he used the drive-through. Ron pulled into the long narrow parking lot and remained at the end so that he could see when Derek's truck exited the other. The smell of hamburgers and grilled onions made Ron hungry. He sat there, growing hungrier until Derek finally drove out.

Ron followed him onto the freeway, keeping his distance. Derek stayed in the right lane and took the first off-ramp onto Clairemont Mesa. He continued until he reached the Top Notch apartments in Tierrasanta. He parked, got out of his truck with the burger bag, and walked up the concrete path between blankets of plush green lawn. Ron didn't dare follow for fear of being spotted in the wide-open space.

Once Derek turned the corner at the end of the building, Ron dashed across the front lawn. He saw Derek walk past the pool to another set of apartments, which appeared to be part of the same complex. Derek walked to the last unit on the bottom floor and knocked. Ron had his camera ready and zoomed in for the shot. When the door opened, Derek held up the white bag, and Ron took several photos in rapid succession. It was difficult to see because Derek blocked most of his view, but the tenant looked like a woman. Derek went inside and the door closed.

Ron waited for a few minutes, trying to decide whether to go closer and possibly get a better photo when he came out. If Derek came out. The only thing between them was the pool, a woman in a skimpy red, white, and blue bikini sunning herself, and an older couple sitting under an umbrella.

Ron glanced around for a better vantage point and a way to get there without being too obvious. Just then, the apartment door opened. Ron took a few more photos, but the angle was not a good one and he didn't expect good results. When Derek started toward him, Ron moved back out of sight and ran across the lawn to his car. He just made it before he saw Derek turn the corner. His heart pounded. He was starting to kind of like this work, because he got to be outside. Anything was better than being cooped up in an office or store. He'd had several not-so-promising jobs lately. He missed his old position at the Park and Recreation Department, but that had been many years ago—before he was forced to leave the state. Ron shook off his thoughts and focused on Derek.

After taking a couple pictures of the complex, he drove past the apartments and onto a side street, anticipating the direction Derek would go. Any other route would put him further into the neighborhood, which Ron didn't think was likely. He was right, a few minutes later Derek passed him. Ron pulled away from the curb, turned right, and followed Derek back toward his house. When Ron was certain where his target was going, he dropped back and waited so he wouldn't be spotted.

Ron called JP and told him what he'd observed.

"How long was he in the apartment?" JP asked.

"Less than five minutes."

"And you couldn't see the woman?"

"Not that well. I took photos, and when we enlarge them, we might get lucky and have one that shows us something. But it doesn't look real promising."

"What's the address? Maybe I can find out who lives there."

Ron rattled it off, but added, "That may not be much help since I don't know the apartment number."

"That's true."

"I guess I screwed up. Sorry."

"No worries. I would've done exactly the same thing you did. The most important thing is that you didn't get caught."

"I was a little worried there for a bit," Ron said. "Do you want me to watch Derek's house again?"

"Not right now. Why don't you go back to the apartments and get the number of the unit? It's unlikely Derek will go back there for a while, so you should be able to move about with ease. Maybe you can even find out who lives there, without being too obvious, of course. There may be a mailbox with a name on it or something. See what you can get."

"You got it, boss."

~~~

Back at the complex, Ron walked across the patio, around the pool, and toward the apartment where he had seen Derek earlier. The older couple had left. The woman tanning was now in a more upright position, and Ron could see she was an attractive brunette in her mid-to-late twenties. She appeared to be texting someone. Two other women sat on the side of the pool with their feet in the water, watching three little boys swim and play.

As Ron walked past, the sunbather looked up from her phone and said, "Well, hello," in a flirtatious tone. Ron decided to take advantage of it and stopped. "Hi there. Is it safe to assume you live here? I mean, since you're out here in the sun, I figured you probably do. Anyway, I'm looking for a new apartment, and I was wondering about this complex."

She laughed. "Yes, I live here. I've been here for three years, and it's a great place to live. As you can see, they keep the grounds tidy. Sometimes they take longer than I'd like to fix things that break, but if it's like plumbing or something, they get right on it. It's a fairly large complex, and they don't seem to have enough workers. Joel, the head maintenance guy, is really good though."

"I do a lot of online tech stuff, and I get a lot of small packages," Ron said. "Do they have mailboxes on each apartment or is there a central drop?"

The woman pointed toward a metal structure about thirty feet away. "That's the mail box for the back buildings. There's another one out front for that building." She pointed forward.

"How about the pool? Does it get very crowded?"

"Not really. Mostly little kids, but there's not that many here. The weekends are a little busier."

"Good. I like to swim in the early morning."

"I'm sure that won't be a problem."

"I think I'll have a look around. I like that end unit right there." Ron pointed to the apartment Derek had been to. "That would be the perfect location. Real close to the pool, and the sun hits it just right."

"Sorry. Ginny lives there, and I'm sure she's not going anywhere soon."

"Does she live alone? Maybe we could share the place," Ron said jokingly.

"I think you're a little late. A man has been staying there for a week or so now. He's older than her, so I don't know what the deal is. He may be a relative. She's not real social, so I don't know her well."

"Is he a big guy?" Ron asked, trying to sound playful.

"Not really. About your size. You might be able to take him," she teased back.

"I'm not much of a fighter. So I guess I'll have to settle for a different apartment." He paused. "I'm Ron, by the way."

"Brianna. Hopefully, I'll see you around."

Ron explored the complex and discovered each building had its own address. The letter on the door of the unit Derek had visited was A. Ron wandered a little more, then made his way toward the mailboxes. On the box for Apartment A was the name *Bloome*.

Chapter 16

Sabre finished her morning calendar, and returned to her office. With everything that was going on—the new cases, staying at JP's house, helping with Morgan—Sabre had gotten way behind on her work and had little time to herself. Morgan was a sweet girl, and Sabre was already getting attached, but she wasn't sure how long she could help. She'd pretty much accepted that she might not be *mother* material. She wasn't sure she wanted to have children. She used to think she would someday, but the older she got, the more she thought she might not want to have any. But right now, she needed to decompress and think about something else.

She opened her computer and started looking at online dating sites. She heard the front door open and Bob speaking to her receptionist.

"Good afternoon, Elaine."

"Hello, Bob. She's in her office. Go on in."

Bob walked in. "I came to pick up the Jordan file."

Sabre barely heard him. Some of the men's profiles were both narcissistic and sexist. "They'll never get laid that way," she mumbled.

"What?" Bob came around the desk and glanced at her computer screen. "Are you looking for a replacement for JP? And does he know?"

"Not a chance," Sabre said.

"That he doesn't know?"

"You goofball. I'm not looking for myself. I'm doing research for the Standish case."

"That's what they all say."

Sabre continued to search on Google. "Do you know what site Laura was on?"

"It was one of the top ten." Bob pointed to the middle of her monitor. "There it is, the second one on that list. But I already checked it. Bill Nesbitt closed his account and took his profile down."

"I'm thinking about joining one or two of these sites to see if Nesbitt responds."

"That's crazy."

"I hate that he's out there looking for new victims," Sabre said.

"So do I, but you need to leave that for the police. They'll find him."

"I just want to see what kind of guy responds. He's probably not the only one getting to kids this way."

"How would you even know what sites to sign up for? He could be on any of them, and there are hundreds, if not thousands."

"You know that how?"

"I'm well-read."

Sabre typed *top online dating sites* into the Google search engine. "Here we go. The one Laura used is number three on this list. I'll try the first two." Sabre clicked on the first URL and started to sign up. "I need to create a new email address just for this."

"I have one. Use it." Bob leaned down and wrote the email address and the password on a pad of paper.

"What do you use this one for?"

"Porn sites."

"Eww! I can't use that. I'll end up with a bunch of porn on my computer."

"I'm kidding. It's an old one I don't use anymore."

Sabre looked up at Bob to see his face. "You'd better be telling me the truth."

"I am."

Sabre typed it in. "I need a username."

"How about *ComeFindMe* or *Waiting4U*?"

"I don't want to sound like a hooker."

"Oh, I've got it. *DazzlingMom* or *TiffsMom*, or whatever you want to call your fake daughter. I assume you'll mention children, right?"

"Of course, but I think I need more than one. Nesbitt likely looks for a full house, in case one doesn't work."

"You're probably right. Your username could be *TwinGirlsMom* or *TripGirlsMom* or—"

Sabre cut in. "I got the point." She typed in *TwinGirlsMom*. "I like that idea. It might even be a bigger incentive if he thinks he can get twin photos."

"Sobs, you don't plan to meet with any of these creeps, do you?"

"Probably not."

"What do you mean *probably*? It's not a good idea."

"I won't unless I'm pretty sure it's Nesbitt."

"Will you tell JP about this?"

"I haven't decided yet."

"Sabre, I think you should."

"He won't like it."

"No kidding." Bob touched her shoulder. "Promise me you'll tell him, or at least me, if you decide to meet anyone."

"Deal." Sabre looked him in the eye when she said it. "Now help me fill in the questionnaire and write a profile description." She opened the list of questions. "I need a title."

"Must Love Children, you know, like the old *Must Love Dogs* movie."

"I like that." She keyed it in. She put her age as twenty-six.

"Really?"

"I want to be old enough to have seven-year-olds, but young enough to still be more vulnerable."

"That makes sense. What's next?"

"Children?" Sabre spoke aloud as she typed her answers. "Two, and they live at home. Religion? Spiritual, but not religious. Political affiliation? Middle of the road."

"That's good; be noncontroversial where you can."

With Bob's help, Sabre continued through the list, trying to answer the questions in a way that would appeal to Nesbitt, based on the information Laura had provided. When it came to the profile description, Bob said, "Let me do this part." Sabre stood up and Bob took over. She read as he typed:

I'm a mother of beautiful, model-gorgeous twin girls. I'm looking for a caring man to share my life. My children are very important to me, and it's imperative for me to have someone in my life who learns to care about them as much as I do and wants to spend time with them.

I am fun, active, and like new adventures. I'm open and honest and expect the same from a mate.

I am financially stable—not looking for a sugar daddy. I want a father for my children, not me.

"What do you think?" Bob glanced up at her.

"It's a little sappy, but it'll do the trick." Sabre tapped his shoulder, and they switched places again. She opened the section where it called for a photo.

"You're not going to upload your picture, are you?" Bob asked.

Sabre hesitated, unsure. "I've heard that most people won't even read the profiles without photos."

"Nesbitt didn't put his on there, and Laura found him."

"That's right, but he wrote something in his profile that made him sound like he was a spy or something. That's why he couldn't use his image."

"Besides, do you think Nesbitt really cares what the mother looks like?"

"Maybe," Sabre said. "Laura is an attractive woman. That might have been the draw initially, and he did need to court her somewhat to get to the kids. But I don't really want to have my picture on there." Sabre jumped up. "I know what to do."

She left the room, returning a few minutes later wearing a blonde wig. "What do you think?"

"You definitely look different, at least at first glance." Bob cocked his head and scowled. "Why do you have a blonde wig in your office?"

"It was here from last Halloween. It's time to bring out my inner blonde woman."

Sabre handed Bob her phone and stood against the wall. "Take my photo, but don't get too close."

Chapter 17

Later that day, JP sat with Conner in the interview room at juvenile hall. "I have some questions, and I need you to be straight with me," JP said.

"Okay."

"What can you tell me about Judd Soper?"

"He's a friend of Bullet's. I don't know him that well. He came over quite a bit, but I never hang around when there's company there. I don't like that guy."

"What about Andy?"

"Same thing. They're jerks, both of them."

"Morgan said someone tried to hug her one night when your mom was having a party. Do you know who that was?"

Conner's face turned red. "I wasn't there, but Morgan said it was Judd. Bullet thought it was a big joke. He encouraged them both to do it. I heard him talking with Judd and Andy and making jokes about 'fresh, young meat.' Then Bullet tried to hug her himself, the night before he left. I wanted to kill him."

"Did you tell anyone that you wanted to kill Bullet?" JP knew from the police report that someone claimed he had. That was part of the reason for the probable cause to search Conner's room.

"I didn't really mean it. I was just angry."

"Conner, you need to be careful about what you say to others. What you say to Sabre or me is confidential, but you can't be saying that to other people or they'll use it against you."

"I don't know if I said it to anyone else, besides my family. I don't think I did." Conner's expression suddenly tightened.

"What is it?" JP asked.

"I told my girlfriend, Emily."

"Did you know she told the investigator what you said?"

"I heard that, but only after that kid, Ben, said something. Ben heard it and was being a jerk about it. He kept asking me who I was going to kill. He made a really big deal of it, and who knows who all he told."

JP got all the information he could about Emily and Ben and wrote it in his notebook. Then he asked Conner again about the night before Bullet left—what happened and who was there. Conner gave the same account the others had. JP had a hunch there was something wrong with the story, but he couldn't figure out what.

~~~

After leaving the building, JP turned his phone on and found three voicemail messages. One was a sales call, which he deleted, one was from Sabre, and the other from Ron. He called Sabre back first.

"Mom and Harley are having a barbeque on Saturday, and they'd like us to come," Sabre said. "Can you make it?"

"I don't have any other plans."

"Great. I'll let her know. Did you talk to Conner?"

"Yes, but I didn't learn anything new. I have a hunch that everyone is lying about that last night with Bullet, but I can't narrow it down."

"Morgan gives the same story."

"I know. It's just that the details are all the same, exactly the same, which usually means they've been rehearsed."

"What do you think they're lying about?"

"I'm worried they're all covering for someone, but I can't figure out what really went down."

"Do you think they're covering for Conner?"

"Or Gene."

"Has Ron learned anything new?" Sabre asked.

"I'm about to call him. I'll let you know." JP hung up and called Ron. "What do you have for me, kid?"

"The name of the woman who lives in the apartment Derek visited is Ginny, and the name on the mailbox is Bloome."

"That's interesting. Maybe it's Derek's sister. Or it's his apartment and a female friend lives there."

"Here's the thing. Someone is staying with Ginny right now, and it's not Derek."

"Did you get a look at him?"

"No, but a neighbor said he's been living there about a week and that he's about my size."

"Thanks, Ron. I think I'll pay Ginny a visit."

Chapter 18

It was shortly after noon when JP drove to Ginny's apartment. He watched for a bit to see if he could detect any movement. He thought he saw some activity near the window. The next step made him nervous, but he decided to go for it. He walked up to the front door and rang the bell.

Ginny opened the door.

"I need to talk to Gene," JP said before she could speak.

The woman seemed genuinely surprised. She paused for a second, then said, "There's no one here by that name."

"Look, Ginny, I know he's inside. Just tell him I'm here."

"I don't know who you are or what you're talking about." She tried to close the door. JP stuck his foot in the opening and held the knob with his hand so she couldn't close it.

"Let him in," a male voice bellowed from a few feet away. "What the hell. He already knows I'm here." Gene stepped forward, and Ginny walked down the hall toward a bedroom.

"Don't just stand there exposing me to the rest of the world," Gene said. "Come in and shut the damn door."

JP looked at the brother he hadn't seen in over twenty years. Gene had a few more wrinkles on his face, but he still had a full head of blond hair with very little gray, and his body was still buff. Gene had apparently continued to work out and stay in shape. JP couldn't decide if he should shake his hand, give him a hug, or punch him in the face.

Gene turned before he could do any of those and led him to the living room. "You've grown up, Johnny."

JP wanted to say *you sure haven't*, but he didn't.

Gene sat in a recliner but didn't raise the footrest. He didn't offer JP a seat.

JP took one anyway, selecting the sofa so he could look directly at Gene. "What are you doing in San Diego?"

"I've been in this city on and off for a while now," Gene said. "What took you so long to come see me?"

"You're still a jerk," JP said. "Why wouldn't you let me know you had kids and that they were living only a few miles away?"

"Didn't know you'd care. You never made any attempt to see me after that visit to Norco prison. Besides, I figured Troy would tell you."

"I don't talk to Troy much, but the times I have, he never mentioned you or your children."

"I'll be damned. The kid can keep his mouth shut. I told him not to tell you, but I figured he would anyway."

"Nope, not a word."

Gene stood and walked to the kitchen. JP watched as Gene reached into the refrigerator and took out a can of Bud Light.

"You want a Bud?" Gene asked. "Or are you still drinking that piss water you call beer?"

"I'm good, thanks."

Gene walked back and sat down. "I'm guessing this isn't really a social call."

"Not really."

"How are my kids doing?"

"How do you suppose they're doing? Morgan has been removed from her home and is living with strangers, and Conner is sitting in juvenile hall."

"I thought Morgan was with you."

"She is, but she doesn't know me from Adam. She must be scared to death. I'm guessing anything you've told her about me isn't too favorable."

"I never said a bad word about you, Johnny, except that you were a pain-in-the-ass. I told her you were a cop, but you were one of the *good guys*. It's not my fault you went to the dark side."

JP wasn't sure he believed that Gene hadn't spoken badly about him, but the kids seemed to trust him.

"How's Conner holding up in juvie?" Gene asked.

"He's surviving, but it's not easy for him."

"He shouldn't be there, you know. He didn't kill Bullet."

"And you know who did?"

"No. I don't know who killed him."

"You were at the party the night before Bullet supposedly left, weren't you?"

"Why do you ask that?"

"Roxy almost spilled it, but Derek was the one who convinced me. He doesn't like to be around your wife when you aren't home, yet he was there that night. He told me he was sick, but I got the feeling he would've had to be dead to still be there. You'll be happy to know you trained your children well though. They both stuck to your lies."

Gene didn't confirm or deny it.

"You're no better than Dad," JP said. "Putting Conner in the middle of your mess, just like Dad did to us. What did you think? Conner's a minor so they wouldn't go as hard on him?"

"You're still an ass, Jackie."

JP hadn't been called Jackie since he was young. He'd only heard it back then when someone in the family was really mad at him. Mostly, they called him Johnny. "That may be, but it doesn't make what you're doing right. Your son is sitting in juvenile hall, awaiting trial for murder, and he's scared to death—while you run around free."

"Free? I haven't been free since I was ten years old. You can take some blame for that. As for Conner, I'd never do to him what Dad did to me."

"Are you saying you didn't kill Bullet?"

"That's what I'm saying." Gene looked straight at him.

"Looking me directly in the eye isn't going to make me believe you. I know that trick."

"And not looking at you isn't going to either, because you don't *want* to believe me. You want to think I'm despicable. Well, maybe I am, but I love my son."

"Then why haven't you come forward?"

"Because I'm still on parole, and in case you didn't notice, I've committed a few violations. I've been trying to find out who the hell killed Bullet. I can't do that if I'm locked up. Besides, I thought you might have come up with something by now."

"Let's assume for a minute that you didn't do it, and that's not to say I believe you, but if you didn't, who did? Do you think it was Conner?"

"No, I don't," Gene said quickly, then paused. "I don't know. He could have, I suppose, if he snapped or something. But it's not his nature."

"But you *were* there?"

"I was at the house when Bullet left."

"Why has everyone been lying about that?"

"Because they thought they were protecting me."

"How about if you tell me the truth about what really happened? Start with the party."

"There wasn't really a party. We were all at home, and the only other person there was Derek. We were grilling some hamburgers when a couple of Bullet's friends came by."

"Andy Rankin and Judd Soper?"

"Yes. Roxy knew them pretty well. Too well. I don't give a rat's ass what she does when I'm away, but she's not doing that crap when I'm around. The woman is a tramp. I wouldn't ever see her again if it wasn't for the kids."

"Why don't you try to get custody of them?" JP couldn't believe he was even asking that, but for a second, he thought Gene might be the better parent of the two.

"What the hell can I do for them? I can't even keep myself out of prison, much less raise two kids."

"You're probably right," JP said. "So, what happened after Bullet's friends got there?"

"I told them to leave, but Roxy and Bullet kept telling them to stay. They even got Muriel to say the guys could stay, and since it was her house, there wasn't much I could do. She didn't want them there any more than I did, but she was pretty afraid of Bullet, and she can't say no to Roxy." Gene took a long swig of beer. "Bullet and his boys were all in the backyard drinking. Derek and I stayed inside and had a few beers, quite a few beers. Derek can get pretty crazy when he drinks too much, and he was puttin' 'em down pretty good. Then Conner came in and said he needed to tell me something."

"What did he tell you?

"Morgan had just told him that when she got up to go to the bathroom the night before, Bullet came in, naked again, and tried to hug her. I tried to keep calm, but I was ready to blow Bullet's head off."

"Did you?"

"No. I jumped up, and Derek grabbed me by the shoulders and told me to think it through. Then he let go of me, and said, 'Hell with this. Let's kick his ass.' So, I did."

"*You* did?"

"Yes. Derek was busy with the other two clowns. We were doing great until Andy pulled a gun."

"What did you do?"

"I gave Bullet one more punch and stopped. Derek backed off, and Bullet told his friends to leave."

"And Bullet? What did he do?"

"The crazy sonofabitch went to bed with Muriel. I'm sure he slept close to his gun, so I let him be. The next morning early, I heard a ruckus in the kitchen. When I got there, Conner was leaving with Morgan. They both looked pretty scared. Muriel was cowering in a corner, and Bullet was ranting at her."

JP just listened, wondering if this was the real story. When his cell rang, he glanced at it but didn't recognize the number, so he declined the call.

Gene continued with his recall of the events. "I grabbed Bullet and threw him against the counter. I was still mad about what he did to Morgan, and now the coward was beating on Muriel. I snapped. I think I broke his nose. Blood was spurting everywhere. I told him to get out and if he ever came back I'd kill him."

"And did you?"

"Did I what?"

"Kill him?"

"No." Gene scowled. "Aren't you listening? I did *not* kill Bullet."

JP's phone rang again. This time it was Sabre. "Hey, kid." He listened for a few seconds, then said, "I'll meet you there."

JP hung up and turned to Gene. "I've got to go. Your child got in a fight."

Gene jumped up. "Is Conner okay?"

"It wasn't Conner. It was Morgan."

"Morgan doesn't fight. What happened?"

"I don't know, but I'm about to find out." JP walked toward the door, then turned back. "Are you going to stick around and help your kids, or are you leaving?"

"You're an ass, Jackie."

Chapter 19

Sabre was already at the school and waiting in front of the counselor's office when JP arrived.

"I don't know anything yet," she said. "A school counselor will see us in a few minutes. They wanted you here since you're the legal custodian."

JP sat down next to her and tapped on the arm of the bench.

"Are you okay?" Sabre asked. "I've never seen you look so uncomfortable."

"I feel like a kid getting called into the principal's office. I've been here too many times. It never came out good. Besides, I'm afraid I might say the wrong thing."

"You'll do fine," Sabre said.

"Can you do the talkin'? You know how to handle these things better than I do."

Sabre smiled and nodded. "We'll find out what went down."

A clean-shaven, African-American man in his mid-thirties came out of the counselor's office. He stood about five-nine, with an athletic build. He approached JP and said, "Are you John Torn?"

JP stood. "Yes, sir, I am. And this is Sabre Brown."

The man turned to Sabre, who had gotten up too. "What is your relationship to Morgan?"

"I'm JP's, I mean John's, significant other and Morgan's brother's attorney."

He extended his hand, first to Sabre and then to JP. "I'm Terrance Godwin, the school counselor. Please follow me."

Godwin led them into a small office. The wall behind his desk had several framed certificates, including master's degrees in education and psychology. The wall opposite his desk was filled with photos of his family, his wife, and two young boys—all in his full view.

"Here's the thing," he said. "Morgan was in a fight with another student, a boy, and we have a zero-tolerance policy at this school. Morgan has been here awhile, and she has never had any problems of any kind. When I checked her records, I saw that a dependency case has recently been filed. I'm hoping you can give me a little background on that."

JP looked at Sabre and she spoke for them. "Morgan was removed from her home last week, and her brother was arrested and put in juvenile hall."

"Did her brother do something to her?"

"Quite the contrary. He was her rock, her safe place to go. Morgan is dealing with a lot of loss right now. She was removed from her mother and grandmother, who are less than appropriate caretakers. Her father isn't around, her brother is in the Hall, and she's living with her uncle, who she met just a few days ago. She has very little to hold onto. We probably should've kept her out of school, but we thought it would be good for her to see some of her friends."

"I feel for her. She's a good kid. I understand that the boy was teasing her about her brother. He called him a murderer. Is that what he was charged with?"

"Yes, but he didn't do it."

"Spoken like a true defense attorney." Godwin looked down at the file on his desk. "The thing is, my hands are kind of tied. Even though this boy has had his share of trouble, and frankly, is a bit of a bully, Morgan threw the first blow. And she got the best of him." His mouth turned up slightly at the corners as he said it, then his face went solemn again.

"With the zero-tolerance policy, I'm supposed to suspend them both. And I certainly can't punish the boy if I don't punish her."

"I'm not suggesting they not be punished, but something short of suspension," Sabre offered. "There are federal guidelines that came down a few years ago that encourage alternatives to suspension."

"I see you've done your homework."

"I deal with children in crises every day. For most of them, suspension from school is the least of their problems, but it certainly adds to their already heavy load. I expect that's probably true of the boy Morgan fought with as well. But I'm guessing that if he really is a bully and got beat up by a girl, the humiliation of facing classmates would be far worse than getting to go home."

"You have a point, Ms. Brown," the counselor said. "Wait here; let me see what I can do." He took the file and left the office.

JP took Sabre's hand. "You're amazing. I'm sure glad you were here with me. I was about to ask the school to give her a medal for beating up a bully. I have to tell you, I'm kinda proud of her."

Sabre shook her head. "Let's not go there."

"I know you don't agree with me, but if putting a bully in his place ain't right, then grits ain't groceries."

"Grits *ain't* groceries," Sabre said with a smirk. "But never mind that. What happens if they send her home today? What does your schedule look like?"

"I'd like to go back and see Gene, but I can't take Morgan with me."

"Bob is covering my court cases this morning, and I don't have anything on calendar for this afternoon. She can go to my office with me, if you're okay with that. I can keep her busy. I plan to go see Conner, but Elaine will be there, and I know she'd be glad to help."

"I'm sure Morgan would enjoy that. I know *I* like hanging with you at your office, so I'm sure she will too." He winked at her.

The counselor returned and interrupted their chat. "Here's what we can do. We're sending both kids home today, but they can come back tomorrow. They'll be given detention, and the amount will be based on the number of fights they've been involved in previously. Since this is Morgan's first offense, hers will be minimal. We'll try to keep some distance between them. Neither is to approach the other. They're in the same class, but the teacher has agreed to keep them apart. Please have a talk with Morgan so she understands this cannot happen again. I went to bat for her on this one, but if it happens again, I won't have a choice."

Sabre and JP both stood and shook his hand. JP said, "Thank you, sir."

"Come on. I'll take you to Morgan. I'm sure she's anxious to get out of here."

Morgan was sitting in the principal's office when they walked in. She was hunched over, and her face was pale. Her damp eyes widened when she saw them. She didn't move, as if she wasn't sure what to do. Sabre approached her and put her arm around the girl. Morgan avoided eye contact and started to cry.

"It's okay, Morgan." Sabre hugged her tighter. "Everything's going to be okay."

They walked out of the school office with Sabre's arm still around Morgan. Once outside, the girl looked up at JP. "Are you mad at me, Uncle Johnny?"

JP reached down and took her hand in his. "No, Munchkin, I'm not mad at you. We'll talk about it later."

Chapter 20

Sabre waited in the interview room while the probation officer retrieved Conner. He walked in with drooping shoulders and sat down in a slump, looking almost broken. The boy had an air of innocence about him that she hoped would help at the 707 hearing, which was coming up in a few days. But she would have to fight like crazy to get him tried as a minor and not an adult.

"I know it's not easy being in here, Conner, but you look more dejected than usual today," Sabre said. "Did something happen?"

"It's just...this place is awful, and I want to go home," he blurted.

"I know. I'm working on it. I wish I had more good news for you. We have your fitness hearing scheduled for next week. At that time, the court will determine if your case should be heard in juvenile court or adult court."

"But I'm only fifteen."

"They'll look at things other than your age, such as your criminal record, which you have none. The judge will also consider your criminal sophistication, the seriousness of the crime, and whether you can be rehabilitated as a minor. I'll fight to keep you in juvenile court, because if you were to be convicted, your sentence would be a lot harsher in adult court." Sabre paused. This was a lot for him to take in. "On the other hand, juvenile courts only have judge trials. But if you're sent to adult court, we could have a jury trial. Then the prosecution would have to convince twelve regular people, instead of just one judge, that you're guilty."

Conner gave her a blank stare.

"I know this is all overwhelming, so we'll take it one step at a time. But you need to know what's ahead."

"But I didn't kill Bullet."

"I know. And your uncle is working very hard to prove it. You can help by giving me more information."

"I'll try."

"For starters, you need to explain why your fingerprints are on the murder weapon."

"Because I touched it."

"When?"

"A couple of days before I was arrested."

"Tell me exactly what happened."

Conner shifted in his seat. "I came home from school and planned to go skateboarding. I grabbed my board off the floor of the closet, and a pair of my shorts fell onto the floor. Apparently, they had been covering the gun because after they fell, I saw the handle. I picked it up and looked at it."

Sabre noticed he called the grip a handle. He apparently didn't know much about guns. "Are you left or right handed?" she asked.

"Right."

"Make a fist out of your left hand and extend your index finger."

Conner followed the directions.

"Now, imagine your left hand is the gun. Now, using your right hand, show me how you held it."

Conner wrapped his right hand around his left fist. "I put my hand around the handle and held it like I was going to shoot something. I pointed it toward the window, at a bird in the tree."

"Did you ever touch the trigger?"

"No. I didn't know if it was loaded, and I didn't know how to check. I had never seen a real gun up close like that before. Lots of my mom's friends have guns, but I've never looked at one of them up close."

"What did you do with it after you pointed it?"

"I looked at the gun real close. It was a little scary, just holding it. It felt heavy in my hand. And powerful." Conner looked both excited and ashamed. "I was afraid Morgan might find it and get hurt, so I stuck it back in the corner of my closet in a shoebox and threw some things over it."

"Did you know where the gun had come from?"

"No."

"Did you ever see it before?"

"No."

"At the time you found the gun, how did you think it got into your closet?"

"I didn't know, but I figured it was my dad's."

"Did you ask him?"

"No."

"Why not?"

The boy shrugged his shoulders. "I don't know. I just didn't."

"Did you say anything to anyone about the gun?"

"I told my grandma, and she just said to leave it alone and not touch it. She said she'd take care of it as soon as she could."

~~~

Sabre returned to her office and found Morgan making copies of documents for Elaine.

"This is fun," Morgan said. "And look, the machine separates the pages and puts them in stacks, and then even staples them. Isn't that cool?"

"Yeah, that's pretty cool."

Sabre had a long talk with Morgan about alternatives to physical confrontations. "You're probably going to get more harassment from students who don't understand what's going on. Conner would not want you getting into trouble over him."

"I know. I won't let them get to me again." The girl looked up at Sabre with sad eyes. "You won't tell Conner about this, will you? I don't want him to worry about me."

"Your secret's safe."

Chapter 21

After leaving the school, JP headed back to his house. There was some information he wanted to gather before he questioned his brother again. JP set up his whiteboard and made a list of suspects. He intentionally left Gene's name off, not because he thought his brother was innocent, but because he didn't want Morgan to see it. Everyone who attended the party was listed. The killer had to be someone who had been at the house and had put the gun into Conner's closet. JP made a spot on the board for questions and started to jot them down.

— *Ask Gene how the gun got there and how long it has been there.*

— *Who else knew the gun was there?*

— *Who else had been in the house after the party and prior to the cops confiscating the gun?*

— *What enemies of Bullet had access to the house?*

The list went on.

JP picked up the phone and called Muriel. She agreed to see him, so he drove over on his way back to Gene's. Muriel was cleaning when JP arrived, and Roxy was asleep.

"Thanks for seeing me on such short notice."

"Anything to help my grandson. How is he?" Muriel led him into the living room and offered him something to drink, which he declined. They sat down.

"About what you'd expect, I guess," JP said. "It's difficult for him."

"I'm sure it is. He's seen his share of criminals in his life, but he's always been able to go to his room and get away." Muriel pushed a strand of hair away from her face. "What can I do for you?"

"I have some questions about the gun they found in Conner's closet."

"What about it?"

"Did you know it had Conner's fingerprints on it?"

"No, I figured it would have someone else's prints and they'd let Conner go."

"I'd like to know why you lied."

"I don't know what you're talking about." She clasped her hands together and twisted them back and forth.

"You said you didn't know the gun was in Conner's closet, but he says you did."

Muriel sighed. "I would've told you about it if I'd known he touched it. He came to me and told me it was there, and I told him to just leave it alone. He said he would, but apparently he didn't. Or maybe he had already touched it."

JP shifted forward in his seat. "Why would you leave the gun in his room?"

"I had planned to remove it when I could get in there without Morgan seeing me. I didn't have a key to their room, and Morgan was always there when Conner could let me in. Unfortunately, the cops came before I had a chance to do anything."

"What were you intending to do with it?"

"I don't know. I hadn't thought that far ahead. But Gene was gone, and I didn't want a gun just lying around. I had no idea it was used to kill Bullet."

"Do you think it was Gene who killed Bullet?"

"I don't know. I'm not sure what he's capable of." Muriel exhaled. "Gene and I have always gotten along. He's the best thing that ever happened to my daughter, and he's a good father—except that he can't keep himself out of prison. He's got a temper, but even that has mellowed over the years. I personally think the guy can't catch a break."

"That's the way it's been all his life." JP instantly wished he hadn't said that out loud. "Did you know it was Gene's gun?"

"No, but I figured as much. I knew he had one because Roxanne bragged about it, but I never saw it."

"Other than the people who were at the party the night before Bullet left, who else had been in the house prior to Conner's arrest?"

Muriel pursed her lips in thought. "Gee, I'm not sure. I remember one of Bullet's friends came by looking for him."

"You mean Soper or Rankin?"

"No, another guy. He's been here a few times. His name is Steve something."

"Did he come inside?"

"No. He came to the door shortly after Bullet left, and I told him Bullet wasn't here, so he left."

"Anyone else?"

"Just Emily, Conner's girlfriend. She's been here a couple of times."

JP asked Muriel a few more questions, then thanked her and left. He arrived at Ginny Bloome's apartment about fifteen minutes later, but no one answered when he knocked. He walked around back and checked for a back entrance. There was none, so he returned to the front and knocked again. Still nothing. He sat down at a table with an umbrella near the pool, where he had a good vantage point of the front door.

After half an hour, JP had finished all the phone calls he needed to make. He walked to the front door and rang the bell again, several times. Then he knocked loudly. He was about to give up when he heard a scuffle coming from inside.

The door opened, and Ginny stood there with messy hair, wearing a rather revealing nightie.

"He's not here," she said before JP could ask.

"I don't believe you."

"Come in and see for yourself."

JP followed her inside and looked around, covering every possible room. Ginny invited him to look in her bedroom and bathroom as well. Gene was gone.

"Where did he go?"

"I have no idea. He didn't leave a forwarding address."

"Did he say anything before he left?"

"He just said he had to go, because if his jackass brother could find him, so could the cops."

Chapter 22

Sabre and Morgan were home, cooking dinner when JP arrived. He gently flicked Morgan on the head. "Hi, Munchkin."

"Hi, Uncle Johnny."

JP liked what he saw in front of him. It felt like they were a family. He put his arms around Sabre and whispered, "You don't have to cook for us, you know. I can always barbeque in a pinch."

"I know," Sabre said aloud. "I only know how to cook a couple of things, so when I reach my limit, you can take over. Besides, this is Morgan's meal. She wanted to make it for you. I'm just the helper."

JP turned to Morgan. "Whatcha cookin'?"

"I'm making chili, Texas style. It doesn't have any beans in it."

"Perfect. I don't like beans in my chili."

"Just like my dad," Morgan said, stirring the pot.

JP's jaw clenched at the comparison to his brother. Sabre noticed and smiled at him, and he felt himself relax.

"Do you want a taste?" Morgan asked. "You can tell me if it's ready."

"I'd love to be your taster."

Morgan took a tablespoon out of a drawer, scooped up some chili, and handed it to JP. "Be careful, it's hot."

JP sniffed at the chili as though it were a fine glass of wine, waved the spoon back and forth, then slowly and deliberately put it into his mouth. He smacked his lips, but didn't say anything.

"Well? Is it okay?"

"That tastes so good it'll make your tapeworm stand up and bark."

"You say a lot of funny stuff, Uncle Johnny." Morgan tipped her head to one side. "Did that mean you liked it?"

"It's perfect, Munchkin. Just like my mama used to make."

"That's because my dad taught me how to make it."

JP gulped a little, and Sabre glared at him. Morgan didn't seem to notice. "Sabre made cornbread, but it's not from scratch. It came in a Jiffy box."

"Hey, don't be a squealer." Sabre made a funny face at Morgan.

"Don't worry, darlin'," JP said with a grin. "I'm not with you for your culinary skills."

"Culinary," Morgan repeated. "That's a cool word. Maybe that'll be my next word of the day." She nodded. "*Culinary*, good word."

~~~

Once Morgan was in bed, JP and Sabre went into his office to discuss Conner's case.

"I'm sorry your brother is in the wind," Sabre said.

"I guess I shouldn't be surprised. I haven't been able to count on him since he was ten." JP paced back and forth in front of the whiteboard. "I was hoping he'd come through for his kids, but hell, he's probably the one who killed Bullet."

"Do you really think that, or are you venting?"

JP stopped pacing. "I don't know. Gene can be such a jerk. If he had to save his own ass, I believe he would let Conner take the fall."

"Here's the problem I have with that," Sabre said. "If Gene killed him, why would he put the gun in Conner's closet? That makes no sense. You can tell he loves his son, and maybe that's not enough to keep him from shifting the blame if he had to. But why would he deliberately frame Conner?"

"Because he's a self-centered jackass."

"I think you're letting old emotions cloud your judgment. Do you really believe Gene would set up Conner for the fall when there was no reason to? He didn't have to bring the gun back into the house. He could've gotten rid of it elsewhere."

"He's pretty attached to that gun. He's kept it for over forty years."

"Do you really think it's worth more to him than his own son?"

"You're probably right." JP sighed. "He had lots of alternatives. It seems the least likely one would be to set up Conner. But that's not enough for me to take my brother off the suspect list."

"I'm sure that's wise," Sabre said. "Where do we go from here?"

JP stood for a long time with his arms crossed and legs spread apart, staring at the whiteboard.

"It has to be someone with access to the house. The first thing I need to do is make sure my suspect list is complete."

"How will you accomplish that?"

"I've been talking to everyone at that house. I saw Muriel again today, and she mentioned that Conner's girlfriend, Emily, had been there a few times. The only other person she mentioned was a friend of Bullet's named Steve, but he didn't come into the house."

"Conner said Emily heard him threaten to kill Bullet," Sabre noted. "I think we'd better see what all she knows."

"Do you want me to interview her?"

"I'll do this one. You can take care of the thugs."

JP returned to the whiteboard and added Emily and Steve and their relationships to others.

"You don't think Emily could have killed him?" Sabre asked. She stared at JP who didn't answer right away. "Do you?"

"I don't know, but she's on the list. Maybe she's a woman scorned. We don't know anything about this girl."

"You're right. If someone set up Conner, they either had to be very angry at him, or not care about him at all."

"That would include Bullet's friends and maybe Emily."

"Or Ben," Sabre said.

"Who's Ben?"

"Ben is a kid who overheard Conner talking to Emily when he threatened to kill Bullet. I'll see if I can get more information about him from Emily."

"On the other hand," JP mused. "If it wasn't a setup for Conner, then the gun was put there just for convenience, and that could be anyone who has been in that house."

"And the most likely?"

"Gene or Conner." JP ran his hand through his hair as he stared at the whiteboard.

"What's on your mind?" Sabre asked.

"Can you stay tonight?"

"Sure. I'd like to take Morgan to school tomorrow anyway, if that's okay."

"She'd like that." He paused. "Muriel mentioned some of the places Bullet hangs out. I'd like to see what I can find out about him and those buddies of his. Would you mind if I went out for a bit?"

"Go ahead. I'm going to crash. Just be careful."

Chapter 23

JP walked into The Conversation bar, a name he thought was a real misnomer. The patrons were not the greatest conversationalists. He took a seat at the bar and ordered a beer. The bartender was in his mid-fifties, short, and slightly overweight. When he delivered the brew, JP said, "I'm looking for a guy named Bullet. Do you know him?"

"Bullet's dead, man. Some kid shot him, did the world a favor. You a friend of his?"

"I wouldn't exactly call him a friend."

"Good. I was pretty sure he didn't have any of those."

"I take it you didn't like him much. Why's that?"

"Because the man had no redeeming qualities of any kind. He treated everyone like crap. He was a rude, angry man, always looking for a fight."

"Did he come in here often?"

"At least two or three times a week, and he was thrown out on more than one occasion. Always came back though, like a bad penny. They practically destroyed the place one night, had a complete brawl going on. The owner finally told Bullet and his buddies they weren't welcome anymore."

"Anyone call the cops?"

"The owner doesn't bring in cops unless he has to. He's a big guy, so he and a couple of his friends took care of the thugs. They never came back, so it was effective."

"Are you talking about Andy and Judd?" JP asked, taking a sip of beer.

"Yeah, that's them. Andy was nearly as bad as Bullet, always in a fight."

"How long ago was that?"

The bartender lowered his head and studied JP. "Are you a cop?"

"No, I'm the private investigator for the kid who is charged with Bullet's murder. I'd appreciate any help you can give me."

"I'm glad to help. Like I said, the kid did the world a favor by getting rid of that scum. Hate to see him in trouble for it though."

"I'm not convinced he did it."

"Everyone who knew Bullet hated him, so if you're looking for someone else who might have done it, you're going to catch a lot of fish in that net."

"How well did he get along with Judd and Andy?"

"Andy seemed to do whatever Bullet told him. He was the meaner of the two, but he never crossed Bullet. Judd was more quiet, but I'm not sure he even liked the guy."

"What makes you say that?"

"Just the way he looked at Bullet with an intense, fevered stare when Bullet wasn't watching, especially when the asshole was rude to women."

After further discussion, the bartender disclosed the name of the bar he'd heard Andy and Judd were now frequenting. JP left his nearly full bottle on the bar and drove to the other dive. As soon as he walked in, he spotted a tall man with a brown ponytail and a tattoo-covered left arm. The guy stood near the bar. JP thought it was Andy Rankin, and when he got a little closer, he was certain.

JP looked around for Judd Soper since the two were never far apart, but he didn't spot him right away. JP continued toward Rankin, not sure what he would do next. On the way over, he saw Soper sitting on a barstool behind his friend. JP took one more step toward them, when he felt a hand on his shoulder.

JP looked up into shark-like eyes in a pocked face. "Hello, Derek."

"I'd stay away from them if I were you," Derek said.

"Why's that?"

"Because they're both trouble."

"I just want to ask them some questions about Bullet."

"They ain't gonna tell you the truth, and if they find out you're Gene's brother, Rankin will kick your ass."

"Why?"

"Because he ain't capable of kickin' Gene's, and you're the next best thing."

"Maybe I'll just ask around and see what else I can find out about Bullet."

"You can't do that either."

"Why's that?"

"Even though everyone who knows Bullet hates him, someone will tell Rankin that you're asking, probably a lowlife who wants to get in his good graces."

"I need to investigate—unless you know who killed Bullet and can fill me in."

"It ain't gonna do you any good to find out if you're dead and can't prove it."

"Is that a threat?"

"I ain't gonna hurt you." Derek paused and stared. "Unless you cross Gene. I'm just trying to keep your ass out of the sling."

"Why?"

"Because Gene needs you to help his kids."

"Where is he?"

"He'll get ahold of you when he can."

Chapter 24

Sabre dropped Morgan at school, completed her morning court calendar by eleven-thirty, had lunch with Bob, then drove back to her office. She read through her files that were on calendar for the next day and prepared for those cases. She had many unanswered emails that needed responses and a 288 motion to draft. By two-thirty she couldn't sit at her desk any longer. She got in her car and drove to see Conner's girlfriend, Emily, who lived about a mile from his family's home. Sabre knocked on the front door, expecting to have to deal with a parent, but found Emily home alone. She was a short, blonde girl with braces who was dressed conservatively in stark contrast to the streak of pink hair on the right side of her head.

"I'm Sabre Brown, Conner's attorney. Can I talk to you for a few minutes?"

"Come in." The petite girl stepped back, brushing long hair off her shoulder.

Sabre entered the living room and glanced around. The furniture was old, but the house was clean. She walked to the sofa and sat down. Emily did the same. "How is Conner?"

"It's rough, but he's handling it."

"It must be just awful for him. I've asked to see Conner, but my parents won't allow it."

"Do they think he's guilty?"

"They don't know, but they're trying to keep an open mind. My dad is better than my mom. He says they have to prove it, and they could be wrong."

"What do you think?"

"I don't think Conner could kill anyone, no matter how mad he was. He's so kind. Once we found a little bird that had been wounded, and he wanted to take it to a vet and get help. But we didn't have to because he held it for a little while, and then it flew away."

"I don't think he's guilty either," Sabre said, "but I need to prove it. That's why I'm here. I need to ask some questions. Maybe you saw or heard something that might help us find the real killer."

"I don't know much."

"Did you ever meet Bullet?"

"I saw him at Conner's, but I never talked to him. I didn't like the way he looked at me."

"Did he ever say anything to you?"

"He just stared at my boobs," Emily said. "He was creepy."

"Did you ever say anything to Conner about it?"

"Yeah."

"How did he react?"

"He just said to stay away from Bullet and his friends. And Conner always made sure I wasn't alone with them. He would usually take me right to his room, and we'd stay in there until I left."

"Did someone from the prosecutor's office come to see you?"

"An investigator."

"Did you tell them that Conner threatened to kill Bullet?"

Emily's shoulders drooped. "They told me I had to tell the truth."

"And you should," Sabre said. "But I need to know exactly what you told them."

"I said we were at school and I could tell Conner was really upset. We went behind the science building to have a little privacy, and Conner started ranting about Bullet. He said he was a scumbag and that he was going to kill him."

"Did you believe him when he said that?"

"No, I just thought he was mad. I've never seen him like that before, but when Bullet was killed I started to wonder."

"How did you know Bullet was killed?"

"Conner told me."

"Did you ask him if he did it?"

"Not exactly. I didn't want him to think I didn't trust him, but then he told me he didn't do it. I wouldn't have said anything if it wasn't for Ben. I don't think the investigator would have even questioned me."

"You mean Ben Thompson?"

"Yes." Emily seemed surprised that Sabre might know about him.

"What did Ben do?"

"He told the cops Conner said he wanted to kill Bullet and that he believed him. Ben made it sound way worse than it was."

"Why would he do that?"

Emily's face reddened with embarrassment. "Ben has wanted to be my boyfriend for a long time. Before Conner and I hooked up, Ben had almost worn me down. I wasn't with anyone, and I had one date with him. It wasn't even a real date, and I didn't really like him. After that one time, he thought he owned me. He started following me around all the time. He was spying on us when he heard what Conner said."

"Did you ever see a gun in Conner's room?"

Emily's mouth fell open, and she quickly closed it. "No, I never saw a gun in his room. I...I...I'm pretty sure he wasn't into guns. He didn't like the idea of hunting or anything. He liked animals too much." She crossed and uncrossed her legs.

"Emily, I need the truth. When did you see the gun?"

She took a deep breath. "It was the last time I was there, just before Conner was arrested."

"Were you there when the cops came?"

"No, it was earlier...that afternoon."

"What exactly did you see?" Sabre asked.

"Conner had told me to pick out a video game. He said they were in the closet on the left side. There was a box on the floor with the videos, and when I picked it up, I pulled a shirt or something up with it. A shoebox fell over, and I heard a slight clunk. That's when I saw the gun."

"Did you ask Conner about it?"

"No. I just threw the clothing on it and set the box back down."

"Did you tell anyone else you saw the gun?"

"No."

"Not even the detective who questioned you?"

"He never asked about it."

Chapter 25

The next morning, Sabre drove to her office. It was the first day she hadn't had court in weeks, so it was a chance to catch up on some paperwork she had to do. She sat down at her computer and responded to emails, then she drafted a change-of-venue motion for dependency court, plus a motion to recuse a judge on a delinquency case.

After several hours of sitting and typing, she stood and stretched, then walked to the copy room and grabbed a bottle of water. When she sat back down, she opened the online dating site where she had posted her profile.

Her receptionist walked in, carrying the mail. "Here you go. It's all opened and ready for you." Elaine saw the dating site open on the monitor and gave her a suspicious look.

"It's not what you think."

"What I was thinking is that if you're done with Cowboy, I'll take him."

Sabre laughed. "No, I think he's a keeper." She explained to Elaine what she was doing and asked her to sit for a bit. "You can help me sort through this stuff. I've been so busy, I haven't even looked at it since I signed up." Sabre signed in, and the site opened to her page.

"Wow!" Elaine said. "You have ninety-four winks, thirty-nine messages in your inbox, and who knows how many matches."

"Is that a lot?"

"You started this less than forty-eight hours ago. Yeah, that's a lot. Where do you want to start?"

"Let's start with the messages."

Sabre read the first one aloud. *"You are stunning. Let's meet."* She laughed. "He gets right to the point." She looked at his age. He was sixty-four. "That's not him," she said.

She opened the next message: *You are the most beautiful girl I've ever seen. We could make beautiful babies together.*

He was twenty-two. Sabre deleted his message. "This will take forever. I think I'll go through them quickly and elimi- nate the ones who can't possibly be Nesbitt."

"Based on what?"

"Age, for one thing. He's not likely to put too young or too old of an age. Also, we know he's about five-ten. So, I'll take out anyone under five-eight or over six-feet."

"That makes sense."

Sabre moved quickly through the messages, glancing at the profiles without reading the descriptions. "That leaves twenty-two messages. Two do not have photos. I'll check those out first, since he didn't put a photo last time."

The first message read: *I think we'd be a good match. We like a lot of the same things. Please respond if you have any interest.*

"He was polite but didn't give me much to go on." Sabre read through his profile description. "That didn't help much either."

"Just leave him in there and come back," Elaine suggested. "What's next?"

"The other one without a photo. His handle is *ImReady.*" Before reading it out loud, Sabre skimmed the message:

Hi TwinGirlsMom,

Please don't skip my profile because theirs no pic but I can explain. I'm a important attorney at a big law firm in town and I don't want clients to see me on here I like to keep my personal life seperate from work. I am attractive man I assure you. you won't be disappointed. As beautiful as you are I'm sure your girls are as you say You are very lucky I hope someday to have children of my own.

Shaking her head, Sabre showed the message to Elaine.

"He sure doesn't write like any attorney I know," Elaine said. "He needs to have someone edit his messages before he sends them. He can't spell, and he doesn't know what a period is."

Sabre read through his profile, which also explained why there was no photo, but he used much better grammar and punctuation. One of his interests was photography. "This could be Nesbitt."

Sabre hit *Reply* and typed:

Hi ImReady,

Thank you for your interest. I'm not concerned about your photo. There are a lot more important things in life than how someone looks. Besides, I'm sure you are as attractive as you say.

Reading over her shoulder, Elaine stuck her finger in her mouth, making a vomiting motion.

Sabre had just looked at the next message when another email came in. "It's from ImReady. That was quick."

"Open it."

They both read the text: *I spend so much time on the computer doing important legal work so I don't like being on here for this. Can we meet? How about dinner tonight at Island Prime? It's a very nice restaurant on the ocean.*

"Seriously?" Elaine scoffed. "Doing important legal work. He doesn't even know what the terms are. This guy is definitely not an attorney, but he did pick a nice restaurant."

"That fits Nesbitt's M.O. too. Bob said he took Laura to a real nice place the first couple of dates. I guess his profession pays well."

Sabre keyed in a response: *I'm sure you're very busy. That's a tough job you have. I'd like to hear more about your work. I'm busy tonight though, and through the weekend. How about coffee at Starbucks on Monday at 1:30?*

"Are you actually going?" Elaine asked.

"What have I got to lose?"

"Oh, I don't know. Your life. Your handsome boyfriend. Your twin girls."

"He's not a murderer. He's a sick photographer," Sabre said. "But I'll either tell JP or Bob. I won't go alone, or they'll both flip out."

Chapter 26

Sabre stood near the pool in Harley's backyard. Sabre's mother and Harley had been dating only a few months, but they seemed to be a good match. She watched them as they moved through the guests, making sure everyone was at ease. It was a beautiful day for a barbeque.

Sabre scanned the yard for Morgan. She was playing with Mandy, Harley's granddaughter on the zipline Harley had made for his grandkids. Mandy was almost five, and Morgan was helping her on and off the zipline. She seemed to be letting Mandy take two turns to her one.

"Your niece is a good kid," Sabre said as JP walked up.

"She's all sweetness and light, that one," JP said. "I'm proud to be her Uncle."

"The sun's about to set," Sabre said. JP stood behind her and wrapped his arms around her waist. They looked at the city and the ocean in the distance. Pink and orange clouds streaked across the sky, where the sun was going down. "What a gorgeous view."

"It sure is." JP was looking at her, not the sky.

She turned, and he kissed her gently on the lips.

"I was talking about the sunset."

"Oh yeah, that's gorgeous too."

Just then, Ron walked up. "Oops, did I ruin a moment?"

"You're good," Sabre said. "Mom seems happy, doesn't she?"

"You know her. If she's entertaining, she's in her glory, and Harley likes to help. They work well together."

"Who all will be here today? Do you know?"

"Just Harley's son and his wife, plus their neighbors, Manfred and Toni." Ron nodded toward a stout, blond man and a woman with short dark hair. "The only one not here yet is Chloe, who's always fashionably, or sometimes unfashionably, late."

"You and Chloe seem to hit it off. Have you asked her out yet?" Sabre asked.

"I'd like to, but it seems kind of awkward since she's Harley's daughter. If he and Mom got married that would make her my step-sister. Or worse yet, what if we started dating and it didn't work out? That could be really uncomfortable at family gatherings."

"You have a point," Sabre said. "What do you think, JP?"

"You never build the outhouse too close to the porch."

"That clears it up," Ron said with a laugh. "Oh, there she is now. I'll see you later."

Ron walked straight to the newcomer, a beautiful girl with big hair. Just before he reached her, a man stepped up and put his arm around Chloe's shoulder. Sabre heard her say "my friend." Ron shook the man's hand, they spoke for a moment, then Ron walked away.

"Looks like that decision was made for him," JP said.

"Maybe it was just as well. When he falls for someone, he falls pretty hard. I'd hate to see his heart broken again, especially with someone who would be constantly there to remind him." Sabre turned toward the expansive view, and they stood for a while with JP wrapped around her. He was more quiet than usual. She turned and stepped back to look at him "Are you okay?"

"Yeah, just a lot on my mind."

"Work?"

"Actually, it's Gene. I need your help."

"What can I do?"

"We haven't really talked about how long you're staying with Morgan and me, and I don't want to be presumptuous, but I need to get out at night and see if I can find Gene."

"I'll be there as long as you need me. Besides, I like taking her to school. She's so delightful that time of morning. She sure is a funny kid."

"She has her dad's sense of humor. He was always the funny one." JP's voice dropped and he muttered, "Let's hope that's all she got from him."

Chapter 27

JP dropped Sabre and Morgan at his house and drove over to Derek Bloome's, only to find his silver Colorado was not there. He drove back to The Conversation bar and found Derek's truck in the parking lot. He wasn't ready for Derek to see him, so he waited outside, watching his vehicle. He'd been there nearly an hour when Soper and Rankin came out of the bar. Rankin pulled slightly to the right as he walked, then overcompensated, swaying as he moved toward a dark Dodge Ram pickup. Soper got in the driver's side and Rankin in the passenger's.

JP was watching the two men so closely he almost missed Derek coming out of the bar. Derek got inside his pickup and followed the Dodge Ram out of the parking lot and onto the street. JP followed Derek. The convoy stayed on side streets until they reached Interstate 8, where Soper headed east.

The three trucks kept their distance for about five miles on the freeway, at which point, Derek sped up and passed the first truck. JP chose to follow Derek, so he did the same. When Derek took Exit 23 to Lake Jennings Park Road, JP followed. They continued on old Highway 80 for about a half a mile, until Derek pulled into The Renegade, a well-known country western bar. Derek exited his truck and hurried inside. JP followed, watching carefully so he wouldn't be spotted, and got a whiff of the steaks grilling on the chuck wagon out back.

JP had not been to The Renegade since it had been remodeled. He was impressed with what they had done—a unique stage backdrop and a charming country feel. It reminded him of the old bars in Texas, and he felt at home. He glanced around, searching for Derek in the crowd and the mass of western hats. Fortunately, Derek was tall enough to stand out, and JP spotted him just before he went out the back door to the patio. Derek walked toward another man standing against the railing. The deck was crowded, making it hard to see who the guy was. JP walked up behind Derek and overhead his conversation.

"I came to give you the heads up," Derek said to other man. "Soper and Rankin are on their way here. At least I'm pretty sure this is where they're headed. I followed them out of the bar, then passed them on the highway. I had no trouble beating them here because Soper drives like an old lady on downers."

JP stepped sideways so he could see who Derek was talking to, although he had a pretty good idea. "Hello, Gene," JP said. "Fancy meetin' you here."

"Dammit, Jackie. What the hell do you want?"

"I want you to help me figure out who killed Bullet."

"I don't know who did it. What do you expect me to do?"

"Man up and help your son!"

"You should leave before those two idiots get here," Derek said to Gene. "They're looking for a fight, and Rankin is just drunk enough to start something."

"Then I'll have to kick his ass," Gene said.

"And violate your parole, get arrested, and go back to prison." JP shook his head. "Derek's right. You need to get out of here. Let's go somewhere where we can talk."

"Just what I want to do—talk to my little brother, the cop. Whoop dee do." Gene raised his beer bottle, mocking him.

"You just might be able to help your son," JP said through clenched teeth.

Gene gulped down his beer and stepped forward.

"Do you want me to stay here and take care of those clowns, or go with you?" Derek asked.

"You don't need to come with me, but don't let those two idiots goad you into anything. It ain't worth it. They'll get what's coming to them."

"Then I think I'll just leave. They can spend the next hour or so trying to find you in this crowd." Derek turned and headed for the door. JP and Gene followed him out.

In the parking lot, JP asked, "Where are you staying?"

"None of your business."

"Did you drive here?"

"A friend dropped me off. What's it to you?"

JP's jaw tightened again as he looked at Gene. "You'd have to get smarter, just to be stupid."

"I'm not the one who lived within miles of his family for years and didn't know they were there."

JP raised his usual soft voice. "Because you kept them from me."

"And I'm not the hot-shot PI who can't get his nephew out of the clink."

"Maybe if his father would try to help a little, instead of being such an ass, we could figure this out." JP lowered his voice back down. "Look, I'm just trying to find a place where we can have a private conversation."

"Why didn't you just say that?" Gene asked. "Let's go to Ginny's. She's not there. I can spend the night and regroup in the morning."

JP didn't know whether Gene had been goading him the whole time, or if his brother was genuinely angry at him. *It doesn't matter* he reminded himself. *As long as he's willing to help.*

Chapter 28

JP had so many questions, he was anxious to get to Ginny's and get some answers. Besides, he had Gene captive in the truck, so he might as well take advantage.

"How and why do you still have Dad's gun?" JP asked, as he pulled onto Interstate 8 and drove west.

"Remember that night..."

"Of course, I remember. How could either of us forget it?" JP growled.

"Don't get your knickers in a knot, little brother."

"Dammit, Gene. You say it like it was some fun adventure we had. That night changed our lives forever."

Gene raised his voice. "Don't you think I know it? Look where it's got me."

"I know life hasn't been easy for you since then," JP said softly. "But maybe you can do something now to help your son. Stop the cycle Dad started." JP paused. "Or maybe Grandpa Torn started. We both know Dad didn't have it so good as a kid."

"Dad's still paying for being born a Torn. I guess we all are." Gene shifted and changed the subject. "How is Conner?"

"So far, he seems to be holding up okay. He's scared. And at first, he was more worried about Morgan than himself, but he feels better now that she's with me."

"That's my son. He's been the father to Morgan that I haven't been."

"Morgan worships you. Her eyes light up when she talks about you. It makes me think you've done something right."

"Not much."

JP didn't want the conversation to get too maudlin. "Conner has a 707 hearing next week. That's when they'll decide if he should be tried as a minor in juvenile court or go downtown to adult court. Sabre will fight like crazy to keep him in juvenile, but not too many murder cases get tried there."

"What's the difference in outcomes?"

"If he's convicted in juvenile court, they won't keep him beyond the age of twenty-five. And even though he would likely go to a pretty strict juvenile camp, he'd get far more services than in state prison." JP thought about how unsophisticated Conner was and what it would do to him to be locked up with hard core criminals. He felt an ache in the pit of his stomach. "As an adult, he could get life in prison."

"How do we keep him in juvenile court?"

"Sabre is gathering all the information she can to use on his behalf—such as school records, information about his character, and his criminal sophistication."

"He has no *criminal sophistication*. He's never done anything illegal in his life. He doesn't hang with rowdy kids or gang members. He can't survive in that world."

"Sabre will do everything she can to prove that."

"And that could make a difference?"

"It's a combination of factors. The court will consider them all."

Gene went quiet.

"What are you thinking?"

"Nothing. I'd just like to help him."

"You can help by answering my questions," JP said. "I thought Dad's gun was gone. What happened? How could you possibly still have it?"

"After I got out of that group home, I went back to where I had hid it. I'd stashed it pretty well in a hole in an old tree, and I almost couldn't find it. But I kept looking, and there it was. When we went back to Texas, I took it with me."

"When I visited you in Norco, you told me you threw it into the ocean near the cliffs."

"Yeah, I lied about that. I didn't want you to know I still had it."

JP hit a pothole and cursed the road. "And you kept the gun all this time?"

"It served as a reminder for me. Whenever I saw it, I'd remember what happened when we were kids, and, believe it or not, it kept me on the straight and narrow."

"Gene, you haven't exactly lived an exemplary life."

"But it could've been a lot worse. What happened when we were kids with that gun changed my whole outlook."

"For the worse. And now it's ruining your son's life."

"I never expected this to happen."

Of course you didn't, JP thought, but didn't say. "What did you do with the gun when you were in prison?"

"Roxy had it most of the time. I put it in a shoebox, all tied up. I don't know if she even knew what was in the box, but she schlepped it from place to place for me."

"How did it get out?"

"I don't know." Gene took a pack of cigarettes out of his pocket and removed one from the pack.

"You're not smoking that in my truck."

Gene grumbled and put it away.

"Whoever shot Bullet had to know about the gun," JP said. "That makes it unlikely it was Rankin or Soper."

"Except Roxy has a big mouth. If she found it, she probably blabbed. She could've told Muriel, who told Bullet, who told his buddies. I don't think either of them are off the hook."

"Or *you* could be lying about the whole thing."

"I could be, but I'm not. I didn't do this one, little bro. I've done some pretty crappy things in my life, but I didn't do this. And I'm sure as hell not going to repeat what Dad did to us."

JP wanted to believe him, but Gene had lied to him in the past so many times. It didn't matter anyway. What mattered was that Gene was willing to help.

"Wait a minute." JP looked toward his brother for a few seconds and then back at the road. "When was the last time you actually saw the gun?"

"A year ago, maybe. It's not like I was planning to use it for anything. I just assumed Roxy still had it in the shoebox in the house somewhere."

"Someone could've taken the gun a long time ago, which means it could be anyone who has been in that house in the last year."

"That opens it up to any of Roxy's friends, and that's a whole lot of suspects."

"Trying to narrow that down will be harder than tryin' to stack BBs with boxing gloves on."

Gene looked at JP with raised eyebrows.

JP realized his comment regarding Gene's wife was not appropriate. "I'm sorry, that was uncalled for."

Gene laughed. "She is what she is. I was over that a long time ago. I was just thinking how much you sound like Grampa Pippin."

JP tried to get the conversation back on track. "There's also the possibility that Conner found the gun, shot Bullet, and stuck it back in his closet," JP said.

"I suppose. But there's got to be a way to stick this on one of those other clowns."

"Gene, we're not going to *stick* this on anyone. We have to find out what really happened. Sabre believes Conner, and she has good instincts. We just need to track down more evidence." When Gene didn't respond, JP asked, "Are you going to help me or what?"

"What do you want me to do?"

"Get me to the people who might know what happened. Get me closer to Roxy's contacts and to Bullet's circle of friends and enemies."

"You're a cop. They'll smell you coming."

JP felt his face heat up. He took a deep breath and said, "Then I guess your prison stench will have to cover it."

After a pause, Gene said, "I'll see what I can do."

"You know this will be risky for you too. There's a greater chance you'll get caught violating your parole."

"Yeah, well, I'm going back one way or the other. I just need to stay out long enough to help Conner."

Chapter 29

Sunday morning, Sabre made pancakes with Morgan's help, then they sat down at the table to eat breakfast with JP. Morgan put a pancake on her plate, buttered it, and waited for JP to finish with the syrup.

"Are you going to save some for the rest of us?" the girl asked, grinning at JP.

"What can I say? I like my pancakes wet." He finished pouring, handed the half-full bottle to Morgan, then mussed her hair. "There you go, Munchkin. Still plenty left, but you don't need any. You're already sweeter than stolen honey."

Morgan smiled, her eyes lighting up. "You sure say some funny stuff, Uncle Johnny."

"So I've been told."

Morgan chattered as they ate, smiling all through the meal.

"You got a smile bigger than Texas. What's that all about?" JP asked.

"I can't wait to see Conner today. I want to tell him all about living here." Morgan got really quiet for a few seconds. "Maybe I shouldn't. Do you think he'll feel bad because he can't be here? I don't want him to feel bad."

Sabre patted her arm. "I think your brother will be glad to hear that you're happy. He'll want to know what's going on in your life. He loves you very much."

Morgan's head bobbed up and down. "You're right, and I love him. I love my parents too, but it's not the same."

"How is it different?" Sabre asked.

"My dad is great and spends a lot of time with us and teaches us things—when he's around. But I know he isn't always going to be there, so I don't count on it. That's just the way it is."

JP shifted in his seat, but didn't say anything.

"What about your mom?" Sabre asked, knowing the subject could be painful.

"My mom is different than other moms. It's important to her to do her own thing. She hardly ever comes to any school things or takes us anywhere. She says we have to be more independent and that she needs to set an example. She says she does that by doing what she wants." Morgan shrugged. "I don't mind, because my brother is always there for me. And most of the time, my grandma is too."

Sabre was frustrated by the plight of this young girl and the lack of parenting she received. It made her even more determined to prove Conner's innocence. Morgan needed him.

"We'd better get moving, or we'll miss visiting hours," Sabre said after a while.

Morgan jumped up, picked up her plate, and put it in the sink.

~~~

Morgan and Conner seemed to be thrilled to see one another. She asked him questions about the Hall, and he answered the best he could, sugar-coating them for her. Whenever there was a lull in the conversation, Conner seemed to know just what to ask to keep it going. Sabre admired the love between them and compared it to her own sibling situation. Conner was like her brother, Ron, always protecting, loving, and teasing her. When Morgan told him about the fight at school, he scolded her a little, but not harshly, and told her never to do that again.

About ten minutes before their time was up, Sabre said she needed to talk to Conner alone, so JP agreed to take Morgan out.

"Bye, Morgonster. Stay out of trouble and no more fights." Conner winked at her.

"You know you're not supposed to call me Morgonster." Tears started to form in Morgan's eyes. "No more fights for you either, and you be good too."

After they left, Sabre noticed Conner's eyes were wet as well. "Are you doing okay in here?" she asked. "Is there anything I should know?"

"Everything is okay. I keep to myself as much as I can."

"Good. We have your 707 hearing this week. I wanted to make sure you understood what's going on. Do you know what a 707, or fitness hearing, is?"

He shrugged. "Just what you told me before. The judge needs to decide if I get my trial in juvenile or adult court, right?"

"Yes. Do you have any questions?"

"Will my mom and dad be there?"

"I expect your mom and grandmother, but I'm pretty sure your father won't be in court."

"That's okay. I'm used to him not being there for things."

Sabre watched his expression as he spoke. He didn't appear to have any malice, frustration, or sadness—much the way Morgan had talked about her father. It just was what it was.

Chapter 30

It was 9:35 p.m. JP sat on the sofa watching an old M*A*S*H rerun, and Sabre was in the office working when the phone rang. There was no ID displayed. "JP Torn," he said, answering the call.

"Hello, Jackie," Gene said. "Come pick me up."

"And take you where?"

"I'll tell you when you get here. Just get your ass over here so we can help Conner."

"Are you still at Ginny's?"

"Yes," Gene said. "And bring some cash—three or four hundred. At least three."

"What the hell?"

"Just do it." Gene hung up.

Sabre walked into the room. "Who was that?"

"Gene. He wants me to pick him up and take him somewhere. He said it would help Conner."

"Do you think it's a good idea?"

"Most of Gene's ideas are bad, but I asked for his help. He has better access to information than I do right now. I've reached a dead end."

"Just be careful."

JP stood up, clipped his holster back onto his jeans, and checked to see how much cash he had—only a hundred and twenty bucks. "Do you have any cash on you?"

"How much do you need?"

"A couple hundred, if you have it."

Sabre never carried a purse so she didn't have to go far to get the money. She reached in her jeans and pulled it out. She counted two-hundred and thirty dollars, and handed it to him without asking what it was for.

JP kissed Sabre goodbye. "I don't know when I'll be back, but I expect it'll be late."

~~~

Gene directed JP as they drove to a neighborhood in El Cajon.

"When do you plan to tell me where we're going? I'd just as soon not go in blind."

"We're headed to a poker game."

"So, that's why I needed to bring cash. What's the buy-in?"

"A hundred and fifty."

"And I needed three hundred so I can pay for yours as well."

"Yeah, I don't have any money."

"That's all I have with me, so you'd better not lose it too quick."

"I won't, little brother. I'm not so sure about you."

JP hadn't played much poker during the last years, but he'd been pretty decent in his youth. Never anywhere as good as Gene though, who could bluff with the best of them and never seemed to have a tell. JP's strength was in reading people. They both had learned the game from their father when they were very young.

"Who are the players?"

"Some of Bullet's cronies."

"Will Soper and Rankin be there?"

Gene hesitated. "No."

"Are you sure?"

"As sure as I can be, but life is full of surprises."

JP hoped he wasn't getting himself into a mess. He didn't trust Gene, and for all he knew, Gene was the one who'd killed Bullet. The only thing JP could hold onto was that his brother seemed genuinely concerned about helping Conner. On the other hand, Gene might have set JP up just so he could play a game of poker.

"How are we going to learn anything at a poker game?" JP asked as he took the onramp to Interstate 8.

"I'll bring up Bullet. There's been all kinds of rumors flying around. I'll see if anyone tries to dispel them. You watch their faces. You're good at that. Give me a signal if something is suspicious."

"What kind of signal?"

"I don't know. You're the smart one. Come up with something. And take the next offramp."

"And if you get a signal, what will you do?"

"I don't know, because I don't know what we're gonna hear." Gene continued to instruct him where to turn.

"So, what's the point of a signal?"

"Don't be an ass, Jack. Just blink at me or something, and I'll know what to do with it."

JP was frustrated with himself for goading Gene, but he just couldn't seem to stop. He and his brother had had this kind of relationship for so long, he didn't know how else to act around him. JP took a deep breath and regrouped. He had to work with Gene on this. He wasn't sure what kind of people he'd be dealing with at this game, and he needed Gene to have his back.

After driving past the address twice, they finally discovered the house was located behind a small apartment building.

When JP parked, Gene said, "Give me my buy-in money. I don't want you paying for me when we get inside. It won't look good."

JP reluctantly gave him a hundred-dollar bill and three twenties. "I want the change, and if you win, I get my money back, plus anything I might have lost as well. You can keep the profit."

"You'll get your money."

Gene knocked on the door, and a dark-haired man with a mustache answered. "Who are you?" The guy spoke in a deep gruff voice.

"I'm Gene. This is Johnny."

JP scowled at Gene, but his brother ignored him. *At least he didn't call him Jackie.*

"Who sent you?"

"Derek."

"Come in." The guy stepped inside, and JP and Gene followed. "I'm Lucky Len," the man said.

"Do they call you Lucky because of your poker skills?" JP asked.

"Naw. I win some. I lose some. They call me Lucky Len because I'm still alive."

"And you shouldn't be?" JP asked.

"Been shot twice, stabbed once, fell off a second-story building, survived a motorcycle crash, and had three wives who didn't seem to like my girlfriends much."

"Dang, that is lucky. I think I'd better watch my cards."

The living room had a poker table with six seats, a bar, a small sofa, and an armchair. No wall hangings of any kind or lighting other than the can fixtures in the ceiling. It was plenty bright for card playing though. A thin man with wild hair and wire-rimmed glasses sat in the armchair with a box of poker chips and a cash bag in his lap.

"It's a cash buy-in. You can get your chips from the Professor." Lucky Len nodded toward the man in the armchair. "It's one-fifty. No more, no less. If you lose that and want to buy in again, you can do it one more time. The game is straight Texas hold 'em, nothing wild, nothing wussy. Small blind is two bucks, big blind four bucks. The Professor will start the deal and the button will move to the left."

JP bought his chips, and Gene did the same.

"I'd wish you luck," the Professor said, "but since I'm in the game and we're playing against Lucky Len and Dean, I'm keeping all the luck I can for myself."

"Who's Dean?" JP asked.

"One of the best players around."

"Why was he invited if he's so good?" JP needed all the information he could get.

"Because, if someone cleans the table, the house gets its buy-in back. And Dean has done that on more than one occasion."

"Good to know," JP said. "Do we have a sixth?"

"Donna."

Gene glanced over. "Pinnick?"

"Do you know her?" JP asked.

"We're acquainted."

"She's quite the gal," the Professor said, but Gene was already walking away. JP followed him to the poker table. They passed a tall man in his early fifties who had just come in and was walking toward the bar.

Gene nodded at him, then stopped. "You must be Dean."

"I am."

Gene reached out his hand, and Dean shook it. "I'm Gene. This is Johnny."

JP shook his hand too. "I hear you're a good player."

"I win some now and again." Dean kept walking.

When he was out of earshot, JP asked, "What's Donna's story?"

"She's a good poker player and can bluff better than most pros. Everyone says she doesn't have a tell. Watch her closely and see if you spot one."

"Will do."

"I'll try to sit next to her," Gene said. "If you can, sit across from us."

"Okay."

"Donna and Bullet go way back. They even lived together for a while, until she caught him cheating."

"Did she actually find him in bed with someone?"

Gene chuckled. "No, cheating at cards. She probably wouldn't have cared less if he went out on her, but she doesn't take kindly to people who cheat at cards. Donna is probably the only person in the world Bullet was afraid of."

"What did she do to him?"

"There's rumors about what happened, but I'm not sure what's true. All I know is that Bullet was never allowed to play in any decent poker games unless Donna was there to keep him straight."

"That's odd. Were they still friends?"

"They had a strange relationship, but Derek said they pretty much hated each other."

"Maybe we can find out tonight what she did to him," JP said. "Maybe she killed him for cheating. How long ago did she catch him?"

"That was ten or fifteen years ago."

"I guess it's not likely then."

Gene cocked his head to one side. "Unless he was stupid enough to do it twice."

Lucky Len walked up to the oval-shaped game table. "You boys ready?"

"Are we all here?" Gene asked.

"Donna will be along any minute. She's never been late to a game, but she don't come early either."

"Does it matter where we sit?" JP asked.

Lucky Len pointed to the chair nearest him. "The Professor sits here, and Donna sits next to him." He nodded toward the chair on his left. "The rest are open. Just take a seat."

The Professor walked up and placed a pile of chips on the table in front of Donna's chair. Then he took his seat and put his chips in front of him.

Gene sat next to Donna's open chair, and JP took the seat across from Gene. Dean returned from the bar with a bottle of beer and took the seat next to JP. Lucky Len sat down between Gene and Dean. JP looked at his watch: 9:59 p.m. The door opened, and a woman walked in. JP was expecting a big, tough gal, but Donna was barely five feet and weighed about ninety pounds. Boney knees showed beneath the hem of her short denim Daisy Duke skirt. A short-sleeved plaid blouse, pink western boots, and a matching pink cowboy hat finished the ensemble on the sixty-something woman.

Donna walked over to her seat at the table, handed the Professor some cash, then sat down. She placed two dollars in chips for the small blind near her stack and said, "Okay, boys, let's put the cards in the air."

Chapter 31

After about twenty minutes, JP had a good read of the players. The Professor pushed his glasses up when he had a good hand, Dean had not revealed a tell, and Lucky Len either didn't know when to fold, or it was part of his game plan to make the others think he didn't. JP wasn't sure, but he was starting to think Len was just a bad player.

JP was down about twenty-five dollars. He hadn't yet been dealt anything worth staying in the game for. Dean, Donna, and Gene had each won a small pot. The betting was still conservative, but JP figured that wouldn't last long. He was right. The raises in the next hand became more aggressive. Dean dealt the cards, JP put in the two-dollar small blind, and the Professor put in the big blind. Each player called. Dean laid the first three cards face up.

JP was far more interested in the dynamics of the players and what he might find out about Bullet than he was in the game itself. The Professor seemed nonchalant and apparently used to losing. Lucky Len was more intense and talked a lot when he was bluffing. Dean and Donna were the most interesting and were also complete opposites. Dean was very focused, said very little even between hands, and seldom changed his demeanor. Donna, on the other hand, talked a lot, but no more or no less when she had a winning hand. JP admired her ability to talk incessantly without interfering with her card game.

JP told a story about a game he participated in when a player was caught cheating. "When he palmed a card," JP said, "Big Joe stood up, grabbed the guy with one hand on his belt and the other on his bicep, carried him outside, and threw him into the swimming pool."

Donna, Len, and the Professor all laughed. "Did he come back in?" the Professor asked.

"Nope. He must've gone out the side gate, because when I went to leave, his car was gone."

"Your bet," Dean said.

JP checked, so did the Professor.

"He got what he deserved," Donna said, as she matched the big blind. "Basic rules of life: You don't talk bad about someone's mama, you don't hurt little kids, and you don't ever cheat at cards."

"I bet you've seen a few cheaters in your time," JP said to her.

"Seen my share. They only cheat once with me at the table."

Gene raised the bet to eight dollars. "Speaking of cheaters," Gene said. "I heard Bullet got shot. Did he cheat at your table twice?"

Donna stared at Gene for several seconds. "I didn't kill him, if that's what you're asking, but I probably would've if I'd caught him a second time." She laughed as if it was a joke, but JP wasn't so sure. He looked around at the others. Dean's face showed the first sign of emotion, but JP wasn't sure if it was hatred, concern, or anger. Perhaps it was frustration because the players were talking too much, but JP thought it had more to do with the mention of Bullet. Whatever caused it, the expression only lasted for a passing second, then it was gone.

Len looked long and hard at the cards on the table and back at his hand, then called the raise. Dean matched the bet. JP and the Professor folded. Donna matched the bet, and Dean dealt the fourth card face up.

"I heard some teenager was arrested for it," Lucky Len said. "It was only a matter of time before someone whacked that guy. He caused trouble wherever he went."

"You weren't a fan, huh?" Gene asked.

"Was anyone?" Lucky Len glanced at Donna. "Sorry, Donna. I know you two once shared a bond."

"We shared a house; we shared a bed; we shared meals. We *didn't* share a bond. He was always a crazy jerk, but he used to be fun. He got worse with age. I put up with all his flaws until he cheated at cards. That was it for me."

"What did you do when you caught him?" JP asked.

Donna put in her bet without raising. "Not as much as people like to say I did." She chuckled. "I did threaten to superglue his dick to his stomach when he was asleep."

JP cringed. "But you didn't, right?"

"No, but Bullet never went to sleep around me again. I guess he wasn't too sure what I'd do."

Gene again raised the bet to eight dollars. Lucky Len folded. Dean matched the bet. "Do you think that kid killed him?" Dean asked Donna.

"I don't have any reason to think otherwise," Donna said. "But it could've been any one of his enemies. That's not a short list."

Donna raised the bet, and Gene upped it again. Dean dropped out. Donna called Gene's raise, and Dean dealt the last card. Both Donna and Gene checked.

Donna showed a queen-high straight. But Gene's hand was better, with a king-high straight, and he won the first decent pot of the night.

JP won a couple of pots in the next hour, but he played so cautiously the winnings were small when he stayed in. *Talk about a big tell.* But JP didn't care. Gene was winning more and bigger pots, and JP was watching and listening. The Professor lost his money and didn't do a second buy-in.

He sat at the table for another ten minutes, then moved to the armchair and fell asleep.

Lucky Len was the next to lose his money, bought in again, and lost it quicker the second time. He moved to the bar and drank. JP was the next to go, but he stayed at the table watching the last three. All were good players, but with different skills. JP couldn't find anything that gave away when Gene or Dean had a winning hand, but after awhile, JP noticed Donna talked just a little faster when she had an advantage. He soon realized Gene had picked up on it too and so had Dean. But Dean couldn't draw a good hand and finally went all-in on a hand with two pair, king high. Gene beat him with aces and eights.

Dean left the house, leaving only Gene and Donna still in the game.

"Do you mind if the kid deals for us?" Donna said, nodding toward JP.

"Nope. I don't mind at all."

JP didn't like being called "the kid." It reminded him of when they were young, and Gene's friends were around. JP was the tagalong. But he looked around and realized he was the youngest person in the room, and being the kid wasn't so bad.

Donna had a larger stack of chips than Gene did when they started playing one-on-one. She had won most of Lucky's money as well as the Professor's. Gene had taken most of JP's, and they had mostly split Dean's. JP shuffled the cards and dealt the first round. Gene won the first and second hands. Donna took the next one, but then Gene won again. The stacks had evened out, and the bets had increased.

JP dealt them each two cards. Donna opened with a twenty-dollar bet. Gene matched.

"You mentioned the list is long for those who wanted to kill Bullet," Gene commented. "Any chance you could share the list with me?"

Donna laid her cards on the table and tilted her head. "Is that what this is about?"

"What?"

"You playing this game. And please don't tell me you're an undercover cop, because I don't need to be busted for some lightweight poker game."

"I'm not a cop. I'm just trying to find out who killed Bullet." Gene put in his forty dollars.

JP dealt three cards face up—the ace of diamonds, the seven of diamonds, and the eight of spades.

Donna picked up her cards, bet forty dollars, and looked Gene in the eye. "Why do you care? Was Bullet a friend of yours?"

"Like everyone else, I hated the guy, even more now that he's dead. The boy they charged with his murder is my son."

JP dealt the next card—a jack of clubs. *A nine and ten in the hole would make a straight,* he thought. He watched their faces to see if he could tell what they had, but neither gave anything away. Donna bet sixty, and Gene raised the ante to one hundred.

Without hesitation, Donna placed another forty dollars' worth of chips in the pot. "And you don't think he shot Bullet?" Donna asked.

"I don't. Do you know any likely suspects?"

"I might know a few worth investigating." She glanced at JP.

"He's good," Gene said.

Donna looked around the room to see if anyone was paying attention to her. Then she lowered her voice almost to a whisper. "You don't have to look too far to find Bullet's enemies." She reached her hand out to JP. "Give me your phone."

JP hesitated. But Gene nodded at him, so JP handed Donna his cell, unlocking it with his thumbprint as he gave it to her.

"You two must be close," she said.

"Brothers," Gene said.

"I never would've guessed." She put her name and number in JP's contact list and turned back to Gene. "Call me ten minutes after we leave. Now, let's finish this hand." She paused. "By the way, I seem to know a lot more when I'm a winner." She smiled sheepishly.

JP dealt the last card—a nine of diamonds. *Now all it took in the hole was a ten for a straight, or two diamonds for a flush.* He glanced back and forth between the two players. Donna bet two hundred. Gene reached for his chips and pushed them to the center of the table. "I'm all in."

Donna did the same, then turned over her cards—a king of hearts, and a ten of clubs. "A jack-high straight."

Gene laid his cards face down on the table. "It's yours."

Donna raked in the pot. "Never play poker when you owe your opponent a debt. My bluff was in my statement, not my cards."

"I know," Gene said and shrugged, "but it was my brother's money."

"I would've given you the information either way, for your kid's sake."

"That, I didn't know."

JP gathered up the cards, leaving Gene's *hold cards* on the bottom, so he could check out what he had. He put the cards together and tapped them on the table so they were in a neat stack, observing the card on the bottom. A ten of diamonds. *So, Gene had a straight too.* With slight pressure from his thumb, JP moved the bottom card so he could see Gene's other hold. It was a queen of diamonds—giving him a flush.

Chapter 32

"You won that hand with a flush," JP said, once he and Gene were driving away. "She got to you when she said she'd talk more if she won, didn't she?"

"Just paying for information."

"With my money."

"Would you rather not get the information?" Gene asked.

"Let's hope she comes through. She probably didn't even give us her correct number." JP drove through the neighborhood toward the freeway.

"Maybe. But like you said, it was your money, so I had nothing to lose." Gene checked the time. "Give me your phone. Let's find out if she wrong-numbered me." Gene put the phone on speaker and placed the call.

"Hello." Donna's voice came through clearly.

"Thanks for taking my call," Gene said.

"Thanks for a good game. You're a worthy opponent."

"So are you. What can you tell me about Bullet's death?"

"I don't know anything about his death, but I know a little about his life. Bullet wasn't loyal to anyone. He didn't care who he hurt or upset." She paused. "Do you know his buddies, Judd Soper and Andy Rankin?"

"Yes, I do."

"They were supposedly his best friends, and neither liked him, especially Soper. He's the quieter of the two, but he hated the way Bullet bossed him around."

"Why would they stick with him?" JP asked.

"Who knows? I'm sure he had something on both of them, but they're all losers."

"Who else can you tell me about?" Gene asked.

"Everyone in that room tonight had a beef with Bullet. The Professor's grandson was working with Bullet for a while, stealing cars. The kid got busted and took a plea, but he didn't give up Bullet."

"How long ago was that?"

"Just a few months, so it's still raw. Rumor has it, the kid isn't doing well in custody."

"Maybe the Professor got even."

"Maybe. Then there's Lucky Len, who Bullet humiliated in a bar last month. They got into a fist fight, but Len didn't stand a chance. Bullet beat him up pretty good, but mostly he threw him around like he was a feather and made him look bad."

"What about Dean?" JP asked. "He didn't seem to have any lost love for the guy."

"Bullet slept with his wife."

"That would do it."

"Anyone else we should know about?" Gene asked.

"That's the problem. Like I said, Bullet didn't care who he crossed, so there's dozens of stories like those."

"That doesn't narrow it down much."

"No, but those are the most recent. If it doesn't help, let me know. I'll give you more names of people who may have older vendettas." Before Donna hung up, she gave the names of the bars where her poker-player friends hung out, as well as their last names.

"Now what?" Gene asked, after he hung up.

"The most likely suspects are still Soper or Rankin since they have been to the house and could've gotten the gun."

"Unless Roxy opened her big mouth about it. If Bullet found out about the gun, he could've stolen it and sold it."

"Wouldn't that be ironic? If Bullet sold the gun to someone who then used it on him?" JP paused. "Too much speculating. We need to see what we can get out of Soper and/or Rankin."

"Leave it to me. I'll get them to talk."

JP frowned. "Let's try a little more interrogation first."

"My way is quicker."

"And against the law, not to mention dangerous," JP added.

He stopped at a light near the freeway, when suddenly a loud gunshot blasted the night. JP's back window shattered as a bullet pierced it. Gene ducked down, and JP hit the accelerator, his heart hammering. Another shot rang out, and the sound of metal on metal rung in his ears. JP passed a Toyota, ran the next red light, and zoomed onto the freeway. He raced down the road, dodging in and out of traffic, doing ninety miles per hour.

When he was sure no one was following, he slowed down, but kept checking his rearview mirror.

"Are you okay?" JP asked.

"I'm fine," Gene said. "What the hell was that?"

"I don't know, but I think we might be plowing too close to the cotton."

JP exited the freeway and soon pulled up to the condos where Gene was staying. When Gene opened the passenger door, the light went on, and JP saw blood all over Gene's shirt.

"I'm taking you to a hospital."

Gene pulled his shirt back, exposing his shoulder. "It doesn't hurt that bad." His brother used the corner of his shirt to wipe away some of the blood so they could get a better look. "It just barely got me. I'll be fine." He stepped out of the truck and walked away.

Chapter 33

Sabre and JP sat outside on the patio, drinking their morning coffee. Morgan was still asleep. Sabre listened without interrupting as JP told her about the poker game and the information they received from Donna. But the shooting afterward unnerved her. "Someone shot at you? Did you report it?"

"I couldn't without getting Gene arrested. He got hit, but he's okay. I didn't even know he was bleeding until I dropped him off. I tried to get him to go to emergency, but he wouldn't. I followed him inside and helped bandage the wound. I think he's okay, but I'll check on him this morning."

Sabre wasn't soothed. "I don't like this one bit."

"I don't like it much either, but we're in too deep now. My only concern is that they might know where I live, and that puts you and Morgan in danger too."

"Did you go anywhere besides the poker game?"

"No."

"So, it was likely a player from the game."

"Unless we stirred someone up asking questions earlier. Nothing much was said at the game, except that Gene was looking for Bullet's killer. We shared a few other things with Donna, but she seems an unlikely suspect."

"What happens now?"

"I need to get my truck fixed."

"Let me know if you need transportation," Sabre said. "I'm going to be in court all morning, but I'm sure Bob can get me around if you need my car."

"You're not afraid it'll get shot up?"

"A little."

Sabre thought about telling JP about her coffee date with *ImReady*, but she decided not to. He was dealing with enough, and he already had plans. Since she didn't have transportation, Bob would have to take her anyway. She wouldn't be alone.

~~~

JP's first stop was to see Gene and check his wound.

"It's no big deal," Gene said.

JP reached to remove the bandage. "We need to change the dressing and put more Neosporin on it, so it doesn't get infected."

"What, are you a doctor now?"

JP pushed back. "Would you rather I take you to the ER and let you explain what happened?"

"No." Gene used his good arm to yank the bloody bandage off. The open wound was about three inches long and a half-inch wide. The bullet had torn off the skin, exposing flesh as it burned across Gene's arm, right through an old tattoo.

"What did the tattoo say?" JP asked.

"Delilah."

JP tipped his head. "That's so like Mom. She's still trying to save your ass."

"Hmph. She woulda taken a bullet for any of her boys." Gene cleared his throat. "Unlike Dad."

"Yeah, Elvis Torn was cut from another cloth."

JP examined the gash more closely, wanting to get off the subject of their parents. "You sure you don't want to see a doctor? Mostly the bullet tore the skin, but there's a couple of spots that got some flesh and could probably use stitches."

Gene looked at his arm and shook his head. "Naw, it'll be all right. Just put some salve on it and cover it up. I've had worse injuries and survived."

JP bandaged the bullet wound again. "I'm taking my truck to get that window replaced. I found someone who can do it this morning. It'll only take about an hour."

"I plan to hit those bars tonight that Donna told us about," Gene said. "And I'll confront Soper and Rankin." He looked at JP. "You gonna take me, or do I need to get my own ride?"

"I'm not letting you go alone. You're liable to get yourself killed."

Gene chuckled. "You may not want to get that window fixed until this is over."

"You have a point." JP's cell rang, and he looked at the ID "Hey, kid, what's up?"

"It's Conner," Sabre said.

JP heard the concern in her voice. "What's wrong?"

"Conner is in the emergency room. He was beat up by another inmate. I'm waiting to go in." Sabre explained what little she knew about the incident. "I'll call you when I know more."

JP hung up and told Gene. His brother asked calmly, "Is he okay?"

"No broken bones, but he's pretty bruised. They won't keep him in the hospital long, but he'll be put back in protective custody for a while."

JP expected Gene to start punching things or threaten to go after the kid who hurt him, but instead he just said, "Poor kid."

"What's going on in that warped brain of yours?"

"Nothin'. I cain't do nothin' about it," he said nonchalantly, his Texas accent a little more pronounced than normal. "Just need to get him outta there soon."

Chapter 34

Since JP had Sabre's car, Bob drove her to the pre-arranged Starbucks meeting a half hour early. They parked around the corner in front of Staples. They didn't want their target to see them together and get scared off. Before they got out, Bob asked, "You ready?"

"I'm ready."

"No, he's *ImReady*. You're *TwinGirlsMom*. You can't pull this off, Sobs, if you can't remember who you are." Bob grinned.

"You're weird, you know that? Let's go."

Sabre looked in the mirror and adjusted her blonde wig. Then they got out, locked the car, and walked up to the front of Starbucks.

"I'll go inside, and you can wait outside at one of these tables," Bob said. There were three large round tables on the concrete slab, set away from the coffee shop. Four more lined the building. "Sit at a table by the window, and I'll be right near you on a barstool, just on the other side of the glass." He pointed inside the café. "I'll sit where I can see your face. Nod at me if he approaches you."

"Won't you be able to see if he approaches me?"

"Yes, but you need to nod if it's the right guy."

"Because so many men will be stopping by." She gave him a sarcastic look.

"You never know. This is your first time out as a blonde."

Bob walked away and Sabre followed.

"What are you doing? I thought you were going to stay out here."

"I decided to get my own coffee. Then we don't have to go through that awkward thing about who's going to pay for it."

"Whatever. But you could've at least got a free cup of joe out of this guy."

Inside, Sabre bought a grande, decaf, mocha latte with half-and-half instead of milk.

Bob got a black house coffee. "Sobs, if at any time you want to get away from him, just give me a sign, and I'll call you."

"Good idea. What kind of sign?"

"I don't know. Rub your ear or bang your head against the window. Just tell me what the signal is."

"I think I'll go with the ear rub. If you see me banging my head against the window, don't bother to call, just come get me." Sabre took her drink outside and sat down at one of the small tables by the window. She could see Bob only a few feet away from her. If it weren't for the wall and window between them, they could've had a conversation.

A minute later, a man in jeans and a t-shirt walked up to her table. "Do I know you?" he asked.

"I don't think so."

"We can remedy that. Would you like a cup of coffee?"

Sabre smiled. "No, thank you. I'm waiting for someone."

"Lucky guy," he said and walked away.

Sabre turned toward Bob and slowly shook her head. Bob smiled and mouthed the word, *Blondes*.

"You look just like your photo." The voice cut into her thoughts.

Sabre turned to see a man in a cheap charcoal suit, a light-blue shirt, and a black-and-green tie.

"Hello," she said.

"It's refreshing to see that you look like your photo. So many women don't."

"I take it you've done this a few times."

"Not that many, but a few." He reached out his hand. "I'm Sam, by the way."

"I'm Say… Shay… Sheila." Sabre couldn't believe she'd almost said her real name. "Sorry, I guess I'm more nervous than I thought I'd be. This is the first time for me."

"I'm glad to be your first," he said with a smile. "I see you already have coffee."

"Yeah, I got here a little early."

"I'll get mine and be right back."

"Go ahead." As he walked away, Sabre nodded at Bob.

Her date returned shortly and sat down across from her. "Tell me about yourself," he said.

"Not much to tell. I'm a working mom with twin seven-year-old girls. They are my world. I keep pretty busy with all their activities, but mostly I've been trying to get them into modeling." She paused, not wanting to come on too strong with the kid thing. "What about you? What kind of law do you practice?"

"I do a lot of different things. I'm a partner in a big firm."

"Do you handle criminal cases?"

"I've done a murder case or two. Some drug stuff. Mostly I do the big medical malpractice cases."

"That's pretty impressive. Can I ask you a question?"

"Sure."

"I have a friend who's involved in a lawsuit with her neighbor."

"What happened?"

"A tree in her backyard fell on the neighbor's house, and she got sued. The prosecutor—that's what they call the attorney on the other side, correct?"

"That's right." He looked directly at her as if he was really listening.

"He said my friend would have to prove it didn't happen. Does that make sense? Doesn't the prosecutor have to prove the case?"

"Yes, he does."

"Beyond a reasonable doubt?"

"That's right."

"She won't have to do jail time if she loses, will she?"

"It's not likely."

Sabre struggled to keep from rolling her eyes. Finally, she said, "It's just not fair."

"Does she have an attorney?" he asked.

"She had one, but he got too expensive."

Sam raised his hand, palm facing her. "Just a minute." He removed his phone from his coat pocket, looked at the screen, then put it up to his ear and said, "What is it, John?" A moment of quiet. "We're not settling for a mere million. Set it for trial." Silence again. "I have to go. Just set the damn thing. They'll come around, or we'll kick their ass in court."

Sabre was pretty certain it was a fake call meant to impress her, not to get away. It didn't work.

Sam returned the phone to his pocket. "Sorry about that. I shut the ringer off, but I could feel the vibration. I get a lot of calls, and technically I should be working. I'll only take the most important ones."

"No problem. I'm sure you're very busy."

"Now, where were we?" Without pausing, he said, "Let's not talk about law. That's what I do all day. I know it's important work, but I just want to relax and get to know you. You said you were a working mom. What kind of work do you do?"

"I'm a waitress. The bad part is that I have to work nights, and I hate leaving my kids with a sitter."

"Nothing wrong with being a waitress. My mom was one for years." He smiled at her. "I drive racecars. I'm not big time or anything, but I've been in a few important races."

Sabre thought she would vomit if he used the words *I* and *important* in one more sentence. He didn't even segue from talking about her to himself. She went with it, and they talked about him for the next ten minutes. She tried once again to get the conversation back to herself and her twins, but within a minute or so, he was telling her about the triathlons he had won. Sabre rubbed her ear, and her phone rang a moment later.

"Is everything okay?" she asked, without saying hello.

"You rubbed?"

"Oh no." Sabre tried to sound startled.

"No? You didn't rub? Never mind then." Bob laughed.

Sabre resisted the urge to glare at him. "Yes. I'll be right there." She clicked off the phone and stood. "I'm terribly sorry to cut this short, but one of my girls fell at school. I need to go." She started to walk away.

"Don't you want my phone number?" Sam called after her.

Sabre waved her hand in the air. "Just message me." She kept walking, turned the corner, and waited at the car. About three minutes later, Bob showed up.

"Did he leave?" Sabre asked.

"Yes. I watched him pull away. I take it, he's not Nesbitt."

"Probably not. He seemed far more interested in himself than he did in my twin girls. I tried baiting him a couple of times, but it never worked. He always got the conversation back to him. One thing's for sure; he's not an attorney, or he's the dumbest one I've ever met. I don't think he knows the difference between civil and criminal court, and he sure doesn't know the standard of proof for a civil case."

"We'll know for certain if it's him real soon," Bob said.

"How's that?"

"I took photos of him, and I'll show them to Laura."

"Look at you, being the little detective."

Chapter 35

JP, Sabre, and Morgan had dinner like a real family. They cleaned up the kitchen, Morgan got ready for bed, and Sabre read her a story. Once she was tucked in, JP came in and told her goodnight. Then Sabre and JP sat together on the sofa, JP with his coffee and Sabre with her herbal tea.

"You got the window replaced?" Sabre asked.

"Yes, but the damage to the body isn't going to be cheap. The dents will need to be fixed, the holes filled, and the whole thing painted." JP paused. "I think it might be time for a new truck."

Surprised, Sabre looked at him. "Really? You've always been so attached to that truck."

"I know, but I kinda been lookin' at a new Chevy Silverado."

"I know." She smiled. She had noticed the ads on the computer screen when he searched. "Do you think you'll get something soon?"

"Once this case is over, I'll start looking."

They sat there together, exchanging stories from the day.

"Is Gene okay?" Sabre asked.

"He'll be fine. He's tougher than a one-eared alley cat. How about Conner?"

"They didn't keep him long in the ER. I went by juvenile hall to make sure he was put in protective custody. He was in a room by himself when I got there."

"How's he handling it?"

"He's scared, but fine with not having to interact with any-one." Sabre wrinkled her brow. "It's unfortunate it happened, but still, the attack might help at the 707 hearing. It could make things worse if they thought he was just in a fight, but the probation officer saw what happened and is willing to testify on Conner's behalf."

"Do you know what prompted the kid to beat him up?"

"No idea."

JP took a sip of coffee. "Gene and I are going to some bars tonight to see what we can find out."

Sabre's lip twitched a little. "Please be careful."

~~~

Their first stop was at the bar where Lucky Len hung out. Lucky was seated at the counter between two men. Behind him stood two others.

"Do you know any of those guys with Lucky?" JP asked Gene.

"The one standing to his left is Skip Evans. I don't know any of the others."

"How well do you know Skip?"

"Well enough to ask him what's going on. He's in construc-tion and gives me work every once in a while. He's a decent enough guy."

They sat at the bar nursing their beers, until Skip walked away from the crowd and toward the exit. Gene followed him outside. JP chatted with the bartender until Gene returned.

"What did you find out?" JP asked.

"Lucky has been braggin' about getting rid of Bullet."

"Did he actually say he shot him?"

"Everything but. He's been saying things like 'He won't ever mess with me again. I saw to that.' And 'He messed with the wrong guy this time.' That kind of stuff."

The bartender overheard their conversation and said, "Smart move. Everyone hated Bullet, and they all keep buy-ing Lucky drinks."

"Is this the first time he's said anything?" JP asked.

"Oh, he's been bragging about it for a week now. Different crowd each time. That's one way to get free drinks and look important."

"You say that like you don't think he killed him."

"I know he didn't." The bartender smirked.

"Why's that?" Gene asked.

"Because Lucky wasn't even in town. He was camping with my sister."

"Was Bullet a regular here?"

"He came in quite a bit. A couple of weeks ago, he and Lucky got into a fist fight out front. Lucky didn't stand a chance. Bullet tossed him around like he was nothing. It was pretty humiliating, so I can see why Lucky wants to brag about getting even. But that's all it is."

"Lucky is a regular too?"

"Yeah, he came in every night until the fight. After that, he didn't return until Bullet had died. I suspect he was too afraid. I don't blame him—Bullet was one mean hombre."

JP put down a twenty-dollar tip. "You hear a lot of talk. Anyone else bragging about doing him in?"

"Thanks," the bartender said, picking up the twenty. "No one is as stupid as Lucky Len, but there is some speculation that it was a jealous husband."

"Dean?" Gene asked.

"You know him?"

"We met once," JP said.

"What is your interest in all this?" the bartender asked.

JP explained that Gene's son was the kid who'd been arrested for the murder and that they were convinced he didn't do it. The bartender seemed sympathetic.

"Do you think it was Dean?" JP asked.

He shook his head. "It could've been, I suppose, but I don't think so."

"Why's that?" JP asked.

A thin woman with bleached-blonde hair took a seat at the bar nearby. "Excuse me," the bartender said and walked over. He drew a tap beer, took the cash she put down, and gave her change. Then he returned. "Where were we?"

"Why do you think it wasn't Dean who killed Bullet?" JP repeated.

"Because his wife has slept with half the bar. Why would he single out Bullet?"

"Dean knew she was sleeping with other guys?"

"There's no way he couldn't know. Everyone knew. But Bullet is the only one who actually threw it in Dean's face. But my money's still on Soper or Rankin, his so-called buddies."

"Why's that?"

"Because neither of them is talking about Bullet at all, and everyone knows how poorly Bullet treated both of them. There was no love lost between those guys."

Chapter 36

The more people JP and Gene spoke to, the less they thought Dean had anything to do with Bullet's murder. The same was true of the Professor who may have been trying to revenge his grandson after Bullet got him arrested for stealing cars. The consensus seemed to be that if it wasn't the kid who'd been charged that killed him, it was most likely Soper and/or Rankin, or some stranger who Bullet happened to tick off. After an hour, they headed back out.

"Will you take me to The Conversation so I can see Soper and Rankin?" Gene asked. "Because if you won't, I have to find another ride. But either way, I'm going now."

"Okay," JP said as they climbed into his truck. "I'll take you there, but only to talk to them. "Don't go all Elvis on me." That's what they called it when someone punched first and asked questions later. Their father, Elvis Torn, was known for that when they were kids. He'd done the same with them when they got in trouble. They often got their punishment before they could explain what happened.

"Dad knows how to kick ass and take names," Gene said. "He might have something there."

"Gene, I mean it. Let me handle this."

"Sure, why not?"

When they arrived at the bar, JP said, "Why don't I go in and see if they're here. Maybe I can get them to come outside and talk to us."

"Good idea."

JP wasn't sure he could trust Gene to wait, but he didn't want him starting anything inside either. JP was nearly to the front door when he saw two men walking across the parking lot toward his pickup. It was Soper and Rankin. JP turned and hurried in their direction. When he was within ten feet, Gene jumped out of the truck and started punching, first Soper, then Rankin.

"Dammit, Gene!" JP shouted. Soper abruptly turned and swung at him, landing a blow to his chin. JP was stunned, but regained his footing quickly and threw punches at Soper, first in the face, then to the gut. Soper kept swinging, but he was intoxicated and not stable on his feet.

Gene had Rankin on the ground and was slamming him with punches to his face and upper body. After a minute, Gene jumped up. "Need help, little brother?"

JP grabbed Soper by the arm, swung him around, and threw him against the back of the car parked next to his truck. He patted him down to make sure he wasn't packing a gun. "I got this."

"I bet they'll talk now," Gene said.

JP turned just in time to see Rankin get up and come at Gene. JP yelled, "Behind you."

Gene spun around, ducking down as he did, and Rankin swung at air. Gene hit him hard in the gut. When Rankin doubled over from the blow, Gene kneed him in the chin, knocking him backward. Gene stepped forward and threw a left hook that landed squarely on Rankin's jaw, sending him to the pavement. Gene's boot came down hard on his triceps.

"What the hell is your beef with me?" Rankin mumbled.

"I have a few questions," Gene said. "Let's start with who shot Bullet."

"How the hell should I know?"

"I'm convinced it was one of you two, just not sure which one." Gene removed his foot from the thug's arm. "Get up. Maybe it'll help clear your brain."

Rankin stood, turned his back as if he intended to step away, then spun and punched Gene with a drunken blow. Gene shoved him against the tailgate of JP's truck. Then he grabbed him by the throat and pressed him hard against the metal.

"You just don't know when to stop, do you?" Gene said.

"I think you poked the bear," JP said.

"The bear better start talking before I shoot the bear." Gene loosened his grip.

"I don't know who killed Bullet," Rankin grumbled. "It was probably that kid of yours. He hated him."

"Everybody hated Bullet, including you. He treated you both like crap, and you just took it. Which tells me he had something on you. Did you decide to cut the ties?"

"Bullet didn't control me."

Gene let go of Rankin and stepped back, still not taking his eye off him. He moved toward Soper. JP backed up. "So much for letting me do the talking."

Gene's face was within six inches of Soper's. He spoke softly. "Who killed Bullet?"

"I don't know."

"Wrong answer," Gene said loudly and grabbed his collar.

"I...I don't know. I thought it was Conner like everyone else."

His brother pulled his arm back with a doubled fist.

"Gene!" JP yelled. "Let me talk to him."

Gene lowered his arm and let loose of Soper's collar. JP moved in as Gene stepped aside. Even though JP was still mad at Gene for starting this ruckus, for a second, JP enjoyed the "good cop, bad cop" routine with his older brother. They hadn't done it since they were little kids, and even then, it was mostly Gene protecting him. Now he felt like he had to protect Gene. But JP didn't know how far Gene would go with this. He still wasn't sure it wasn't all a big game to him. Maybe this was just a show to cover what Gene had himself done.

"Did you kill Bullet?"

"No," Soper said.

"Was it Rankin?" JP asked.

"I don't know."

"What do you mean, you don't know?" Rankin yelled.

"I wasn't with you every minute. I don't know. I just know I didn't do it."

"You ass," Rankin mumbled. "You had more reason to kill him than I did. At least I wasn't lusting after his girlfriend."

"What do you mean?" JP turned to Rankin.

"Nothin'."

JP spun back to Soper. "Is he talking about Muriel?"

"I guess."

"What does he mean?" JP asked.

"Muriel's a nice lady, and I didn't like the way Bullet treated her. That's all."

"Enough to kill him?"

"No," Soper said, shaking his head and wrinkling his brow.

"Did you know there was a gun in the house?" JP asked.

Soper hesitated for a second. "Everyone knew the gun was there. Roxy always wanted everyone to know how tough her husband was. She bragged about it."

"What did she say?" JP asked.

"She said Gene had a gun, a snub nose. She said he was always a tough guy. She didn't know for sure what happened, but she was convinced that Gene killed someone with that gun when he was just a kid."

Gene pounded his fist on the side of the truck.

"Take it easy," JP said. "I don't need any more dents." He turned back to Soper. "Did you ever see the gun?"

"Yeah, just before Gene came back. Roxy brought the box out, opened it up, and took out the gun."

"What kind of box was it in?"

"Just an old shoe box, pretty beat up. It had rubber bands around it, but most of those broke when she started to take them off."

"What did she do with it?"

"She showed it to us, then put it back in the box. Andy wanted to buy the gun from her, but she said she couldn't sell it because Gene would be furious."

"Was that the only time you saw it?"

"Yeah, but she talked about it sometimes. I figured Gene was carrying it when he was home."

"Did you ever *see* Gene with the gun?"

"No, I just figured he'd have it on him."

"Did you ever see anyone else with the gun besides Roxy?"

"No," Soper said, but not before he flinched slightly.

Chapter 37

Sabre and JP sat in the back of the courtroom as Morgan's case was called. Bob was at the counsel table. Next to him sat Roxy and her attorney, Richard Wagner.

"I understand the mother is going to enter a plea," Judge Hekman said. "Is that correct, Mr. Wagner?"

"That's correct, Your Honor." Wagner stood up. "She's accepting jurisdiction, but would like to set disposition over to another date."

"Will it be contested?"

"Possibly."

"Are you asking for a trial date?"

"No, Your Honor. We have reason to believe the case may settle before then, but I can't be certain. My client is already involved in parenting classes and is waiting for the social worker to set up therapy for her. Her household has changed considerably. With Bullet gone, his friends left as well. The father and his buddies are no longer at the house, and Conner is in custody. The only people remaining in the home are my client and her mother."

The judge looked at County Counsel Linda Farris. "Has the mother been visiting Morgan?"

"There have been two visits arranged for her. She appeared for both, but she was late for the Sunday one and missed half the visit."

"Was it set too early? Or was she in church?"

"It was at noon, Your Honor, and the mother overslept."

Hekman looked at Roxy. "Is that correct, ma'am?"

"Yeah, but I had trouble sleeping that night. I had a migraine, and every time I'd get to sleep, the neighbor's dogs started barking. It was morning before I finally got to sleep."

Judge Hekman shook her head and addressed Wagner, her attorney. "Counselor, make sure your client understands the importance of visiting her daughter—and on time."

"Yes, Your Honor."

The judge heard the plea and set the case for a dispositional hearing to decide where Morgan would be placed. JP had already agreed to keep her if she wasn't returned to her mother. He didn't want her placed into foster care, but that would all be decided at disposition. In the meantime, the temporary orders were to leave Morgan with him. He was used to having her around, and for the first time, he realized how hard it would be when she left.

"What are you going to do now?" Sabre interrupted his thoughts.

"Gene's meeting me at home to hopefully narrow the suspect list. Unless you need me to go to Conner's 707 hearing."

"There's nothing to be gained by that. Your time is better spent finding out who really killed Bullet."

"What are your chances of getting him tried as a minor?"

"I don't know. I've got some good arguments. There's new legislation that isn't in effect yet, but it might help. And frankly, Conner getting beat up without provocation just might put us over the top."

"They don't know why that inmate started pounding on him?"

"No idea. Conner didn't even know him. Maybe it was a gang initiation thing. The boy is a gang member. His father's in Donovan, and he's a gang member too. Who knows why boys do what they do, and nobody's talking."

~~~

Before Gene arrived, JP did a little investigation into Calvin Greene, the gang member who beat up Conner in the Hall. He was not surprised at what he found. He wrote the list of suspects on his whiteboard, then sat back and studied them. When Gene knocked, JP answered the door.

"Come on in. I just finished the suspect list. I'm hoping we can narrow it down."

"Okay."

"You know Conner has his 707 hearing today?"

"That's right," Gene said. "Do you think he'll win it?"

"They're tough, but Sabre thinks they have a chance."

"I hope so. He'll never survive in real prison. He's too much like his Grandma Delilah."

"She was a good lady," JP said softly, then quickly changed the subject. "Do you know a guy named Otis Greene?"

Gene looked JP straight in the eye. "Maybe."

"What kind of debt did you get repaid?"

"I don't know what you're talking about."

"Don't BS me. Otis Greene has a son named Calvin, the kid who attacked Conner. It must've been a doozy of a debt for him to put his son in jeopardy to repay it. You had Conner beat up, didn't you?"

"I did what I had to do."

"You're crazy. It could've backfired and got Conner in more trouble."

"You told me he had to look weak or vulnerable. I knew exactly what Conner would do. He's not a fighter."

"Is this how you justify what you did? If he serves time as a minor for your crime, you don't have to feel so guilty?"

Gene clenched his fist but didn't say anything for a few seconds. When he spoke it was in a calm, soft voice. "How about if we figure this out so you can stop blaming me?"

JP considered calling Sabre to tell her what Gene had done, but decided against it, afraid it might hinder her at the 707. He sat down at his desk and looked at the list of names on the whiteboard. Gene sat on the sofa doing the same. Neither of them too happy with the other. JP had written every possible suspect on the board:

Gene

Conner

Judd Soper

Andy Rankin

Donna Pinnick

The Professor

Dean

Lucky Len

Roxy

Muriel

Derek Bloome

Ginny Bloome

Ben

EmilyMorgan

"Nice list, Jackie, but why is my name at the top?"

"Because you're still my number one suspect."

"So, they *are* in order? I'll tell you again, I didn't do it." Gene pounded the arm of the sofa. "Why would I be helping you find the killer if I already knew who it was?"

"Oh, I don't know, maybe to throw me off your trail, so you can pin it on someone else? That stunt you pulled last night was a prime example. I doubt we'll get anything more out of those two clowns."

"I'll get something out of them if you let me," Gene muttered. His voice grew louder and more disturbed. "You still have Conner at the top. So he's your second choice?"

"No, but I need to leave him there because the evidence is against him."

"I just don't want you wasting time looking at us when you could be finding the killer."

JP stared at Gene. "I don't believe you've been completely forthright with me. What I don't know is whether you're covering for yourself or for Conner." JP shook his head. "I wouldn't have you around, helping me, if I didn't really need your insight on some of these suspects."

"I wouldn't be here if my son wasn't in the Hall, so I guess I need you too. Let's figure this out, then we can go back to being estranged brothers again."

JP strode up to the whiteboard and crossed out Lucky Len. "I think it's safe to cross him off since he has an alibi."

"Why is Morgan on the list?" Gene asked.

"She had access to the gun and reason to hate Bullet. Although she's very resourceful, by all accounts, she was never at the scene of the crime." JP crossed Morgan off, then Dean too. "I think we can stop wasting time with him. From all we've learned, he's unlikely."

"You still have a pretty long list."

"Now that we know Roxy showed the gun to Soper and Rankin, the suspect list could include anyone that has ever been in the house, making this list meaningless." JP stood back, looked at the whiteboard again, then turned to Gene. "Unless you have a better idea, it's all we have to work with. We need to whittle away at it, until we get it narrowed down." He crossed off Emily and Ben. "From what Sabre discovered, those two are unlikely."

"I'll see what I can find out about Donna and the Professor," Gene said. "Maybe we can get them off the list."

"Just stay away from Soper and Rankin. I'll deal with them."

"Whatever you say, little brother."

"I mean it, Gene. You'll end up back in prison, or worse—dead."

"I'll be back in prison soon enough anyway."

"You're so damn pig-headed."

"We're both from the same gene pool," his brother said. He pointed to the whiteboard. "You can take Ginny off. She has no motive. She didn't even know Bullet. The only reason I was staying at her house is because she was doing a favor for her brother."

JP crossed Ginny off the list.

"While you're at it, you might as well take Derek off," Gene added. "I'm not saying he wouldn't kill Bullet, he probably could have. But there is no way he would let Conner go down for it."

"Why not?"

"Because he likes the kid. Besides, he owes me big time. I saved his life, not once, but twice."

"Which is a good reason why he may have killed Bullet as a favor to you. Or to protect you if you were involved. I think I'll leave him on the list for now."

"Whatever you may think, Derek knows I love my son more than my own life."

JP looked into his brother's eyes, trying to see the good behind them, but all he saw was their father. Gene resembled Elvis a little too much, not only physically, but personally too. JP couldn't get past it. "I wish I could believe that."

Chapter 38

When Sabre walked into the delinquency courtroom for Conner's hearing, the bailiff said, "Good morning, Ms. Brown. I'll get your client."

A few minutes later, the bailiff seated Conner next to Sabre at the defense table. He had a black eye, cut lip, and swollen face. Deputy District Attorney Benson sat to their left with the probation officer. Judge Gerald Feldman took the bench. When Feldman looked at Conner and studied his injuries, Sabre saw a moment of empathy pass across the judge's face. Then he glanced at Conner's arm in the sling. "Is it broken?"

"No, Your Honor," Sabre said, "but his shoulder was dislocated."

The judge's face tightened. He was obviously not pleased with what had happened. "Are you ready, counselors?"

DDA Benson and Sabre both stated their readiness. Benson had initiated the fitness hearing. She alleged that the minor was at least fourteen years old and was charged with murder, an offense covered by Section 707 (b) of the Welfare and Institutions Code.

"Although Conner Torn is only fifteen years old, he's charged with the heinous crime of murder," Benson began. "The evidence will show that Torn would not be amenable to the care, treatment, and training available through the juvenile facilities, based on the following criteria:

"Number one is the degree of criminal sophistication exhibited by Torn. He planned a very sophisticated crime. He was filled with rage, talked about killing him, then followed his victim and shot him.

"Second, the defendant would not have the time to be rehabilitated before the expiration of the juvenile jurisdiction if he were tried as a minor. We will present evidence through expert testimony to those criteria.

"Third, it is true that Torn has no previous delinquent history that we have been able to determine. However, the crime was premeditated and committed with no remorse.

"The fourth criterion is to show that previous attempts by the court to rehabilitate the defendant have been unsuccessful. However, since there have been no previous crimes for which he was convicted, there have been no attempts to rehabilitate.

"Which leads us to the fifth criterion, the circumstances and gravity of the alleged offense. It doesn't get graver than murder. And in order for this crime to have been executed, it would have taken very careful planning."

"Thank you, Ms. Benson," Judge Feldman said before the DDA could continue. "Now that we're all aware of the requirements for a fitness hearing, let's proceed. Please call your first witness."

"Of course, Your Honor," Benson said. "I would like to call Marcia Woolard."

A woman—about fifty-five with short blonde hair and oval glasses—took the stand, and the clerk swore her in.

"What is your profession, Ms. Woolard?" Benson asked.

"I'm a San Diego County probation officer, and I work with juveniles. Conner Torn is one of the minors on my caseload."

"Where did you receive your training?"

"We'll stipulate as to Ms. Woolard's training, Your Honor," Sabre said.

"Ms. Benson?" The judge looked over at the DDA.

"So stipulated." Benson turned to her witness. "How much experience do you have as a probation officer?"

"I worked with adults for five years, and for the past twenty-two, I've been working as a PO in juvenile court."

"And in that time, how many investigations have you done?"

"Over a thousand."

"Have you specialized in any particular area?"

"Homicide."

Sabre started to tune out. She wasn't going to question the PO's ability or her experience since neither was an issue. Woolard continued to testify, and Benson entered the probationary report into evidence.

"I stipulate to the report, Your Honor," Sabre said. "As long as it's not submitted for the truth of the matter asserted."

Benson turned to her witness. "In your opinion, did this homicide appear to be planned in advance?"

"The victim, Carroll Hall, was badly beaten, then shot and left by the roadside to die. Perhaps it was a fight initially, or an act of passion, but at some point the suspect had to make decisions. Also, it appeared that Conner had to have followed or chased Hall to the hillside where he was shot."

In her attempt to prove Conner's unfitness for juvenile court, Benson continued to question Woolard to show that a homicide had been committed and that it took careful planning.

After a few more minutes, Sabre stood and began her cross-examination. "Carroll Hall had the street name of Bullet, correct?"

"Correct."

"And that name was used throughout the report?"

"Yes, that's correct."

"Bullet was a fairly large man, correct?"

"Yes."

"According to the report, he was about five-eleven, weighed two-hundred and twenty pounds, and was very muscular, correct?"

"Yes."

"And Conner Torn is about the same height, but nearly a hundred pounds lighter, right?"

"I don't know his weight," Woolard said.

"Would you say he is thin, Ms. Woolard?"

"Yes, he's thin."

"Objection," the DDA said. "It appears that Ms. Brown is trying to fight the merits of the case and the factual issues, which should be left for the trial."

"Your Honor," Sabre objected, "the prosecutor is attempting to show what a sophisticated criminal my client is, which is irrelevant if my client isn't physically capable of committing the crime."

"He is physically capable of shooting the gun," Benson argued.

"Which, in and of itself, does not show planning or criminal sophistication."

The judge raised his hand in a motion to stop. "I got your point, Ms. Brown. Let's move on."

Sabre turned to the witness. "You testified that Bullet was beat up and then shot, correct?"

"That's correct."

"Was there anything in the reports that indicates that the beating and the gunshot were done by the same person?"

"No."

"Did Conner have marks on him when he was arrested to make you believe he may have been in an altercation?

"No, but it was almost a week later when he was arrested. He could have healed by then."

Sabre could have expounded on the size difference and the damage Bullet would have done to someone Conner's size, but she had made her point to the judge. That's all she needed to do here. She moved on. "Conner has no criminal record, correct?"

"Not that I was able to find," Woolard said.

"And you've done a thorough investigation, correct?"

"Yes, of course, but he has lived in other states, which sometimes takes a little longer to find."

"How old is Conner?"

"Fifteen."

"And he has lived in California for just over four years, correct?"

"That's correct."

"So, you haven't found any convictions since he was ten or eleven years old, right?"

"That's right."

"And he has no arrests in California, correct?"

"Correct."

"Are you aware of any other crimes that Conner has either planned or committed?"

"No."

"And he has never received a referral for misconduct in school, correct?"

"That's correct."

"And he gets average or better grades?"

"About average."

"Does Conner have any record of fighting in school?" Sabre asked, changing tactics.

"No."

"Any history of violence of any kind?"

"Not that I'm aware of."

"Can you tell the court what happened to cause Conner's present injuries?"

Woolard glanced at her report, then up at Sabre. "There was an altercation in the Hall with another inmate."

"When you say 'altercation,' do you mean a fight or an attack?"

Woolard hesitated. "It was more like an attack on Conner."

"Where did the attack happen?"

"In the hallway on the way back from lunch. Calvin Greene, another inmate, came up alongside Conner, called him by name, and when Conner turned, Greene punched him in the face."

"Did Conner fight back?"

"No."

"In fact, Conner raised his arms and put his hands out, palms open, in an attempt to protect himself, is that correct?"

"Yes, that's correct."

"Did Greene stop after one punch?"

"No, he slammed Conner against the wall and hit him twice more before the probation officers were able to break it up."

"Did Conner get punished for this *altercation*?"

"The Hall has a zero tolerance for fights."

"So, that's a *yes*?"

"Yes."

"But Conner didn't fight, correct?"

"That's correct, but both boys were put on room confinement."

"And while on room confinement, they're not allowed out of the cell for education or programming, correct?"

"That's correct."

"Ms. Woolard, did Conner's behavior in the *altercation* show criminal sophistication?"

Woolard shifted in her seat. "No, but it doesn't mean he couldn't shoot a gun."

Sabre continued questioning for another thirty minutes, and when she made her argument, she used the incident to show that Conner was not a hardened youth. She also pointed out all his good behaviors and argued that he was too young. "Your Honor, I understand that the present law is set at the age of fourteen to be considered for adult court.

But as I'm sure the court is aware, there is a bill before the Assembly right now, SB 1391, attempting to change that age to sixteen. In all likelihood, it will pass in the next few months."

"Your Honor," DDA Benson said, "that's all well and good, but that is not the law today. The court needs to follow the law that is presently in effect."

Sabre was going to argue, but before she could say anything, the judge spoke. "I'm well aware of the law, Ms. Benson, and my duty to abide by it."

"Since the present law gives this court the discretion," Sabre said, "I would ask that you consider why the legislature is proposing the change, primarily the issues pertaining to the ability of these young minds to rehabilitate and their decision-making process at this age. I have submitted the arguments with my pleadings."

"Thank you, counselor," the judge said. "Anything further?"

Benson made one last argument to have Conner tried as an adult.

Sabre felt reasonably good about the way the hearing progressed. The prosecution didn't have any real compelling evidence to show her client was unfit for juvenile court, but the burden was on her to prove that he was, in fact, fit. It was a difficult burden to meet, particularly with a crime such as murder. Sabre just hoped she had done enough.

Judge Feldman said, "Thank you, counselors. I'll take this under advisement and let you know when I've made my decision. This court is adjourned."

Chapter 39

JP was about to go see Derek Bloome when his cell rang.

It was Gene. "You can take Donna and the Professor off the list."

"Why's that?" JP asked.

"Trust me, they didn't do it."

"That's just it, Gene. I don't trust you."

"They didn't do it. They both have alibis."

"Where were they?"

"I checked out both of them, and they couldn't have done it."

JP rolled his eyes and left them on the list.

"You're not taking them off, are you?"

"Not unless you tell me why."

Gene sighed. "They were together, and the Professor had a heart attack. Donna took him to the hospital and stayed with him. When the Professor's wife got there, Donna left, but that was long after Bullet was killed."

"Why didn't you just tell me that?"

"Because it's more fun yanking your chain."

"You're so annoying you could make a bishop kick in a stained-glass window." JP shook his head even though Gene couldn't see him. "What are you doing next?"

"I have a few other things to check on. They may take a while."

"Where are you?"

"I'm out gathering information."

That was vague. "I wish you would tell me where you are in case something goes wrong."

"Nothin's gonna go wrong."

"Gene, stay away from Soper and—"

"Sorry, bad connection." The phone went dead.

JP was anxious to solve the case and get Gene out of his hair. It was bad enough that he couldn't find who killed Bullet, but he had to babysit his brother and parent his niece. He kind of liked taking care of Morgan, but Gene? He'd had enough.

~~~

Ron Brown sat watching the apartment where Judd Soper lived. The lights were on and the front curtain was open. Ron could see a football game playing on the large-screen television. Every once in a while, Soper would come into view and watch a few minutes of the game. After a fifteen-minute lull, Soper came into the room, carrying a plate of food. He sat down with his back to Ron, eating and watching the game.

Ron kept thinking about Addie, a policewoman he'd met on a case Sabre was involved in. He had finally worked up the nerve to ask her out, and she'd said yes. It had been difficult to find a time that worked for both of them, but the date was all set for that night. When JP called earlier and asked for his help, Ron had been tempted to say no, but he needed the work and JP needed help. Right now, he regretted the decision. Addie seemed to understand when he'd told her, but he didn't want this thing to end before it even started.

After an hour, Soper shut off his television, stood up, and left the room. A few minutes later, he walked out the front door toward his pickup, which was parked a few cars away. Ron tailed Soper all the way to The Conversation.

Such a creature of habit, Ron thought as Soper parked and walked into the bar. Ron followed. He had an advantage on Soper because they had never met. He could watch him without Soper knowing. JP had been adamant about not getting too close to either him or Rankin for fear of what they might do.

Soper took a seat with Rankin and two other guys. The table was about ten feet from the bar, so Ron parked himself on a barstool and ordered a beer. He had a good view of Soper and Rankin, but he couldn't hear anything that was said. JP had also given strict orders to not get too close to either man. He sat nursing his beer as the thugs powered down two bottles each.

Rankin answered a cell call, then said something to the other men, and walked toward the front door. Two minutes later, Soper guzzled the rest of his beer and did the same. Ron was suspicious about why they didn't leave together, but he followed them out anyway.

Ron was careful when he opened the exterior door, looking around for anyone who might be lurking. No one was there. He couldn't see either Soper or Rankin, but Rankin's truck was still in its parking spot. Worried, Ron hurried to his car, still glancing around. Just before he reached it, Rankin stepped out from behind a van and punched Ron in the face. He fell backward and hit his head on the pavement. Rankin kicked him in the leg.

"Stay away from me, punk."

Ron scrambled to get up, and Rankin's heavy boot came at him again. This time in the shoulder. Ron yelped with pain. His eye was already swelling shut and his head hurt, but he tried to stand. When he saw Rankin come at him again, he rolled under the van instead. Rankin's foot got him again just before he got fully underneath. He scooted toward the middle where he couldn't be reached.

Ron heard someone yell, "Leave him alone." He couldn't see the man, but he recognized the voice. Rankin's footsteps clicked across the pavement, then Ron heard a commotion that sounded like another fight just a few steps away. Ron couldn't see what was going on. He scooted toward the opposite side of the van and looked out. Three men moved across the lot, but he couldn't tell who they were. He heard the sound of an engine, and about a minute later, Rankin's truck drove away.

Ron reached for his cell phone, but it wasn't in his pocket. He looked back under the van, but it was too dark to see. As he scooted back across to the other side where he came in, he felt around but didn't find it. Once out from under the van, he tried to stand up, but he felt dizzy and faint. He stayed on the ground, searching for his phone where the scuffle had started.

There were no lights in this part of the parking lot and little light from the moon. Ron's head throbbed, but he kept feeling around. As he neared a pickup next to the van, he saw a dark spot by the tire. He crawled over and retrieved his phone. It wasn't busted.

Ron called JP. "Rankin just beat me up."

"Where are you?"

"At The Conversation bar."

"Do you want an ambulance?"

"No. I'm a little dizzy, but I won't get up. I'll just lie here until you come." Ron heard JP's truck engine start up.

"I'll be right there. I'm less than five minutes away."

Ron breathed a sigh of relief.

"I'll put you on speaker, and I want you to stay on the line. Okay?"

"Okay."

"Where are you hurt?"

"My head, my leg, my face, my shoulder, my pride."

"Do you think anything is broken?"

"I haven't a clue."

"Are you bleeding?"

"A little."

"Is Rankin still there?"

"No." Ron hesitated. "But JP, I think Gene is with them."

Chapter 40

Sabre and Morgan sat at the table, playing a board game called Four Square. "Gotcha," Morgan said.

"You're pretty good at this," Sabre said.

"I was the champion at home." Morgan grinned.

"Well, champ. I'm afraid it's bedtime."

"But Uncle Johnny isn't home yet."

"He's working late and may not be home for hours. You'll see him in the morning."

Morgan reluctantly stood and walked toward her room.

A few minutes later, Sabre tucked her in. As part of their ritual, Sabre sat on the bed, and they talked about their days. Each one told the other something that happened. There were no rules. It could be a funny story, or something happy or even sad, or maybe just an interesting event. Sabre wasn't sure how it had started, but they had done it every night since Morgan had moved in. It was her turn to go first. Sabre struggled to find something that wasn't depressing or inappropriate to share with a ten-year-old.

"We had a singing telegram at court today," Sabre said. "A man came in with a bunch of balloons and sang to an attorney who was having a birthday. She was really embarrassed."

"Did he give her the balloons?"

"Yes, and a present."

"What was the present?"

"I don't know. She didn't open it in front of us," Sabre said. "Your turn. What do you have to share?"

"Another kid said something about my brother today, but I didn't get in a fight."

"That's a good thing. I'm happy to hear you controlled yourself."

"Sabre," Morgan said, chewing at the side of her lip.

"What is it?"

"Will things ever be like they were?"

"Sweetie, life changes constantly, and things are never the same today as they were yesterday. But even when things seem really bad, they always get better with time."

"Will I ever be back with my family, and will Conner ever be home again?"

"I can't say for sure, but your uncle and I are doing everything we can to get Conner home. Unfortunately, these things take time, and when you're young, it seems even longer. As for going back to your mom—is that what you want?"

"I love my mom, but it's better when Daddy's home. I feel safe when he's there, and I'm not afraid to go to sleep at night."

Sabre let her talk as long as she needed, then kissed her goodnight, and shut off the light. She hated when children felt this kind of grown-up pain, caused by the adults who were supposed to protect them.

Sabre fixed herself a cup of herbal tea and signed into her online dating site. She went straight to her inbox to check her messages, moving through them and eliminating the ones that weren't the right age or height. Then she started to read the profiles of those left. She was getting faster at this, but it was still time-consuming. She was so glad she wasn't doing this for herself, or she would've given up already. She had little patience for this sort of thing.

She read one that made her laugh. She saved it so Bob could see it. It read:

I'm looking for someone to have sex with. If you're still interested after that statement, please read on. I'm in a long-term relationship which I have no intention of ending. It has grown cold, but she's a wonderful woman. If you're looking for someone to have fun with, without any worry of commitment, please message me.

A new message pinged in her inbox. It lacked a photo, so she opened it immediately. It read:

Hello there. You have a lovely smile and a great profile. We seem to have a lot of common interests. I bet you are amazing. I'd like to know you. I'm Bill and do you have kids?

A tingle ran up her spine. A man named Bill who'd asked about her children. He either hadn't read her profile, or he was trying to sound as if he hadn't noticed the kids. Either way, he was a likely candidate. She clicked on his profile and found he was thirty-five years old. Still promising.

His profile description read:

I do not have a photo posted because of my work, which, unfortunately, I cannot disclose here. I travel a lot, often internationally, with my career choice. It's intriguing and rewarding, but it does limit me.

I'm fun, adventurous, physically fit, and my mother says I'm handsome. Let's get together and you can tell me if she's right.

Sabre hit reply and typed:

Hi Bill,

I'm intrigued by your profile. Yes, I have two beautiful girls who are very important to me. So, if you asked that question because you don't want to be around children, then we wouldn't work. However, if you do like children, I'd like to get to know more about you.

Sheila

Sabre decided to stay with the name Sheila even though it wasn't what she'd initially planned.

The rest of the emails held little hope. She checked the matches the computer had generated, then ran a discovery for new matches for herself. The criteria she used was minimal, no photo, age, or height. The search returned pages of matches. She went through about ten and gave up. She had emails to answer for work and reports to read for the next day. She switched to her work inbox and started through those.

About ten o'clock, she closed her mailbox and checked the dating site again. Only one message, and it was from Bill.

I love children and don't have any of my own. How about dinner tomorrow at 7:00 at George's in La Jolla?

Sabre responded:

How about coffee at 1:30 tomorrow afternoon at Starbucks at 4380 Kearny Mesa Road?

Sheila

She waited a few minutes but got no response. Sabre shut down her computer and sat down to watch a movie. She was tired, but she knew she wouldn't be able to sleep. She hoped JP would be home soon.

Chapter 41

JP found Ron sitting against the tire of a pickup truck. "Dang! He did a number on you. Do you think you can stand?"

"I think so."

"Let me help you up, so we can see how bad you are." JP bent down to help him.

"Better come at me from the other side. That shoulder is pretty sore."

JP switched over and put his arm around Ron to brace him. "Are you still dizzy?"

"Things are spinning, just not quite as fast."

"Can you put weight on your leg?"

Ron gingerly shifted his weight. "I don't think it's broken, but I'm sure I'm going to have a bad bruise on my thigh. It's tender as hell."

"Can you walk?"

"I could, if you'd stop the world from moving."

JP helped Ron to his truck. "I'm taking you to the hospital. You may have a concussion, and you need to get that cut stitched up."

"No. I don't like hospitals. And they'll ask a bunch of senseless questions." Ron moved his arm, checking his range. "The arm is good. I don't have anything broken. Please take me to your house."

"Sabre's there, and she'll be mad at both of us for not calling an ambulance. Then she'll make you go to the hospital anyway."

"You have a point. It'll be easier dealing with the hospital than my sister."

On the way, JP called Gene's cell phone and got no answer. That wasn't a surprise, because Gene often didn't answer. But at this point JP didn't know if Gene was in cahoots with Soper and Rankin, or if he was in trouble.

~~~

"What happened?" the young, male doctor asked.

"I came out of a bar and someone didn't like my looks," Ron said. "So they tried to change them."

"He got you pretty good."

"You should see the other guy."

"Did you get in a few punches?"

"Nope, not a scratch on him."

"So, you were mugged?"

"I guess you could say that."

The doctor gave Ron a thorough examination and sent him for x-rays.

While he was gone, JP called Sabre and told her what had happened. "Before you say anything, I know it was stupid, and I won't put him in that position again. He's coherent and has no apparent broken bones. Ron's getting x-rays right now."

Sabre took it better than JP expected her to. "I need to see him, but Morgan's asleep and I can't leave her here alone. Maybe I could get someone to come over and stay with her so I can go to the hospital."

"If that doesn't work, I'll come home." JP hung up and tried Gene's cell again. No answer. He hoped Sabre was able to find a babysitter, so he could go check on Gene. The more he thought about it, the more upset he got at his brother. JP had warned Gene not to approach those guys, but for all he knew, they were working together.

He called Sabre back. "Don't worry about asking anyone to babysit. I'm coming home. You can sit with Ron."

~~~

While Sabre waited in Ron's ER room, she took out her iPad and checked for messages. She had one from Bill that read: *I'd rather do dinner.*

She responded: *I'd rather do coffee.*

When Ron was wheeled back into the room, she closed her tablet.

"JP called you, didn't he?" Ron asked.

"Yes, and I'm glad he did."

"You didn't need to come here. I'm fine."

She looked at his bandaged face. "Yeah, I can see that." The nurse parked Ron in the room, hooked him back up to his monitor, and left.

"They took x-rays and did an MRI on my head. The doctor will be here eventually to tell me the results, but I'm pretty sure I don't have anything broken."

"Are you still dizzy?"

"Not so much."

"What happened? JP only gave me the highlights."

Ron told her the whole story. "And don't blame JP because I got sloppy. He warned me about getting too close, and I blew it."

"Because you're not trained to do this job. He never should've put you on it."

"Sis, please. I'm a big boy. I can make my own mistakes. I've already discussed this with JP, and I'm going to continue. But I plan to get some training."

"I wish you'd just find some other kind of work. I don't need both men in my life risking theirs."

"Yeah, sure. I'll just be a surgeon or an airline pilot. Or, I know, a male stripper. I haven't decided which."

Sabre smiled, then changed the subject. They continued to chat for nearly an hour before the doctor came in.

"Hi, doc," Ron said. "You're still here, I see."

"The important thing is that you are."

"You're a hoot."

"Yeah, my day job is stand-up comedy. I just decided to do this ER thing on the side for fun. I even thought about going to med school, but I don't have the time."

Sabre laughed, a good feeling after a long stressful day.

"Am I going to live?" Ron asked.

"Probably longer than you should," the doctor said. "If your goal is to leave this world, today is not your day." He looked at Ron's chart. "No broken bones, no brain damage, and no brain bleeds. But you'll be sore for a while. You have some pretty nasty bruises, but those will go away in a week or so. If headaches persist more than forty-eight hours, or if you get nauseous, you need to come back in. Your face should heal just fine without stitches. You may want to come up with a good story about how you got the black eye. It could make for interesting conversation."

"Does he need any prescriptions?" Sabre asked.

"Just some Ibuprofen and a self-defense course."

Chapter 42

The next morning, JP called Gene's phone again. No answer. He called Ginny.

"No, I haven't seen him in a couple of days," she said, sounding sleepy. "But that's not unusual."

"I'm sure it's not." JP asked her to let him know if she heard from his brother, then hung up.

Sabre walked into the kitchen. "That coffee smells so good."

"It's leaded. If you drink it, you could fly to work instead of drive. I can make you some decaf."

"I'll drink my tea instead, but thanks." Sabre put water into the tea kettle and turned it on. "Still no word from Gene?"

"No. And I wouldn't think anything of it if Ron wasn't pretty certain it was Gene's voice he heard last night. The problem is, I don't know if he's in trouble or scheming with Soper and Rankin."

"Why would he do that?"

"I don't understand why my brother does most of the things he does. He could be trying to get information out of them, because he thinks one of them killed Bullet. Or he conspired with them to kill Bullet, and he's snowing me. Everywhere I go and everyone I talk to leads me to another dead end. I'm starting to think they're all in on it. One big conspiracy and Conner got caught in the middle."

"If Gene's in trouble, you need to help him."

"I know. He just makes me mad. He's like a dime holdin' up a dollar."

Sabre chuckled. "I don't even know what that means."

"He acts like he's tryin' to help, but he gets in the way more than he helps. It's bad enough trying to figure out this mess, but then I have to worry about him on top of everything else."

Sabre put her arms around his neck and kissed him lightly on the lips. "I wish I could make it all better."

"You already do. I couldn't make it through this without you. You've been incredible the way you've taken care of Morgan."

"You'd do the same for me and my family."

JP pulled her closer and gave her a sweet, long kiss.

"Mushy, mushy," Morgan said, walking into the room.

They all laughed.

"You weren't here to tell me goodnight, Uncle Johnny. If you're going to be a responsible parent, you have to change your game a little," the girl teased.

JP tousled Morgan's hair. "I have a lot to learn about this parenting thing, but I can tell you this, Munchkin. As long as I got a biscuit, you got half."

"Thanks, Uncle Johnny, but I don't like biscuits much. Would you share a donut with me if you had one?"

"You bet. Now, eat your breakfast, so we can get you to school."

"Can you take her this morning?" Sabre asked. "I need to stop by my office and pick up a file before I go to court. I can take her if you're busy, but we'd be a little rushed."

"I can do it." He turned toward Morgan. "That's what a *responsible* parent would do."

~~~

When Sabre met up with Bob at court, she told him about what had happened to Ron.

"Will he be all right?" Bob asked.

"Yes, he's home resting now. I talked to him on the way to court."

"Good. Ron's a nice guy. I'd hate to see anything happen to him."

"I'd never forgive myself if something happened when he was working for me or JP. I wish he'd find some regular work, but he's talking about getting some investigative training."

"If he likes the work, that's not a bad idea. JP knows what he's doing, and he could train him right." Bob motioned to the bench in front of Department 4. "Let's sit. There's a hearing in there right now."

"All my cases are here this morning," she said, sitting down.

Bob joined her. "Any new prospects in your search for the perfect man?"

Sabre scowled. "I found one without a photo, who likes kids, and his name is Bill."

"You think he didn't even change his name?"

"He may have changed his last name, but Bill is pretty common. Why not use it? It might even be his real name."

"Have you communicated with him?"

"We're having coffee today at one-thirty."

Bob's jaw tightened. "Why didn't you tell me?"

"I just did."

"Only because I asked."

"I just got the confirmation this morning, and I planned to tell you. Are you available to be my bodyguard and photographer?"

"I think so." Bob pulled his calendar from his coat pocket and looked at his schedule. "I'll be there. By the way, have you told JP yet?"

"No, but I will."

"When?"

"I don't know. He has a lot on his mind right now. His brother appears to be missing."

"What do you mean by *missing*?"

"He hasn't heard from him since yesterday afternoon."

"He hadn't heard from him for over twenty years before. Why is he in a panic about twenty-four hours or less?"

"Because of what Ron witnessed last night. There was a third guy with those thugs, and he thinks he heard Gene's voice." Sabre touched Bob's arm. "Don't worry. I'll tell JP about the dating site soon."

Chapter 43

"Do you have everything you need?" JP asked.

"I think so," Morgan said.

"Your backpack?"

"Check."

"Your lunch?"

"Check."

"Your homework?"

"I didn't have any."

"You may need a light jacket," JP said. "It's a little chilly out. I'm sure it will warm up, but you might need it this morning."

"I'll get one."

"I need to check something really quick, then I'll be ready."

Morgan went to her room, and JP fired up his computer. He was getting impatient waiting for it to boot up when he spotted Sabre's laptop on the small desk in the corner. He walked over and opened it up. He was pleased to see she hadn't shut it down. This would be a lot quicker than waiting on his slow machine.

He didn't want to close anything she'd left open, in case she needed it later, so he looked at the address windows to find where to click another one. Her computer was set up a little different than his, and he was no expert. He read the tabs for the open sites. The first was Inbox. He knew that was her email. The next one was LexisAdvance.com, which

Sabre had told him was a legal-research site. The last was an online dating site.

More research? He hesitated, then opened it.

A profile was open, displaying a photo of what looked like Sabre in a blonde wig. *What the hell?* He enlarged the photo and confirmed his initial suspicion. He read the profile. Everything was made up, and she claimed to have children. *Why?* He clicked on the Inbox and saw a message from someone named Bill. It read: *I love children and don't have any of my own. How about dinner tomorrow at 7:00 at George's in La Jolla?*

Sabre, who was using the name Sheila, had responded: *How about coffee at 1:30 tomorrow afternoon at Starbucks at 4380 Kearny Mesa Road?*

Bill: *I'd rather do dinner.*

Sheila: *I'd rather do coffee.*

Bill: *Coffee then—at Starbucks.*

JP couldn't get himself to read anything more. He took his notebook out of his pocket and wrote down the time and address. A loud sound emanated from his computer, indicating it had opened. He minimized the dating site on Sabre's laptop, closed it, and walked to his desk in a daze. He was confused, shocked, and hurt. The last thing he expected was for Sabre to cheat on him.

Morgan returned to the room. "I'm ready, Uncle Johnny."

"Huh?"

"I'm ready."

JP stood for a second, paralyzed with anger and frustration. "What's the matter?"

JP shook his head, took a deep breath, and said, "Oh, nothing. Just a little frustrated. It's not about you." He touched Morgan lightly on the top of her head. "Let's go, Munchkin."

The ride to school was quiet. JP tried to engage, but his mind kept going back to the messages on Sabre's computer. He tried to think of all the reasons she might be on a dating site, but he kept coming back to the one that hurt the most. He had always had a jealous streak that was hard to control, but he had been better with Sabre. He had trusted her, and that made this news even harder.

JP stopped the truck in front of the school.

"Are you sure you're okay?" Morgan asked.

He forced a smile. "I'm fine. Just some bothersome work stuff."

After Morgan got out, he decided to go see Soper and Rankin. If he concentrated on finding Gene, he hoped it would get his mind off of Sabre.

His first stop was at Derek Bloome's house. Derek answered the door with sleepy eyes and no shirt. "Is it morning already?"

"It's past morning," JP said.

"Come in. I was about to make coffee. But if it's past morning, maybe I'll have a beer." He walked to the refrigerator. "Want one?"

"No thanks. Have you seen Gene?"

"Not since day before yesterday."

"He may be in trouble."

"Gene's always in trouble. You need to be a little more specific."

JP told him what had happened to Ron. "I'm headed to see Soper and Rankin, but I doubt if they'll tell me anything. Still, I can't just ignore this."

Derek put his beer back in the fridge. "Let me get my shirt. You might need some help."

JP was a little surprised by the offer, but he didn't mind the backup, especially from a guy Derek's size.

"Any idea how to handle these thugs?" JP asked.

"I only do things one way. I ask 'em right out. If I think they're lying, I'll apply a little friendly persuasion. I guess I do it two ways, because sometimes I apply the persuasion first."

"How about if I do the askin', and we hold off on the *persuasion*?"

"It's your party," Derek said.

As they got into JP's truck, he said, "I thought we'd start at Rankin's house."

"He may not be there, but I know where Soper will be."

"How do you know that?"

"He plays poker with some suckers every Wednesday, starting about six in the morning."

"How long do they play?"

"Until Soper takes all their money." Derek looked at his watch. "Which is probably pretty soon now."

"And you know that because...?"

"I used to play too, but I got tired of Soper's cheating. The thing is, he didn't need to cheat. They're all such bad players, he could win anyway. Some of those old guys are pretty decent folks, but they sure can't play poker. One guy is nearly blind, can barely see his cards, but he still plays. Soper don't care. He'll take advantage of anyone."

"Lead the way," JP said.

They arrived at the poker-game house just as Soper was leaving. JP stopped his truck in front, and they both climbed out. Soper was walking toward them. He moved past a red Ford Focus parked in the driveway. Derek's gait was a little faster than JP's, putting him a step ahead. Driven by anger at Sabre and concern about his brother, JP picked up his pace and passed Derek. He stepped up to Soper and without any warning punched him in the face knocking him back against the parked car, stunned and dazed. JP hit him again before the thug could get his balance and strike back. JP then grabbed Soper's shirt with his right hand. As he pulled him towards him, he used his left hand to grab the back of his left shoulder and spun him around. JP wrapped his right arm around Soper's neck and used his left hand to assist in applying pressure in a cop's restraining hold. Quickly JP jammed his hand in the small of Soper's back, and took a small step back, leaving Soper's feet in place and keeping him off balance.

Soper tried to pull JP's arm down away from his neck. He tried to kick, but was too far off balance. Soper turned his head in an attempt to relieve the pressure and squirmed to get away. JP applied a little more pressure, gaining complete control, and then directed Derek to check him for weapons.

It all happened so fast, Derek was shocked, but he did what he was told. "Nothing there."

"Where's Gene?" JP asked Soper.

"I don't know."

JP tightened his hold once again. Soper's hands were still on JP's arm and he made one more attempt to loosen his grip, but he had less leverage and strength. When he gave up, JP let up a little, trying to keep himself in check because he realized his anger was getting the best of him.

"He can't talk if he's dead," Derek said calmly.

"He soon will be if he doesn't start talkin'," JP said, and gave him another squeeze.

"Okay," Soper muttered.

JP loosened his hold slightly. Soper tried to pull away, so JP tightened it again.

"You're not too smart, are you?" JP said. "In a few seconds you'll be unconscious. Your choice."

"Okay, okay," Soper gasped.

"What have you done with Gene?"

"He's with Andy."

"Where?"

"I don't know."

"Why is Gene with him?" JP was frustrated that he still didn't know whether Gene was a captive or a willing participant.

"Andy is tired of all the snooping around you two are doing."

"Why? Because he killed Bullet?"

"No." Soper said. "I don't know. He might have, but he just doesn't like people in his business."

JP gave Soper another neck squeeze. "That's not good enough. Tell me where they are, and I'll ask him myself."

"I told you, I don't know."

JP squeezed again for just a second. He knew the limits on the hold. It wouldn't take but a few more seconds for the man to lose consciousness. Soper gasped. "Okay, okay. They're in a round-the-clock poker game."

"What does that mean?"

"They tag in and out."

"Right," JP said. "And I'm the King of Denmark."

"It's true," Soper said.

"You expect me to believe Gene is playing cards with Andy? He doesn't even like the guy. He sure as hell isn't going to tag team with him in a card game." As JP said it, he wondered if it was true. He didn't really know Gene or what he might be doing. For all he knew, Gene could have killed Bullet and was letting his son take the rap. JP was afraid to trust him.

Soper insisted he was telling the truth and tried to explain where the guys were. But it didn't make a lot of sense, and JP knew Soper would call and warn Andy if they let him go.

"How about if you just take us there?" JP said.

Soper acquiesced. JP turned to Derek. "Can you take care of him?"

"Give me a second."

Derek walked toward Soper's truck, which was parked on the street nearby. He opened the tailgate, climbed into the bed, and searched through the junk until he found a piece of rope. When he returned, JP let go of Soper's neck and pulled the man's arms behind his back for Derek to tie up.

"Do you know how to do it?" JP asked

A split second later, Derek was done. "I roped a few calves back in the day."

As they walked to JP's truck, Derek mumbled, "So much for askin' questions first."

"You can't get lard unless you boil the hog."

"And I thought your brother was the bad ass."

"We both had a good example to follow," JP said, thinking about his father.

Chapter 44

Sabre had chosen the same Starbucks where she'd met the first online dating guy. The setup was good, because Bob could sit inside and see everything that went on without Bill knowing he was being watched. Bob could also get photos without being obvious. She and Bob rode together, parked far enough away, and walked up separately, in case her date got there early.

Sabre went into the coffee shop first and stood in line. Bob came in and waited for someone to get between them, then stepped into the line. Sabre ordered a sugar-free hazelnut mocha breve decaf. It was colder outside than it had been in a while and the sky was threatening rain, but Sabre liked her spot outside, so she sat there anyway. Using the window as a mirror, she adjusted her blonde wig, then checked her phone for the time. It was 1:18 p.m. Bill wasn't due for another twelve minutes.

She glanced in the window at Bob. He nodded toward the other chair. She moved, giving Bob a better vantage point for photos, assuming that was what he wanted. He casually gave her the thumbs up.

Sabre wrapped her hands around her cup and sipped it slowly. At 1:33, a man meeting the general description of Bill Nesbitt walked up.

"Sheila?" he asked.

"Yes, you must be Bill."

"I am. It's a pleasure to meet you. You're even more beautiful than your photograph."

"And you are definitely more handsome than the silhouette they have posted in place of your picture."

He laughed and sat down.

Sabre picked up her cup to show him she already had coffee and subtly nodded at Bob. "I got here a little early. I've never done this before, and I didn't want to go through that awkward thing about who pays."

He smiled. "First dates are tough."

"Feel free to go get something to drink."

"Actually, I've been drinking coffee all morning. I'm already over-caffeinated."

Sabre watched his demeanor. "You were rather mysterious in your profile about your profession. What is it you actually do?" He appeared smooth and self-confident. This was definitely not his first rodeo.

"I can't say too much, but I gather information and analyze data that helps protect you every day."

"Protects me?"

"Not just you—all Americans. Sometimes it's very dangerous." He paused. "I've already said too much. What do you do?"

"Nothing quite as exciting. I'm a waitress, but more importantly, I'm a mom."

"I remember reading that in your profile. Twin girls, right?"

"Right. They are my pride and joy, and they're so beautiful. I'm trying to get them into showbiz. They've already done a few gigs, some modeling and a little acting. I think they have a real chance to make it big."

"Are they identical?"

"Yes, and they love it. They love playing tricks on people. They think they fool me sometimes, but I can always tell which one is which. But enough about that. What do you like to do in your spare time?"

"I used to play a lot of softball, but work travel keeps me from joining a team."

"I've played a few softball games myself. It's a fun sport."

There was a moment of silence, then Bill asked, "How do you do that?"

"Play softball?"

"No." He laughed. "How do you tell your girls apart?"

"By their mannerisms. The differences are very slight, but I've watched them for seven years now, and I'm probably the only one who can see it."

"How do you know they haven't gotten mixed up somewhere along the way?"

"Because one of my daughters has a small mole behind her ear that even they haven't discovered. I'll tell them someday, but for now, I'd just as soon let them think I'm more clever than they are."

"Good move."

There was a moment of awkward silence, which Sabre quickly filled. She needed to be interesting enough for this guy to want further contact. She hoped his interest in the twins was enough, but she had to be certain. "We can't talk about your work, and mine is boring, so tell me about your family. Do you have siblings?"

"I'm an only child. You?"

"I have one brother. We're pretty close." She gave him a brief description of Ron and some of the antics he'd pulled when they were young. Bill laughed and appeared to be having a good time.

The conversation continued for another fifteen minutes, often leading back to her make-believe twins.

Bill reached across the table and touched Sabre lightly on her hand. "I don't know about you, but I feel a connection. I'd like to see you again." He withdrew. "Would you have dinner with me tonight?"

Sabre smiled. "I'm afraid I can't tonight. The girls have a school thing." She wanted to keep the invitation open, but she needed time to confirm with Laura Standish that this was Bill Nesbitt. "Would tomorrow night work?"

"That would be fine." He smiled. "Is it too soon to ask for your phone number?"

"A little, but why don't you give me yours. When I'm ready, I'll call you. Where would you like to meet tomorrow?"

"Do you like seafood?"

"I love it."

"How about Ironsides on India. Do you know the place?"

"I've never eaten there, but I know where it is, and I've heard good things. Does seven work for you?"

"Perfect." Bill gave her his phone number. As she typed it into her contact list, he said, "I don't blame you for being cautious, but you'll soon find out I'm harmless." He winked and got up to leave. "See you soon."

Sabre waited until he drove off in his white Mazda, before she stood up and went inside.

"Did you get some photos?" she asked Bob.

"I got some good ones."

Sabre told him about the next date and getting his phone number.

"Are you crazy?"

"I'm not going to see him again. I need you to contact Laura and find out if this is the right guy. If he is, I'll give the information to the social worker, and they'll contact the proper authorities. Otherwise, I'll cancel."

Chapter 45

Derek pushed Soper into the backseat of JP's truck and crawled in beside him. JP checked his phone for the time. It was a few minutes after one. He turned to Derek. "I have somewhere I really need to be at one-thirty. It's important. Can I drop you and Soper off at your house? It won't take me long."

Derek frowned and didn't respond.

"It's really important or I wouldn't ask you to wait."

"More important than finding Gene?"

"It feels like it at the moment."

"Okay, but I can't put up with this jerk too long, so you'd better hurry."

~~~

JP parked his truck between two others in the Starbuck's parking lot. He kept his distance, but with his binoculars he could see everything. He hoped Sabre wouldn't show up. His heart pounded when he saw her walk around the corner in a blonde wig. He zoomed in on her face. It was Sabre. She went inside the coffee shop. His first instinct was to protect her; his second was to leave and never look back. He fought both urges and waited, wondering if he should go inside. When he saw Bob enter the store behind her, he felt relief that she wasn't alone. A few minutes later, Sabre walked out and took a seat in front of the big glass window. It wasn't long before he noticed Bob sitting inside where he could see Sabre. JP sighed. *Bob was keeping an eye on her.*

He was glad Bob was there, but his thoughts soon turned to anger at him. *Some friend.* No matter how angry he got at Bob for betraying him, he was still thankful he was there to protect Sabre.

When a man walked up and sat at her table, JP slammed his fist on the steering wheel. He felt no pain in his hand, but he thought his heart would break. He wanted to start his truck and drive away, but he froze. He couldn't get his hand to turn the key. Something kept him there—his need to protect her. He had an overwhelming urge to go punch the guy. Heat burned through his body, and his hand shook when he started to open the door. He pulled it shut.

Maybe it's innocent, he thought. *Maybe I'm overreacting. We've never actually said we were exclusive.* JP shook his head. *Of course, we're exclusive. She knows how jealous I get. Maybe I've been expecting too much. Maybe she needed a break. Now she's practically living with me. I never should've asked her to help me with Morgan. I've been such an idiot. Why would she want me, an old guy? She's so young and beautiful. She could have anyone. I'm such a fool.*

The longer JP sat and watched, the angrier he became, not only at Sabre, but at Bob for knowing what was going on and not telling him. But mostly he was mad at himself for falling so hard and being such an idiot. When the man reached over and touched her hand, JP couldn't take it any longer. He took a deep breath, started his engine, and slowly left the parking lot, hoping not to draw Sabre's attention. Within a few blocks, he was on the 163 highway, headed north, passing everyone. He was nearly to the Poway offramp when he realized he was traveling ninety miles an hour. He slowed down and called Sabre, expecting her voicemail, but instead she answered.

"Hi, baby," she said.

When he heard her voice, he felt sick to his stomach and had to swallow before he could talk. "Where are you?" he asked.

"Bob and I are just leaving Starbucks on Kearny Mesa Rd. Where are you?"

"I have to take care of something with my brother. Can you pick up Morgan from school?"

"Sure."

"I don't know when I'll be home. Is that a problem?" He tried not to sound upset, but he couldn't get himself to say any of the things he would normally tell her. He just wanted off the phone.

"It's fine. I don't have any plans."

"Thanks."

"Be careful."

"Yeah."

JP was already hanging up when he heard, "I miss...."

But he didn't want to hear it. He didn't believe it. He hated asking her to help him right now. He didn't want to ask her for anything ever again, but he couldn't leave Morgan alone and he had to find Gene.

In a fog, he almost passed the turn to Derek's house. JP tried to get his mind off Sabre. But the more he thought about finding Gene, the angrier he became. He couldn't trust his brother. He couldn't trust Sabre, and he couldn't trust what he might do right now. But he had to get it together. He needed Gene to help clear Conner. JP called Derek to let him know he was just a few blocks away. As JP pulled into his driveway, Derek came out of his house with Soper still tied up.

They drove east on I-8. Soper said the place was in Crest, but he didn't know the exact address. Twenty minutes later, they were in the small community of Crest, but it took Soper nearly an hour to find the home where the supposed round-the-clock poker game was being held. The last half-mile was a dirt road, leading to a house that sat all by itself, surrounded by trees. All they could see was a chimney.

"That's it," Soper said, nodding toward the bricks that stood just barely above the tree line.

JP stopped the truck among some trees, where he assumed he couldn't be seen from the house. "I'll walk up there and see what's going on," JP said. "Can you keep an eye on Soper?"

"Sure can," Derek said.

"If I'm not back in ten minutes, come get me."

"What should I do with him?"

"You'll figure something out."

"It's just a poker game," Soper said. "Let's all go."

JP ignored him, got out of the truck, and walked toward the house, staying back far enough that he wouldn't be seen. He snuck up to the side of the house with an open window. He peeked inside and saw a man he didn't recognize asleep on the bed. JP worked his way around to the next window, but the shade was closed and he couldn't see in. He turned the corner and came up the back of the house to the kitchen. No one appeared to be in there, but he could hear voices coming from a room nearby. He listened carefully, trying to discern any familiar voices, but he couldn't. He had to get closer. As he rounded the next corner of the house, he spotted another open window, stepped closer, and looked in. Gene, three other men, and one woman sat around a card table. Beyond them was the front entrance.

Just then there was a knock. Everyone, except Gene and the woman, looked toward the door.

"Who the hell is that?" A portly man reached for his hip. JP assumed he had a gun, but the guy didn't produce it.

"Maybe someone ordered pizza," a thin man with a long beard said.

"There's no cell reception here." The portly man stood and walked to the front, keeping his hand on his hip. He opened the door, and Derek stepped inside.

"What are you doing here?"

"I need to talk to Gene."

"Come back tomorrow. We finish at noon." The man walked to his seat, picked up the cards, and dealt a round of Texas hold 'em. Gene folded and walked out the door with Derek.

JP hurried around to the front. "What the hell are *you* doing here?" Gene asked Derek as JP approached. Gene turned toward him. "I might've known this is your doing."

"The real question is, what are you doing?" JP stepped into Gene's personal space, feeling his neck muscles tighten. "All of a sudden you're buddy-buddy with Rankin?" His voice escalated. "You said you'd help Conner. Instead, you're off playing poker. You *are* your father's son."

JP fought the urge to punch Gene. He could feel his pulse pound and adrenaline rush through his body. He took a step back and turned to walk away.

"You're a real ass, Jackie," Gene said.

JP turned and said the worst thing he could think of. "You're just like him."

In a flash, Gene's fist slammed into JP's nose. They were far enough apart that he didn't get the full impact of the punch, but it was enough. JP tasted blood.

"You shouldn't have done that," Derek said, shaking his head.

JP reacted with a blow to Gene's beer-weighted belly. For a second, the punch seemed to take Gene's breath away. JP hesitated, then followed with a blow to his chin. But Gene had rocked back, and it only grazed him. Gene was quicker than JP gave him credit for. His brother came at him with several quick, snapping punches.

JP had a sensation of increased strength as he swung at Gene, but he felt edgy. His mind flashed back and forth between the times Gene had protected him and the anger that had built up over the years. Then he visualized the strange man talking to Sabre, and he hit Gene again. The second blow felt sluggish, and he knew it as soon as he let loose. Gene grabbed him and threw him to the ground like he had so many times as kids. They struggled, rolling around on the dirt, both exhausted.

JP looked up to see the poker players standing near the house, money changing hands as the spectators placed bets on a winner. JP and Gene lay still for a second.

Derek reached down to help Gene up.

Gene put his right hand up in a dismissive motion. "I'm good." He sat up, as did JP, but neither stood. The crowd returned to the house. The brothers just stared at each other for several seconds. Finally, Gene said, "I think Soper killed Bullet. I was trying to get Rankin to spill."

"Sabre is cheating on me." JP didn't know why he chose to say that, but it just came out. He did know that the fight with his brother was long overdue.

Chapter 46

Sabre picked up Morgan from school and drove to Bob's office. Morgan settled into the conference room and started her homework, while Sabre met with Bob and Laura Standish. Bob had gathered five other photos of men who looked similar to Bill and had them all on the screen with an image he'd taken at the coffee shop.

"I want you to look at some photos and see if you recognize any of these men."

"The cops already showed me hundreds of photos," Laura said. "I found nothing."

"Please give this a shot." Bob turned the computer screen around so it was facing Laura.

Her face lit up. "That's him—the fourth one." She pointed at the photo of Sabre's date. "You found him."

"We did."

"Where is he?"

"We don't know, but we're reporting the information we have, and I'm sure the cops will contact you real soon."

~~~

Still lying on the ground, JP asked Gene, "Do you think you can get Rankin to talk?"

Gene shook his head. "I had already given up on him. I was just hangin' around to finish the poker game. I don't think Rankin has any real loyalty to Soper, so I'm guessing Soper either didn't kill Bullet, or if he did, Rankin doesn't know what happened."

"Maybe it was Rankin."

"I don't think so. He had no real motive."

"But Soper did?"

"According to Rankin, Soper was in love with Muriel. I knew he cared about her, but I had no idea how much. Soper didn't like the way Bullet treated her. That last beating may have been the final straw."

"Does Muriel love Soper?"

"I never saw anything that would confirm that, but what do I know? I didn't know Soper was obsessed either."

The stout poker player with the sidearm came outside. "You gonna finish this game, Gene?"

"Let Rankin handle the rest. It's his stake anyway. I've got to take care of some unfinished business." Gene turned to JP. "Can you give me a lift?"

Derek helped them both to their feet. JP brushed the dirt off his clothes, as he started to walk. He looked at Gene. "If you want to ride in my truck, you need to dust yourself off."

When Gene saw Soper tied to the truck, he asked, "Do you want me to interrogate him?"

"We've already tried," JP said. "He's not talkin'. He's tighter than a tick with lockjaw."

"What are you gonna do with him?"

"I think we'll leave him here," JP said. "He can finish your poker game."

Derek laughed. "They won't let him play. They don't put up with cheaters."

"Untie him and let him loose. He can be Rankin's problem."

When Derek let Soper go, he walked toward the house without saying a word or looking back. The three men got in the truck, and JP drove away.

He didn't want to go home to Sabre, but he didn't feel right leaving Morgan there with her either. His niece wasn't Sabre's responsibility. That was all on him.

"What now?" Gene asked.

JP glanced at his brother. "You look like hell."

"You have more blood on you than I do."

"Yeah, but half of it's yours."

"If it's all right with you, Derek, maybe we can go to your house and clean up."

"You bet. I might even have a few shirts that'll fit you shrimps."

"Good. After that, I think I'll have another talk with Muriel. See if she knows anything more that might help us nail Soper."

"If you don't mind, I'd like to tag along," Gene said. "I'd just as soon not see Roxy, but if we're lucky, she may not be there."

"What if she's having one of her sex parties?"

"You up to kickin' some more ass?"

"If I have to." The truth was, JP wouldn't mind at all. He could use another punching bag right now, and the gym was out of the question.

"Muriel may be more forthcoming with me," Gene said. "We've always had a good relationship."

"You're more than welcome if you think it'll help."

"Bullet didn't usually mess with Muriel when I was around."

"Why's that?"

"Because he was a coward."

"*Anyone* who'd beat up a woman is a coward, but why was he afraid of you?"

"I threatened to kick his ass if he didn't leave her alone."

"And did you?" JP turned to his brother.

"No, but I would've if he hadn't left that morning." Gene looked JP straight in the eyes.

"Dammit, you're lying to me. You're trying too hard to hold my gaze. Remember, I know that trick."

"Okay, I knocked him around a little, but I didn't kill him."

JP still didn't trust Gene completely, but he hoped being around him more would convince him one way or the other. If Gene had killed Bullet, maybe he'd finally tip his hand.

Chapter 47

An hour and a few bandages later, JP and Gene arrived at Muriel's house. Before they went in, JP asked, "Do you think Roxy could've killed Bullet?"

"Hell, no," Gene said.

"You seem pretty certain."

"Roxy is a lot of things, but she's no killer."

"She's the only one who had real access to the gun. She could've put it in Conner's room."

"Why would she?" Gene stared at him. "She had no reason to frame Conner."

"I don't think she would plant it so they would arrest Conner, but she might've thought his room was a good hiding place. Then the cops found it before she could move it."

"What possible motive could she have for killing Bullet?" Gene asked.

"He was naked and trying to hug Morgan for starters." JP bristled at the thought.

"Roxy doesn't think there's anything wrong with being naked or hugging. I doubt that hugging naked would set her off. Besides, I don't think she even knew about it."

"What if she did? And it did set her off?"

"Brother, you're under the mistaken view that Roxy cares about her daughter. Roxy only cares about Roxy. And you give her too much credit for being able to plan the murder. She would've had to actually go somewhere to shoot him. That would take too much effort on her part. Roxy wouldn't bother, not when she could be partying instead."

"Why do you stay with her?"

"For my kids." Gene reached for the door handle.

The contradictions his brother presented baffled JP. Gene couldn't stay out of prison or stop making bad choices, but it appeared he loved his children. If only he could do what was best for them on a regular basis. But maybe he just couldn't. Maybe his need for adventure was stronger than his need to be stable. JP saw so much of their father in Gene.

"Besides," his brother said, "after Conner put a lock on their room, Roxy couldn't get inside. She didn't have a key. Conner wouldn't give her one, because he didn't trust her not to leave it lying around."

"Who had keys?"

"As far as I know, just Conner, Morgan, and..." He didn't finish his thought.

"And you?"

"Yeah, I had one."

JP took a deep breath. "Gene, did you put the gun in Conner's closet?"

"No. I did *not* put the gun in Conner's room. I did *not* kill Bullet. I do *not* know who did. How many times do I have to tell you?"

"Until I believe you."

"When do you suppose that'll be?"

"When I find out the truth."

Gene got out of the truck and slammed the door.

"Hey! Don't take it out on my truck."

They walked up to the front door in silence. Gene knocked, then he opened it and stepped inside.

"Muriel, it's me, Gene."

Muriel nodded at JP but beamed at Gene. She embraced him and said, "Good to see you."

"You too, Muriel. Is Roxy around?"

"I'm afraid not. She'll be out for a while."

"Good," Gene said. JP was convinced he meant it.

They all stood in the entry, and Muriel made no move to invite them to sit. "How's Conner's case coming along?" she finally asked.

"That's what we're here to talk about," JP said.

"I've already told you everything I know."

"Conner's in big trouble," Gene said. "The only thing that can save him is if we find out who really killed Bullet. I don't believe Conner did it, and neither do you."

"You're right. I don't." Muriel's shoulders tightened, and her lips trembled slightly. "Did something happen? Are they trying him as an adult?"

"We don't know yet," JP said.

Muriel sighed. "I want to help, but I don't know what else I can tell you."

JP ignored her comment and asked, "When did Soper leave this house the morning Bullet left?"

"Maybe an hour or so after Bullet. Andy left too."

"Did Soper know Bullet beat you up that morning?"

"Yes. He came into the kitchen to get coffee and saw me cleaning up the bloody mess."

"Tell me exactly what happened. How he reacted. What he said and did."

"He was pretty upset. He pounded his fist into his hand, making a loud popping noise. It startled me. I must've cowered, because he apologized and gave me a hug." She paused as if she had remembered something.

"What is it?"

"He said, 'That's the last time.'"

"Why didn't you tell me this before?"

"I'm sorry. I had totally forgotten it. I was pretty dazed. Bullet had hit me hard and slammed my head against the cabinet." Muriel took a breath. "Besides, I don't think Soper killed him."

"Why's that?"

"Because I asked him right out."

"And he said no?"

"That's right," Muriel said. "He said he didn't do it."

"Why would he admit to killing him?"

"He admitted that he beat Bullet up that morning, but he swore he didn't shoot him."

JP turned to Gene. "Did the two of you do that together?"

Gene put his hands up, palms out. "No. Soper wasn't with me, and Bullet hadn't been touched when I found him."

"How much damage did you do?"

"He was bleeding, and his face was cut up pretty good. He must have been swollen and bruised when Soper got to him."

"Was he still able to walk?"

"I didn't hurt his legs, just his face and head, and a few punches to the gut."

JP couldn't let go of Soper as a suspect. "Maybe when Soper found Bullet and saw he was already beat up, he decided the only way to avenge Muriel was to finish him off."

"Or maybe he just took the credit to look good for her," Gene said.

Muriel's eyes focused on the floor for several seconds.

"Did you know he was in love with you, Muriel?" JP asked.

"I had a hunch, but I never encouraged it. Do you think you can pin it on Soper?"

JP wrinkled his brow and stared at Muriel. "I don't want to *pin it* on anyone. I want to find out who actually killed Bullet so Conner can be cleared. I think you've been around Gene too long. You sound like him."

"I'm with her on this one," Gene said. "They're pinning it on Conner right now. I'd rather it was someone else, innocent or not."

"That's all I meant," Muriel said.

"Yeah, I got your point," JP said. "Maybe we can at least cast reasonable doubt. Neither of them can account for their whereabouts, and both have a motive, but the gun was found with Conner's fingerprints."

"That damn gun," Gene said. "I should've left it where I dumped it forty years ago."

"What will happen to Conner if they convict him?" Muriel asked.

"That depends on which court hears the case," JP said. "We're still waiting on the 707 ruling from the judge."

"He's only fifteen. Surely they'll try him as a minor."

"I'm afraid it's not that simple. Very few fifteen-year-olds are tried as minors for murder. The odds are against him."

Muriel's face turned pale and she looked weak. JP realized she had helped raise the boy, and Conner must be like a son to her. But son or grandson—he was a big part of her life.

Chapter 48

It was nearly seven, and Sabre hadn't heard from JP. She'd left only one message. She knew he was busy and probably wouldn't get back to her for a while, but it didn't keep her from worrying. She had dinner with Morgan, then they watched a movie. When it was over, Sabre said, "It's bedtime."

"But Uncle Johnny isn't home yet."

"I know you like to tell him goodnight, but I don't think he'll be here for a while. Remember, I told you he has to work late sometimes."

"I know, but when he comes home, tell him I said he was neglecting his parental duties."

"I'll do that."

Sabre sat with Morgan on the bed, and they talked about their days. Then she tucked her in and left the room. She called JP again and left a voicemail: "I just put Morgan to bed. I'll wait up for a while, but please call when you can, even if it's late. I know you're probably somewhere that you can't call, but I'm a little concerned. I don't like the riff-raff you're dealing with, and you seemed preoccupied this afternoon when we talked. Please be careful."

~~~

JP entered the house as quietly as he could. Louie ran up to him, wagging his tail. JP got down on one knee and rubbed the dog's face, then scratched his head and neck. "Want out, boy?" he asked softly. Louie wagged his tail faster. JP opened the slider and let him outside, leaving it open so Louie could return when he was done.

Meanwhile, JP got a can of beer out of the refrigerator and popped it open. Then he removed his jeans and slipped on a pair of sweats from the laundry room. Louie ran back inside, and JP closed and locked the door. JP heard something creak. He stood still, hoping it wasn't Sabre getting up. He wasn't ready for any kind of confrontation. After a few seconds with no further noise, he sat and gulped down the beer. Leaving the can on the end table, he stretched out on the sofa, pulling the knitted blanket over him. His mother had made the blanket for him many years ago. For a few seconds he felt her love, but it soon turned to loneliness. He wished he could talk to her again. He could use some motherly love right now. Louie jumped up and laid with his head against JP's feet.

JP tried to sleep, but he kept tossing and turning. Finally, after what seemed like hours of fidgeting, he dozed off.

~~~

He awoke to the light coming in the window and Sabre kissing his cheek.

"Good morning," Sabre said.

Startled, JP jerked at the sound of her voice.

"What's the matter?" Sabre asked. Then she saw his bruised face. "What happened to you?"

"I found my brother."

"And he beat you up?"

"I held my own."

JP sat up slowly. His body ached. Between the pain in his gut, his throbbing nose, and his anger at Sabre, he could barely move. Sabre touched his shoulder, and JP flinched and pulled away.

"Are you okay?"

"I'm fine, just sore."

"Do you think you should go to the doctor?"

"I said I was fine," he snapped.

Sabre took a step back, looking hurt and worried. "I'll make some coffee," she said and left.

JP hobbled to the bathroom, far more sore and stiff than he expected. By the time he took his shower, he had started to limber up. Morgan was still not up when he returned to the living room. Sabre handed him a cup of coffee.

"Thanks," he said softly. "I have to go out, and I'd rather Morgan didn't see my face this way. Can you get her to school?"

"Sure. Do you want some breakfast?"

"I'm not hungry." He gestured with his cup. "This is enough."

"We had a breakthrough on the Standish case yesterday. If you can sit for a minute, I'd like to tell you what happened."

"What's the Standish case?"

"It's not one you're working on, but I'd like to tell you about it."

"I don't really have time." JP stepped back and picked up his jacket. "I have to go. You can tell me later." He walked out the door without kissing her goodbye.

~~~

Sabre stood, dumbfounded and a little angry, but mostly she was concerned for JP. There was obviously something he hadn't shared with her, and she expected it had to do with his brother. It had taken him a long time to share what had happened to them as children, and now he was clamming up again.

Chapter 49

Sabre walked outside to meet Bob when he arrived at juvenile court.

"You look kind of down this morning," Bob said. "Is everything okay, Snookums?"

"I don't know. It's JP."

"Did he freak out when you told him about your date?"

"I didn't have a date, and no, I haven't told him."

"Why not?" Bob asked, talking over her.

"Because I've hardly seen him. He came in late last night and slept on the sofa. He had been in a fight with his brother, I think. This morning, JP hardly said two words to me, then he cleaned up and left."

"Siblings," Bob said. "That's why I try to avoid mine."

"I just don't know what to do for him."

"Probably the best thing is to let him be. He'll work it out."

"Right."

Two men in dark suits walked past Bob and Sabre and entered the courtroom.

"Do you know those guys?" Sabre asked.

"Never seen them before. Probably a couple of hired guns. I hope they're not involved in one of my cases. It's a pain working with lawyers who don't know this system. They get paid big bucks to come here, and we have to lead them around, showing them the ropes. We do all the work, and they get the fat paycheck."

"I didn't mean to get you on your soapbox."

Sabre and Bob watched as the two men showed identification to the bailiff working the metal detector. The bailiff stepped outside and pointed toward Sabre and Bob.

"I think they're looking for you," Sabre said. "What have you done?"

"He didn't point at me," Bob said. "He pointed at you. Do you want to make a break for it? I think we can get away, or at least have a high-speed chase. We could make the six o'clock news." Bob was still rambling when the men approached.

"Are you Attorney Sabre Brown?" the shorter of the two men asked.

"Yes, I am."

The man reached into his jacket pocket and retrieved an ID with his photo. He showed it to Sabre. "I'm Agent Roy Nakai. I'd like to speak to you about a case you're involved in. I was informed we could use an office in the back."

"Sure." Sabre glanced at Bob, rolled her eyes, and walked inside with the two agents.

One of the bailiffs took them to the sergeant's office. Sabre felt nervous, like the first time she'd been called into a judge's chambers.

"What's this about?" she finally asked.

"Have a seat," Nakai said. Sabre sat down and so did he. The other agent remained on his feet. "I understand you represent the Standish children."

"I do. Has something happened?"

"The children are fine. We received a report yesterday that you met with a guy named Bill. He has several aliases, one of them is Nesbitt."

Sabre gave a sigh of relief. "Yes, I had coffee with him."

"Why?"

"Because I thought he might be the same guy who had taken nude photos of my clients."

"Did you realize we had an active investigation going on?"

"I assumed so, but I also have an active juvenile court case that I needed to investigate."

"I understand."

The other agent spoke in a harsher tone. "We recently commenced a sting operation, but so far, he hadn't responded to any of our profiles. You could've interfered with that."

"I'm sorry, but I still have to investigate my case."

"It's not your job to solve crimes."

He was trying to intimidate her, but she didn't back down, even though she realized she'd gone a little too far. "Don't tell me how to do my job, and I won't tell you how to do yours."

Nakai shook his head at the other agent and turned to Sabre. "What's done is done. Apparently, you were appealing enough to the suspect to get a response."

"I guess so, which is kind of creepy." Sabre still wasn't sure what they wanted from her. "Did you catch him?"

"Not yet. We don't have his address. Everything he used on the site was bogus, but we understand you have another date with him for dinner tonight."

"Yeah, but I don't plan to go."

"We would prefer that you did. All you have to do is show up, so he doesn't get spooked. We'll make the arrest. We may even catch him before he sees you. Either way, we don't expect him to be armed or dangerous, but we won't take any chances. You don't need to be afraid."

Sabre wasn't afraid, at least not until he said that. "Of course. I'll be glad to help get him off the streets."

When the agents left, Sabre found Bob and told him what was happening.

"Look at that. My little Snookums is a spy. Can I go?"

"I think you better sit this one out. If they see you hanging around, they're liable to arrest you for stalking me."

Sabre's phone vibrated. She removed it from her pocket and smiled. "It's JP," she said to Bob, then stepped away before answering the phone. "Hi, babe."

"Hi," JP said. Sabre's heart sank. Something was definitely wrong. JP always started his conversations with, "Hey, kid," or something more intimate.

"I've been asking too much of you lately," JP said. "I've been giving it a lot of thought. You don't need to keep staying at my house to help with Morgan. I'm arranging for a babysitter."

"It's not a problem. I have something I need to take care of this evening, but it won't take long. Then I can come over."

"That won't be necessary."

"Yes, it is. I love being with Morgan, and I want to help you when I can. I know this is important to you."

"It's important that I show the court I can handle this parental thing. Isn't that right?"

"It is, but having me help is still handling it."

"Just do your thing. I got it covered." He hung up.

Sabre's shoulders drooped as she walked back to where Bob was sitting on a bench in front of Department One.

"What's wrong?" Bob asked.

"I'm not sure, but I think JP may be breaking up with me."

"No. That doesn't make sense. What did he say?"

Sabre summarized their conversation.

"He's not breaking up with you. But there is something going on, and it seems to be tied up with his brother. Family issues can be very draining. You just need to be supportive and remember that JP is crazy about you. I don't mean to scare you, but he may be pushing you away because he's in some kind of danger."

"I thought about that. But I'd rather he break up with me, than get hurt... or worse." She shuddered at the thought of something bad happening to JP.

Chapter 50

While getting dressed for her encounter with Bill Nesbitt, Sabre realized she was more nervous than if she was going on a real first date. But instead of being excited, she felt nauseous. She was glad she didn't have to actually eat dinner. She wished JP could be there. It would make her feel safer. She picked up the phone to call him, then returned it to the counter. Even if he wanted to join her, which he probably didn't, he'd be too busy.

Sabre squared her shoulders, retrieved her phone, and drove to Ironside Fish & Oyster. She glanced around but didn't see Bill or either of the FBI agents. The restaurant was one large room with lots of tables and a long bar that ran nearly the full length of the room. Rows of light bulbs highlighted the hundreds of bottles on the wall. At the end of the bar was an employee shucking oysters under a sign that read: *Shuck Me, Suck Me, Eat Me Raw*. The modern look, sprinkled with old nautical décor, plus the tall painted warehouse-like ceilings somehow matched the millennial clientele. She chuckled to herself—that was her generation. She fell right in the middle of the group, but she suddenly felt older than her peers, though she wasn't sure why. She shook off her silly thoughts and walked over to the front desk to see if Bill had already signed in.

"May I help you?" the hostess asked.

"I'm meeting someone here. His name is Bill." She realized she didn't have a last name to give. "Party of two."

"Do you have a reservation?"

"No. Maybe. I'm not sure."

"I'll check." The hostess looked at her computer screen. "No reservation." Then she looked at the sheet in front of her. "He hasn't signed in yet. Would you like to be added to the waitlist? It'll be about ten or fifteen minutes."

"That would be fine."

Sabre turned to walk away and nearly bumped into the couple standing behind her. Agent Roy Nakai caught her eye for a split second, then turned away. He was with a woman about ten years younger than him. Sabre wondered if the woman was an agent too. She turned without speaking and walked to an open bench near the entrance.

Sabre found herself fidgeting, so she stood up. She checked her phone for the time. Five minutes had passed. Bill was three minutes late. Sabre walked along the end of the restaurant, looking at the odd things on the wall. She stopped and counted the rows of light bulbs over the bar—five rows of fifteen large bulbs. Then she turned and went back. There wasn't a lot of waiting room, so she stepped outside. Roy Nakai and the woman with him followed. Another eight or ten customers milled around outside waiting for their tables. Sabre checked her phone again—eight minutes late. She wondered if she had been stood up. He couldn't call to tell her he was running late or to cancel because he didn't have her number. She'd just have to wait.

Five minutes later, Bill hurried toward her. "You're still here. I was afraid you might be gone."

"I realized you had no way to contact me, so I thought I'd give you another two minutes." Sabre chuckled, but it sounded stilted. She hoped Bill didn't notice.

He laughed. "I'm glad you thought I was worth the fifteen minutes. Shall we go in?"

"I put your name on the list. They should be calling us anytime now."

"Good. I didn't make a reservation." He looked around. "But I guess I should have. I didn't expect a crowd on a weeknight."

"Bill, party of two," came over the loudspeaker.

"That's us," Sabre said.

As they made their way toward the door, the female agent went first so she was a step ahead of Sabre. Nakai stayed several feet behind them. When they reached the door, the woman turned and said, "Bill Wright...."

Bill's eyes scanned his surroundings as if looking for a way out. He suddenly bolted to his left, nearly knocking Sabre down. Nakai blocked Bill's exit, grabbed his arm, and swung him around, throwing him against the wall.

"You're under arrest for violation of Penal Code Section 311, distributing child pornography."

Sabre wanted to give Bill a good kick in the crotch before she left, but decided against it. He would get his in prison. She walked quickly to her car, got inside, and sighed with relief. She was glad it was over and that she hadn't messed it up. She'd been afraid Bill would detect her nervousness, which was all mixed up with the contempt she had for him. But he must've thought it was first-date jitters. Sabre wanted to vomit at the thought.

She reached for her cell and called JP. He didn't answer.

Chapter 51

After she got to her condo, Sabre tried calling JP again. Still nothing. She wanted to talk to him and tell him about her day, but more importantly, she needed to know he was all right. She missed Morgan and wanted to tell her goodnight, but she had no way to reach her either.

Frustrated, and a little angry, Sabre got in her car and drove to JP's house. His truck was in the driveway and lights were on in the house. She called again, but got no answer. She rang the bell.

JP opened the door. "What are you doing here?"

"I called, but you didn't answer your phone."

"Sorry."

Just then Morgan stepped into the room. She ran up to Sabre and hugged her. "You're home. And just in time to tuck me in."

Sabre looked at JP. "Do you mind?"

"Of course not."

Morgan gave JP a hug. "Goodnight, Uncle Johnny."

"Goodnight, Munchkin."

Sabre followed the girl to her room as she chattered about her day.

"Uncle Johnny said you weren't coming home tonight, but I knew you would."

"I'm afraid I can't stay, but I wanted to tell you goodnight. Now, hop into bed."

"What interesting thing do you have to tell me about your day? You get to go first tonight."

Sabre chose her words carefully. "I was able to help get a real bad man arrested today."

"What did he do wrong?"

"He hurt some little girls, but now he won't be able to do that anymore."

"Did you see him get arrested?"

"Yep. They put handcuffs on him and everything." Sabre didn't want to get into details. "What can you tell me about your day?"

"It wasn't as astounding as yours...."

"Is *astounding* your word for the day?"

"Yes." Morgan giggled. "Did I use it right?"

"Yes, you did. Tell me what happened that wasn't as astounding."

"A fireman and a firewoman came to our school and talked to our class. They told us all kinds of cool things, then they let us get in the big truck and see all the equipment. They even put the siren on for a few seconds."

"Wow! That does sound pretty astounding."

"Yeah, and the fireman is our teacher's husband and he gave her a kiss when he left. Everyone laughed, but he just smiled and waved to us."

"That's quite a story, but it's time to go to sleep."

"Can you please stay the night?"

"I'm sorry, but I can't tonight. I'll see you real soon." Sabre tucked Morgan in the way she liked her to.

"Don't tell Uncle Johnny, but you're better at tucking than he is."

"Did your mom or dad tuck you in at night?"

"Mom never did, but Daddy would sometimes. Mostly Conner did, but when he wasn't home, Grandma would. I miss my dad a lot, and Conner too. Do you think we'll ever be back together again?"

"I don't know, sweetheart. When unusual stuff happens in life, things seldom ever return to the way they once were. But I've found that most of the time they turn out even better in the end. I promise you, I'm doing everything I can to make your life and Conner's better."

Sabre kissed Morgan on the cheek. She hated to leave her, suddenly realizing how attached she had become to this sweet child. She left the room and found JP sitting on the sofa.

He stood up. "I'll walk you out."

Sabre glared at him. "I guess that's your way of saying I need to leave."

"It's late."

"JP, what's going on?"

"Nothing."

"Did I do something wrong?"

"I don't know. Did you?" Before she could answer, he said, "I'm just tired and real sore. I'm frustrated because I don't seem to be making any headway on Conner's case, and I still don't trust my brother. Once trust is broken, it's very difficult to get back."

She had no idea what he was trying to say, except that she wasn't sure he was still talking about his brother. "What can I do to help?"

"Nothing." He took two steps toward the door. "We'll talk tomorrow. Maybe I'll have something on the case by then."

JP walked silently with her to her car, opened the door, and stepped back. "Goodnight," he said, crossing his arms.

Sabre wanted to kiss him and hold him, but his body language told her to back off. She feared reaching out and being rejected. Something was terribly wrong. She got in the car without touching him.

Chapter 52

JP drove Morgan to school in silence. Just as they pulled up to the entrance, Morgan asked, "Are you mad at Sabre?"

JP was a caught off guard. He was fit to be tied, but he wasn't about to tell Morgan that. "Why would you ask?"

"Because she didn't stay with us last night, and I'm pretty sure she wanted to."

JP didn't respond.

"Is she mad at you?"

"I don't think so," JP said, knowing he lacked conviction.

"What did you do, Uncle Johnny? Did you do something stupid?"

"No!" JP said, more emphatically than he intended.

"What happened to you? Your face is still jacked up. Did you get in a fight?"

"It was a work-related accident," JP said with a wink. "Now get off to school. You're about to be late."

JP drove to Derek's house to see Gene. They had to do something that would shed light on Bullet's killer. So far, all they had managed to do was eliminate their suspect list—almost everyone except Gene and Conner. Maybe he couldn't find the killer because he wasn't willing to look in the right direction. Gene seemed to be trying hard to help find the real killer, but JP knew that's exactly what he would do if he was guilty.

Derek was gone when JP arrived. Gene invited him in and offered a cup of coffee.

"No, thanks. I've had my caffeine limit."

"Want a beer?"

JP lifted a single eyebrow. "No, thanks."

JP watched to see if Gene would get one for himself, but he didn't. They sat at the kitchen table, empty-handed. JP felt out of ideas too, so he came back to the most logical one. "I still think Soper killed Bullet, but he continues to deny it."

"Maybe I can convince him," Gene said.

"I don't think so. I had him in a carotid hold, and he didn't give. I could've killed him."

"But he knew you wouldn't. You're not that kind of guy. He might not be sure with me."

"That's not a good idea, Gene."

"I'd rather kill the guy than see my son go down for it."

JP shook his head. "Even if Soper's dead, Conner will still get convicted of shooting Bullet."

"I don't plan to kill him. I just have to convince Soper that I would." Gene stood.

So did JP. "I'm going with you."

"No, I'd better do this one alone."

"How will you get there? You don't have a car."

"Okay, you can drive, but you're waiting outside."

"Don't tell me what to do." JP held back a smile as he followed Gene out.

Soper lived in El Cajon in an area JP wasn't familiar with. Ron had been there and done surveillance on Soper, but this was JP's first time. He drove through an older neighborhood with small houses and manicured front lawns. JP surmised that most of the homes were probably owner-occupied. He wondered if Soper's parents had once lived in the house.

JP turned onto Soper's street. He rolled to the end of the cul-de-sac, turned around, and parked just short of the front yard. The dead-end street was not as well-kept as the surrounding area, and Soper's yard was by far the worst. His house was in dire need of a new paint job too.

When JP parked, he again asked Gene, "You sure you don't want backup?"

"I don't need backup with that punk."

"You don't have a weapon, do you?"

Gene's brow furrowed, then he scoffed. "Don't be silly; that would violate my parole."

"Right, and this isn't."

Gene exited the truck, and JP stayed behind, watching as his brother knocked on the door. When Soper opened it, Gene pushed him inside and slammed the door behind him. JP waited, wondering every few seconds if he should go in. He didn't want Gene to get hurt, but more likely, he didn't want him to kill the guy or do permanent damage. Finally, JP couldn't take it any longer. He opened his door to get out, then spotted Gene casually walking to the truck.

"I see you're still alive," JP said.

"Yep." Gene didn't offer more.

"Did you get anything out of Soper?"

"No."

"Is he still breathing?"

"Just barely. The guy either didn't do it, or he's dumb as a rock for not telling me. I could've ended his miserable life."

"Maybe he knew you wouldn't."

"You think I'm going soft?"

JP shrugged. "I don't really know you."

They sat in silence for a few seconds. "I still think he did it," Gene said. "But he won't break. Any ideas?"

"Not any good ones."

Just then Soper rushed out the door and dashed toward them, bellowing something they couldn't understand.

"We may want to leave," Gene said.

"What did you do to him?" JP started the engine. "He looks madder 'en a centipede standing barefoot on a hot rock."

JP sped off, but Soper followed. Within a couple of blocks, JP could see the other truck getting close.

Chapter 53

Sabre walked into the attorneys' lounge and found Bob perusing the day's petitions.

"Are you on detentions?" Sabre asked.

"Yes, but there's not much," Bob said. "That abandoned-baby case that's been in the news is here."

"I haven't been watching much TV lately. What happened?"

"Someone left a baby in a Walmart store. He was only a few days old. They can't find the parents."

"Don't they have the incident on camera?"

"They've been able to figure out that some woman brought him in under her sweatshirt, then left him in a crib that was set up. They don't have any good facial shots apparently. She kept her hair in her face and was always looking down."

"I'll never understand people," Sabre said. "Why would anyone leave a baby at Walmart, of all places?" She paused, but she didn't expect an answer. "Any record of a birth that matches the child?"

"Not yet. It looks like she delivered him outside a hospital. Either that or traveled a long way in two days. They've checked every hospital in a five-hundred-mile radius." Bob looked through the rest of the papers in the bin. "That's about it. What's on your calendar this morning?"

"I have two review hearings in Department One, and Conner's case is on calendar. The judge has made a decision on the 707."

"I hope you win."

"Me too. There's no way that kid should be tried as an adult."

"Do you need me to cover anything in Department One?"

"I don't think so, but I'm headed over to see Conner now. Mike's bringing him in. The hearing itself should be pretty quick."

Sabre walked across the lobby to the interview room. Sabre checked each empty room, then entered the one marked *A* to wait for Conner.

Three minutes later, a deputy brought him in and hand-cuffed him to the bench.

"Thanks, Mike."

Mike nodded and walked out, locking the door behind him.

"Hello, Conner. Are you doing okay?"

"Yes, ma'am."

"Have you had any more problems with other inmates?"

"No, but I'm pretty much by myself. It gets lonely, but it's better than getting beat up."

"I think that's the best we can do for now. Do you know why you're here this morning?"

"They just said I had court."

"The judge has made a decision on whether you will be tried as an adult. He'll give his ruling this morning."

"Then what happens?"

"If we lose, they'll give us a court hearing downtown. Then we'll appear there for a preliminary hearing, which will likely be set for a jury trial."

"And if we win?"

"We'll still set it for trial, but the case will be heard here in juvenile court in front of a judge only. If we lose here, your sentence will be a lot shorter than adult court, and you'll be placed in juvenile facilities with better programs."

Conner seemed to understand, or at least he nodded as if he did. He had little expression on his face, and Sabre wondered what was going through his mind. She couldn't believe this young man had killed anyone and her heart ached for him. If he was innocent, as she believed, how could this poor teenager possibly understand why he was wrongly accused and how much his life would change? Even if he had killed Bullet, Conner would still be in a lot of turmoil. What could have pushed him to that breaking point? Either way, she felt bad for the boy. Unless JP could find something more, she might not be able to help him.

"Conner, I need to ask more questions. Are you up to it?"

"Yeah."

"When did you put the lock on your bedroom door?"

"About a year ago—when Morgan got afraid because guys were running around the house naked."

"Who had keys to the lock?"

"Just me, Morgan, and…"

"And who?"

"My dad. But he wouldn't have put the gun there."

"Why do you say that?"

"Because he loves me, and he has always tried to keep me out of jail. He knows how awful it is."

Sabre hoped he was right, but she couldn't be sure, especially after what JP had told her about Gene and their father.

"I know he loves you, Conner, but sometimes adults make stupid mistakes too."

"It wasn't him."

"Conner, whoever did this had to have access to your room on at least one occasion after the murder. Did your mom ever go in there?"

"Not after I put the lock on. I made it clear that no one could come in."

"And your mom didn't have a key?"

"No."

"Do you think Morgan would've let her in?"

He shook his head. "I'm pretty sure she wouldn't have."

"But you gave your dad a key. Why?"

"Because I trust him, and he'd never let anything happen to Morgan. I wanted him to be able to get in, just in case I wasn't home and one of those creeps tricked their way past Morgan."

"Do you know if any of those creeps got in?"

"I don't think so. Morgan was very careful."

"But you didn't trust your mother enough to give her a key?"

"Not because she'd do anything bad, but she's careless. And she never thought her friends did anything wrong. My mom means well, but she likes to party, and when she gets drunk, she doesn't use her head."

"Did anyone else ever come in your room?"

"Emily did. But only a few times, and I was with her."

"And the day she saw the gun, did she say anything to you about it?"

He shook his head. "I didn't even know she saw it."

"Conner, I want you to visualize everything that happened from the time Emily came into your room."

"Okay."

"When she went to the closet, what were you doing?"

"I was taking a video game out of the machine. Emily went to the closet to pick out a new game. She doesn't like the war games, so I told her to get a game she liked. She came back with the box and picked one."

"Was she carrying a purse or any kind of bag with her?"

Conner thought for a second. "She had her backpack."

"Did she usually have a backpack?"

"I think so."

Chapter 54

Sabre Brown for the defendant, Conner Torn, who is present in court," Sabre said when her case was called.

"Marge Benson, deputy district attorney, for the people."

Judge Feldman got right down to business. "After careful consideration of the evidence provided me regarding the fitness of this young man to be tried in juvenile court, I have come to the following conclusions. Conner Torn does not seem to have a high level of criminal sophistication for his age. Although his father has spent much of his life in custody, it doesn't appear that he has taught his son the ways of the street. Among other things, I have considered the fight that took place in the Hall, in which Conner was not only an innocent victim, but unable to defend himself." The judge looked at the DDA, who was fidgeting in her seat. "Before you object, Ms. Benson, I have considered many other things as well: his school record, the family dynamics, his lack of a criminal record, his demeanor, and the crime itself."

It sounded like the judge was ruling in Conner's favor, but he wasn't done with his comments and Sabre kept waiting for the "but."

The judge paused for a few seconds, and Sabre thought *here it comes*. The judge continued. "I did not consider SB 1391 in making my ruling. As I'm sure you all know, that bill to raise the age for a fitness hearing, from fourteen to sixteen, has passed both the Assembly and the Senate and sits on the governor's desk for approval. I have only considered the merits and evidence of this particular case."

Conner seemed to be holding his breath. Sabre wondered if he understood what the judge was saying.

"Under the present law of Welfare and Institutions Code 707, I find the defendant fit to be tried in juvenile court."

Sabre gave a sigh of relief and smiled at Conner. Then she whispered to him to make sure he understood. "We won. You'll be tried here in juvenile court. That's a really big win."

Sabre looked up at the judge. "Thank you, Your Honor. We'd like to set the matter for trial."

They went off the record while Sabre and the DDA agreed on a date that worked for the court. The trial was set about a month out. Sabre made another attempt to have Conner released, but it was denied.

"That's a long time," Conner said.

"I know it seems like it, but we need time to prepare your case," Sabre said. "You have to go back to the Hall now, but I'll come on Sunday. Morgan has been asking to visit again." Conner didn't smile, but she saw his eyes light up a little. "Has anyone else been to see you?"

"My mom hasn't, other than that one time. Grandma comes a lot, but I still don't know where Dad is."

Sabre whispered, "I haven't seen your dad, but I do know someone who has. Your dad would come here if he could. He's trying to find out who killed Bullet."

Sabre wondered if she'd said too much. She hadn't mentioned Gene before, because she didn't want to tell Conner anything he might have to keep secret, or for him to get caught in a lie. When Conner smiled, she was glad she'd told him what she had.

"If you can pass the word, please tell him I miss him, and I know he didn't kill Bullet."

Sabre thought it was an odd thing to say, but she didn't push Conner to explain.

~~~

JP sped away from Soper's house, only to see that Soper was still following him.

"He's gaining on us," Gene said, looking back.

"He ain't gonna make me run like a scalded dog," JP said. Just then a shot rang out, and they heard the clang of metal on metal.

"You might want to re-think that," Gene said.

"Damn! He hit my truck. Hold on."

JP pressed the gas and squealed around the corner. He was heading west and looking into the blinding sun. Houses flashed past. JP raced through the neighborhood, gaining distance between them and Soper, who hadn't turned onto the same street yet. JP made another right and quickly discovered it was a narrow alley with a dead-end. He slammed the brakes, threw it into reverse, and backed up. "Can you see him?"

"Not yet," Gene said. "I take that back. There he is."

JP shifted again and took off down a different street, but he had lost ground. Another shot rang out. It missed. JP accelerated, wanting to get away before someone got shot, but afraid he might hit a pedestrian.

JP tossed Gene his cell phone. "Call 9-1-1."

"I'm not calling the cops. They'll take me in. Just lose him."

When they had three or four blocks between them, JP turned right, made a quick left, and then another right.

"I can't see him," Gene said.

"Good."

JP had finally reached an area he was more familiar with. Businesses had started to appear. He pulled into an Arco station and drove behind it, where his truck couldn't be seen from the street.

"I think we lost him," JP said. "Give me my phone."

"Are you calling the cops?"

"I need to report this. A madman is driving around shooting at people."

"He's only after us, and he probably doesn't know where you live—which means he'll come after me."

"Does he know where Derek lives?"

"I don't know. I doubt it."

Just as Gene handed JP his phone, it rang. It was Sabre. He considered answering it, but then hit the button declining the call.

"Have you confronted her?"

"I've been busy."

"Are you sure she's cheating?"

"Yes."

"How do you know?"

"I saw her messages from some guy on a dating service, and I went to their meeting place. I saw them together."

"Were they intimate?"

"No, but it looked like a first date."

"Then maybe there's still time."

"Why would she join a dating service if she wasn't done with me? She deserves better anyway. I'm too old for her."

"Sorry, bro," Gene said, sounding sincere.

JP swallowed and took a deep breath.

"Dump the bitch," Gene said. "Let's go out tonight and find some ladies. We could both use the comfort."

Chapter 55

Bob was waiting for Sabre when she came out of the delinquency courtroom. She must've looked happy, because he said, "You won, didn't you?"

"We did. Conner will be tried as a minor. That is huge! We still need to find out what really happened, but no matter what, he won't be spending the rest of his life in prison."

"That's great, Sobs."

"I know." Sabre removed her cell phone from her pocket. "I have to call JP and let him know." She hesitated.

"What's wrong?"

"JP won't answer my calls, and he hasn't returned any either. He won't talk to me, so I don't know what's wrong." She started to put her phone back, then stopped. "I'm calling him." She waited as it rang four times, then left a voicemail: "Hello, JP. The judge just gave us a ruling on the 707 hearing. Please call so I can tell you what happened."

Sabre hung up. "If he wants to know what happened, he'll have to call me."

She and Bob finished their morning calendar, but Sabre kept thinking about the conversation she'd had the night before with Morgan, as well as what Conner had told her earlier.

"Want to go to Pho's?" Bob asked.

"I need to see *your* client, Morgan. I have to ask her some questions about when Bullet was killed. Do you want to tag along?"

"Does that mean we're not eating?"

"It means I'm not eating at Pho's. You can do what you want."

"What the heck. Let's go. I'll even drive."

"It's a deal, but you'll have to stop at In-N-Out to pick up lunch for Morgan." She winked.

"I'll make the sacrifice."

They walked to Bob's car. He removed files from the front seat and tossed them into the back, where they landed on a pile of other folders.

"Nice filing system," Sabre said.

"I thought so. It's very handy."

When they drove off, Bob asked, "Do you want me to talk to JP and see if I can find out what's going on?"

"No, he'll think I sent you. I don't want that. He'll come around."

When they arrived at the school, Sabre and Bob went into the office and signed in. The receptionist recognized Sabre.

"Hello, Ms. Brown. Are you here to pick up Morgan?"

"No, but I brought her lunch." She nodded toward Bob. "This is Bob Clark, Morgan's attorney. We need to talk to Morgan, and the timing worked, so we thought we'd eat lunch with her. I've already checked with her teacher, and she offered her classroom so we could have some privacy."

The receptionist handed her two nametags that said *Visitor*. "You know the way."

Morgan was excited to see Sabre and even more excited to get the burger, fries, and vanilla shake. "I hope you don't mind sharing your fries with me," Sabre said. "I know you usually can't eat them all."

"Totally," Morgan said. She looked at Bob. "You can have some too, if you want."

"Thanks, but I have some." He picked up the burger bag and grinned.

"Want to see my science project?" Morgan asked Bob. "It's a volcano. Sabre has already seen it."

"Sure," Bob said.

Morgan led Bob to a long counter at the back of the room with rows of handmade volcanos. Bob picked hers out and bragged on the quality. Morgan beamed.

She showed Bob a chart with lots of stars after her name.

"You're pretty good at this being-a-student-thing. Do you like school?"

"Yeah, it's fun. I like my teacher, and I've made some friends here."

"You two better come eat," Sabre said. "The food is getting cold."

They all sat down and ate their lunch, with idle chitchat between bites. Sabre let Morgan finish her food before she started questioning her.

"I have to ask you something, and it's very important that you tell me the whole truth. It could be a big help to Conner. Can you promise to tell me the truth?"

"I promise."

"I need to know exactly what happened when Bullet left your house, from the time you woke up, to when Conner was arrested. Please think carefully about those few days."

Morgan closed her eyes, exuded a calm focus, then opened them. "I got up and I was hungry, so I went to the kitchen. I heard Bullet shouting, and I saw Grandma on the floor. She had blood all over her, and it scared me. Before I could see anything else, Conner grabbed me and took me to our room. I waited for the yelling to stop. It seemed to go on for a long time. It got quiet once, and I thought it was over, but then it started again. I could tell Bullet was really mad. I stayed in the room for maybe another hour after it stopped, just to be sure."

"Did Conner stay in there with you?"

"Only for a little while. I didn't want him to leave, but he said he had to talk to Daddy."

"Did he come back?"

"He came in once and told me to stay in the room until there was no more noise in the house and I was sure the fighting had stopped."

"Did you hear more fighting?"

"No, but I heard that my dad whipped Bullet pretty good before he left. The next thing I saw was when Bullet jumped on his bike and took off. I could see that from my bedroom window. Shortly after that, I heard the garage door open and a car leave."

"Do you know who was in the car?"

"No, but it must've been my dad—and maybe Conner. When I finally came out, the only one left was my mom, and she was still asleep."

"Did you see your mom?"

"No, but she had to be there. She never gets up early after a party."

"What did you do then?"

"I ate some cereal and watched TV."

"When did your grandma come home?"

"I don't know exactly, but Mom was already awake, so it must've been after one o'clock."

"You saw your mom before your grandma came home?"

"Yes. Mom came into the living room, and she was already dressed. She talked to me for a minute and then went back to her room. It wasn't long after that when Grandma came home."

"Who else came into the house that day?"

"My dad returned just before dark. I don't know when Conner came because I was already asleep. He was the last one."

"You saw your dad that day?"

"Yes. I was already in my room, and he came and knocked on the door."

"I thought he had a key."

"He does, but he never came in without knocking."

"Was that the last time you saw him?"

"No. I saw him the next morning. Grandma made pancakes, and Conner and I were eating. Daddy was drinking coffee, and Derek came by. They went outside and talked, then Daddy came back inside, went to his room, and got a bag." Morgan's eyes looked sad. "He told us he was leaving. He said he didn't know how long he'd be gone, and if anyone asked, to tell them he'd left a few days earlier and was in Donovan."

"Did you know he wasn't really going to prison?"

"No."

"Why do you think he told you to say he had left a few days before?"

"Sometimes my family has secrets, and it's easier to just do as they say."

Morgan looked conflicted, so Sabre moved on. "The other guys, Judd and Andy, did they return that day?"

"No."

"Did they come back any time before Conner was arrested?"

"They could've when I was at school, but I didn't see either of them." She paused, remembering something. "Judd showed up one day and talked to my grandma for a little while. He didn't stay long."

"Is there any chance Judd could have gotten into your room while he was there?"

"No." Morgan shook her head vehemently. "I'm sure of it, because I went to my room right after he got there, and I stayed until he left. Besides, it's locked."

"And your grandma doesn't have a key?"

"No."

"And you never saw your dad, Judd, Andy, or Derek again?"

"Nope."

"Who else came to your house after that?"

"Emily was there once. No, twice. She came by with Conner the next day, but she waited for him while he got something from our room, then they left. The next time was the day Conner was arrested. She came home with him after school. They were in the room together for quite a while doing homework."

"Were you in the room?"

"I was helping Grandma in the kitchen."

Sabre had a thought. "Did your grandma ever come into your room to tuck you in—between the time Bullet left and Conner was arrested?"

"Only once, I think." Morgan closed her eyes to focus. "It was the same day Bullet beat her up. The day he left."

"And she never came into your room after that?"

"No. I'm sure of it. Conner was home every night until he was arrested, and then I left too. It was only a couple of nights."

"If she didn't have a key, how did your grandma get in that last time?"

Morgan smiled. "We have a secret code so I know it's her. She knocks once, and if I'm alone, I knock back once. Then she knocks four times and I let her in."

"What does your grandma do when she tucks you in?"

"She reads to me. The books sound better because of the way she talks."

"Your grandma has a beautiful accent," Sabre said. "After she reads to you, then what?"

"She usually stays until I fall asleep, then she leaves."

"Does Conner know your grandma comes in the room?"

"I don't think so. It would be okay if he did, but it's fun to have a secret with Grandma."

"Morgan, do you like Emily?"

"Yeah, she's nice. She always says 'Hi' to me, unlike some of my brother's friends."

"But none of them were there after Bullet was shot, right?"

"That's right. Conner hasn't had anyone over for quite a while. Except Emily."

Chapter 56

Sabre called JP and, just as she expected, he didn't answer. She didn't like that he was hanging out with his brother, and she didn't like the things that had been happening on this case. She hoped JP wasn't in trouble. But something else was going on. JP was acting different than she had ever seen before. He was angry, and it seemed to be directed at her.

When the phone beeped, she left a message: "JP, I really need to talk to you about Conner's case. The judge made a ruling on the fitness hearing, and I have information that might help find the killer." She started to hang up, then added, "I think I know who killed Bullet. Please call as soon as you can."

It wasn't long before JP called back.

"Everything okay?" Sabre asked.

"I can't seem to make any headway on this case, and it's driving me mad." His voice was stilted and cold.

"I may be able to help. First, we won the 707 hearing. Conner will be tried in juvenile court."

"That's great news, Sabre. Good for you."

"It wasn't just me. I hate to say it, but I think it helped that Conner got beat up in the Hall."

"You can thank Gene for that."

"What are you saying?" Sabre asked. "Never mind. Don't tell me. I don't need to know that."

"Then I won't," JP said. "I still think Soper is the killer. I'm considering taking another shot at questioning Muriel. Something's not right. She knows more than she's telling."

"You think she would protect Soper over her grandson?"

"Only if she thinks Conner won't get punished. I should tell her we lost the 707 hearing and he's facing life in prison. That might shake her."

"Let me tell you what I found out from Conner and Morgan." Sabre summarized what she'd learned, and gave him her theory of the case.

"You're a genius, kid." His voice sounded normal, soft and loving. For a second, Sabre felt like her JP was back, but then he seemed to harden again. "I'll get right on it."

"Call me as soon as you know something," Sabre said.

She waited for a response, but her phone was silent. He had already hung up.

~~~

JP and Gene drove to Muriel's house, determined to get the truth.

"Back so soon," Muriel said, as they entered.

"Yes," Gene said. "There's something you need to know." He walked into the living room.

Muriel's eyes widened as she followed. "What is it?"

"The judge ruled against us on the 707," JP said. "Conner will be tried as an adult."

Muriel staggered to a chair and sat down. "Oh no. That's not fair." She lowered her head and covered her eyes.

"You're right. It's not fair." JP sat down across from her. "Especially since he didn't do it."

Muriel dragged her hands from her eyes to cover her mouth. Her words were muffled, but understandable. "And you know who did." It was more a statement than a question.

"Yes, we do," JP said. "You want to tell us what happened?"

"I didn't mean to kill him." She started to sob. "I just wanted to scare Bullet enough so he would leave us alone."

"What happened?"

"When he left, I was so angry. I was in pain, and I was so tired of living in fear all the time. I went to Roxanne's room and got Gene's gun from the box. At first, I just planned to have the gun with me, in case he came back. Then I started thinking that if he came back and I shot him, the kids would witness it, and I didn't want that. So, I decided to go after him and scare him. I never planned to kill him."

"How did you know where he was?" JP asked.

"He took his camping gear, so I figured he was at this place he always went. We used to go there quite a bit, so I knew how to find the spot. It's not a real campsite, just a secluded chunk of government land."

"Had he set up camp when you found him?"

She shook her head. "He still had all his gear on his bike when I got there. He was just sitting there on a rock, holding his head. I got the feeling he was in pain. When he turned around, I saw his face looked pretty bad, like someone had beat him up."

"Did you know he and Gene got in a fight before he left?"

"Yes, but he had blood everywhere. I think someone else got to him too."

Muriel stopped talking and looked into her lap.

JP prodded her. "What did Bullet do?"

"He wasn't exactly happy to see me. In fact, he was furious. He yelled, 'What the hell are you doing here? Did you come to finish the job Gene started?' I tried to talk to him, but he jumped on his bike and drove off. I followed him. When he got near the highway, he stopped. I don't know why, but he got off his bike. I parked too, then grabbed the gun and got out of the car. I took one step toward him, pointing the gun the whole time."

"Did you say anything?"

"I said, 'I don't ever want you at my house. If you come back, I'll kill you. You're never going to hurt me or anyone I love again.'" She paused.

Gene cut in. "And then you shot him?"

"No. He said something like, 'You don't scare me with your little toy pistol. You don't have the guts to kill me, or you would've done it already.' Then he suddenly came at me. He grabbed my hand that held the gun and punched me in the face with his other one. I fell back against the car. I felt the jolt of the gun in my hand as it went off. Bullet staggered back a couple of feet and collapsed to the ground."

JP waited. Muriel didn't say anything.

"Then what?" he prompted.

"I stood there for a few seconds, trying to figure out what had happened. There was blood all over his neck, face, and chest. I couldn't even tell where he'd been hit. At first I was afraid to get too close for fear he would grab me, but he wasn't moving at all. Finally, I reached down and checked for a pulse. There was none. So I took out his cell phone and called 9-1-1. Using my best American accent, I told them I was driving by and saw what looked like a man on the ground by his motorcycle. Then hung up and drove off. About a mile down the road, I threw the phone into the canyon."

Gene started to say something, but JP waved him off. "How did the gun end up in Conner's room?" JP asked.

"I was afraid someone would find it if I put it anywhere else. I knew the gun was important to Gene, so I didn't want to throw it away. I knew no one had a key to Conner's room, and I only put it there until I could figure out what to do."

"You have a key to his room?"

"No. As far as I know, only Conner and Morgan have keys." Gene didn't correct her.

"How did you get in?" JP asked. But he thought he knew, based on what Sabre had told him.

"Morgan and I had a secret knock so she could let me in when Conner was gone. That night, Conner was out somewhere, so I took the gun in my book bag and hid it in the corner of their closet after Morgan fell asleep. After that, I never was able to get back into the room without Conner there. Then he got arrested, and they found the gun."

"Dammit, Muriel!" Gene shouted. "Why did you let Conner take the blame? He's your grandson, for God's sake."

"I just got scared, and Gene, you're always saying they don't do anything to these kids when they get arrested. They just slap them on the wrist."

"He's not going to just get a slap on the wrist," JP said, struggling to control his fury. "If Conner was convicted as an adult, he could've been sentenced to life in prison."

"I would've never let that happen." Muriel tilted her head. "Wait a minute. I thought you said he would be tried as an adult."

"I lied. We won the 707 hearing. But even if he lost in juvenile court, he would've spent years in custody with gang members, murderers, and other violent offenders. Incarceration is never a picnic."

Muriel dropped her eyes again. "I know. I feel terrible for what he has already gone through. How do I get him out of juvenile hall?"

"We'll start by talking to Conner's attorney. She'll know the best way to handle it."

JP called Sabre and told her about Muriel's confession.

"I'll call and get an appointment with DDA Benson," Sabre said. "Can you bring Muriel in to give her statement?"

"Just let me know when and where."

JP hung up. They waited in silence until Sabre called back.

"We're meeting in thirty-five minutes with Benson and her investigator," Sabre said. "Is that enough time?"

"We'll be there."

~~~

Sabre was concerned about JP's behavior. He hadn't sounded angry this time, like he did the last time they spoke, but there was still no affection in his comments. She had to find out what was wrong. She decided she'd insist on having that conversation soon.

She called Bob on her way to the DDA's office and told him about Muriel. "You know what that means, right?"

"That you're going to win?"

"I meant that Conner will be released, and you'll get another minor to handle if they file on him too."

"Do you think they will? He wasn't in as much danger as Morgan."

Sabre sighed. "His grandmother let him take the rap for a murder, and his father is likely headed back to prison. His mother is a mess and hasn't done any of her programs yet. Yes, I expect they'll file on him."

Chapter 57

Sabre saw JP pull into the parking spot next to her and felt a twinge of excitement—as she always did when she saw him. She stepped out of her car, hoping to get a warm greeting. But because of the way he'd been acting lately, she braced for more detachment.

JP climbed out, and so did Muriel. "Have you two met?" JP asked, without any other acknowledgment.

"We haven't," Sabre said.

JP introduced them, and Sabre thanked her for coming.

"Am I doing the right thing?" Muriel asked in a soft voice.

The question struck Sabre as odd, but then she realized Muriel was asking her as an attorney. "You're doing the right thing for Conner. I'm his attorney, not yours, so I'm not comfortable advising you. But your grandson doesn't deserve to be behind bars."

Muriel didn't respond.

"You said it was an accident, right?" Sabre prodded.

"Yes, it was." Muriel's voice rose a little.

Sabre's instinct was to tell her not to talk until she had spoken to an attorney. Then she thought of Conner. "Just tell the truth."

"Will they arrest me?"

"Maybe."

Muriel gasped.

Sabre touched her on the shoulder. "I can't be certain, but I expect they won't arrest you today. They'll question whether you're trying to cover for your grandson. They'll do their own investigation after you make your statement, then decide what to do."

They stepped inside the DA's building before anything more was said. Muriel turned to Sabre and asked, "Is Conner okay?"

"For now. He doesn't know anything about this yet. I didn't want to get his hopes up about being released, until we know more."

They walked in silence to the conference room, where they met up with Marge Benson and her investigator, Larry Villareal.

"This is my investigator, JP Torn," Sabre said. "And Conner's grandmother, Muriel Roberts."

"Hi, JP," Larry said. "Nice to see you again."

"You two know each other?" Sabre asked.

"We worked together back when we were both rookies at the sheriff's department," JP explained.

"Let's do this," Benson said abruptly.

Muriel told her account of the events with few interruptions from the DA. When she finished, Benson questioned her mostly about her motives, and Villareal asked about physical details—the campsite location, the area of the shooting, and where she threw the phone. All Muriel could remember about the crime scene was that she stopped in front of a speed-limit sign. The investigator also asked questions about the make and model of the gun. Most of which she couldn't answer. Muriel described it as a "small gun with a real short barrel."

Benson cut back in. "Did Conner hide the gun for you?"

"No," Muriel said indignantly. "He had no idea I put the gun in his room. Even after he found it and came to me."

"He saw the gun and told you about it?"

"Yes, but I didn't realize at the time that he had touched it. I had wiped off the gun so it wouldn't have my fingerprints. I never thought Conner would find it, much less touch it."

"Did Conner go with you when you went after Bullet?"

"No, I went by myself."

Sabre was irritated that Benson was trying to implicate her client, but she had known that would happen. She hoped Muriel could stick to her story and not sound like she was waffling.

The DDA switched tactics. "How is your health, Muriel?"

"My health?"

"Are you well?"

"I'm fine."

"When was the last time you went to the doctor?"

"I don't know exactly. It's been years—at least five, maybe six. I don't get sick much."

Where was she going with this? Sabre tensed with uncertainty.

"And you have no heart problems?"

"No."

"Cancer?"

"No. There's nothing wrong with me."

"Do you mind if we check your medical records?"

Muriel glanced around, as if looking for answers. Sabre understood her confusion. By now, she realized Benson was searching for a reason Muriel might take the blame for Conner, but Sabre couldn't help her.

"It's fine," Muriel said. "But I don't really have any records. I don't think I've ever been to the doctor here in San Diego."

"Did you go to the doctor when Bullet beat you up?"

"No."

"There's no medical record of him ever hurting you?"

"No, but plenty of people saw what happened."

"Including Conner, who has already told the police that," Sabre said.

Benson asked a couple more questions, then looked at her investigator.

"I'm good," he said.

"Thank you, Ms. Roberts, for coming in. We'll be in touch. Please do not leave the jurisdiction."

"I'm not going anywhere," Muriel mumbled. She followed Sabre's lead and stood too. Once they were outside, Muriel asked, "Can I go home now?"

"Yes," JP said. "I'll take you."

"Then what?"

"They'll investigate and see if your story checks out to their satisfaction," JP said.

"Will they let Conner go?"

"If they're satisfied that you killed Bullet, and that Conner didn't help you," Sabre said, "then the DDA will file a motion to dismiss the charges against him."

"Please tell him how sorry I am," Muriel said with wet eyes.

When they reached the car, Muriel climbed in, and Sabre hoped for a few minutes alone with JP.

"I can pick up Morgan from school," she said.

"It's okay. I can get her." JP turned and got in his truck.

Chapter 58

Sabre woke Saturday morning still wondering what had gone wrong with JP. She checked her phone to make sure she hadn't missed a call or text from him. There was nothing. She had fought the urge to stop in and see him the night before. She'd thought about going over just to see Morgan, but even though she missed the girl, it was JP she longed to see and talk to. He would've known it too. She took a deep breath and decided to put it out of her mind.

She dressed and went for a long run along the bay. The sun was shining, people were picnicking, and crew teams moved gracefully through the water. She did her best to just be in the moment and enjoy the sights, sounds, and smell of the salt water. When her mind found its way back to JP, she forced herself to think about something else. It worked some of the time.

After her run, she took a shower and drove to see Conner. She had to let him know what was happening. She didn't want him to hear it from Roxy or Muriel first—if they happened to visit.

Conner's shoulders drooped as he entered the interview room. When he sat down across from Sabre, he slumped in the chair, rather than sitting up straight, as he had the first few times she saw him. The Hall was taking a toll. Sabre hoped her news would help bring him out of his funk, but she knew his grandmother's involvement would hurt him as well. Nevertheless, it had to be done.

"Conner, we found out who murdered Bullet."

The boy's eyes lit up, and he sat up straighter in his seat. Then his shoulders dropped again. "It wasn't my dad, was it?"

"No, but it was someone close to you."

His brow creased. "Who?"

"I'm afraid it was your grandmother." Sabre quickly added. "It was an accident."

Conner stared at his hands for several seconds, then a pinched, painful expression filled his face, and his eyes overflowed with tears. "But how...why...why would she leave me in here?"

Sabre told him what had happened and did her best to explain how afraid Muriel had been. She also pointed out that his grandmother had thought he wouldn't get much punishment. Even as she said it, she didn't expect Conner to understand. *She* certainly didn't. But it was his grandmother and he loved her, so the betrayal was personal for him. This was what Sabre hated most about working with children—watching them get their hearts broken by the people they loved and trusted. It never got any easier.

After Conner composed himself, he asked, "Does that mean I'll get out of here?"

"We have to wait until the DA's office investigates. Hopefully, they'll be able to substantiate the evidence and realize you aren't guilty. If that's the case, the district attorney will set a hearing. The worst-case scenario is if they don't believe your grandmother. Then you'll have to stay here until trial. But we have a good case, and I think we could convince the judge that you're innocent." Sabre wanted to give him hope, but she knew how risky it was if the DA decided to prosecute Conner. She had a good defense, but that was no guarantee.

"Did they arrest Grandma?"

"No."

"Will they?"

"Probably."

"How long before we know what they're going to do?"

"We won't hear anything over the weekend, but I'm hoping they'll set a hearing on Monday or Tuesday. If they decide not to dismiss your case, we'll ask for a speedy trial and get into court as soon as we can. You have a constitutional right to that. We haven't been rushing it, because we didn't have a good defense up until now."

"So, how long?"

"Three or four weeks probably."

Conner gave a heavy sigh. "That's a long time in here."

"I know, but for now, let's hope for the best." Sabre's heart ached for this young man, and anger festered against the adults in his life. "I know it may not seem like much from where you're sitting, but there are a lot of people who care about you, and we're working hard to get you out. Please try to be strong, if not for yourself, for Morgan. She needs you, and she loves you—as she would put it—to the moon and back. She's a special little girl, and I know you've had to be more of a parent sometimes than a big brother, but don't give up now. We're almost there."

"Is Morgan coming to see me tomorrow?"

"I'll make sure she gets here." After she said it, Sabre realized she didn't really have control over Morgan. But she couldn't believe, no matter what state of mind JP was in, that he'd deny the girl a visit with her brother. But then, she didn't really know what was going on with JP these days.

The first thing Sabre did when she left the Hall was call JP. He didn't answer so she left a message: "I just saw Conner and told him about his grandmother. He took it pretty hard. He asked about seeing Morgan tomorrow at visiting hours. It's important that he gets to see her, and I'm assuming you're okay with that. I'll gladly pick her up and take her. Or if you'd prefer to do it, that's fine with me. Please let me know how you want to work it. I think they both need the visit."

Sabre hung up, let out a long breath, and decided that was the last call she would make to him if he didn't get back to her. She was done. If JP wouldn't talk to her, she'd call Bob and ask him to ensure that his client got to visit with her brother.

Chapter 59

By five o'clock that night, Sabre still hadn't heard from JP, so she called Bob.

"Hi, Snookums," he said. "What's up?"

"I need you to see that Morgan gets a visit with Conner tomorrow. The session starts at ten-fifteen. Can you do that for me? Morgan will be disappointed if she doesn't get to see him, and Conner needs the visit as well."

"You can't get her there?"

"No, it's not that. I think JP plans to take her, but I'm not sure because he hasn't answered my call."

"What the heck is up with you two?" Bob asked.

"I wish I knew, but he has completely shut down. I'm done trying to get through to him, but I don't want it to affect Morgan or Conner."

"I'll see that Morgan makes the visit."

~~~

Bob started to call JP, then decided to make a personal visit instead. They'd been friends for a long time, longer than JP and Sabre even. He was the one who'd introduced them, and he knew how happy they had been together. He owed it to both of them to see if he could fix this. Either way, he had to deal with his client, and Morgan was with JP. He stopped at the store and picked up a six-pack of beer on the drive over.

JP and Morgan pulled into the driveway just as Bob arrived.

Morgan jumped out. "Hi, Mr. Clark."

"Hi, Morgan."

"We spent the day in Julian. It was fun. I'd never been."

"Did you eat some apple pie?"

"We sure did. That was almost the best part."

"What was better than Julian apple pie?"

"The horseback ride. Uncle Johnny took me to the stables, and we got to ride for a couple of hours. It was stupendous."

"Stupendous, huh?"

"Yeah, that's the word of the day," JP said. "What are you doing in this neighborhood?"

Bob lifted the six-pack. "I thought maybe you could use a beer."

"As a matter-of-fact I could. Come on in."

Once inside, Morgan went to her room, and JP and Bob sat outside to drink.

"So, what really brings you here?" JP asked.

"Sabre said Conner was looking forward to seeing Morgan tomorrow, and she wanted me to make sure his sister got there. Sabre called and left you a message, but she hadn't heard back."

"We had pretty bad reception in Julian, especially on the trail. When I got home, I was going to let her know I hadn't forgotten about the visit, but then you showed up. Now, you can take care of it."

"You doing okay?" Bob asked.

"I'm fine. But it's been a rough couple of days." JP paused. "This case has gotten to me. I recently discovered I'm an uncle, and then I'm suddenly thrust into a parental role. I see my brother, who hasn't been around in nearly twenty-five years. I've been trying to figure out if I can trust anything he says. Meanwhile, he gets me punched, chased, and shot at. He's my big brother, and I'm not even sure I like the guy."

"Yeah, that's a lot. It might be easier if you had Sabre to help you."

"She doesn't need me or my problems. It's unfair to expect her to stick around this old guy, especially now with Morgan in my care. Sabre needs to find a younger man."

"What the hell's the matter with you?" Bob said. "Sabre is crazy about you."

"I know she's your best friend and..." JP stopped and shook his head. "Let's just drop it. Okay? By the way, I don't think I ever thanked you for taking Morgan's case. She's a handful, but she's awful special. She sure didn't deserve to be living in that environment. I want to pummel my brother when I think about it sometimes, but the truth is, things seemed to be better over there when he was around. Unfortunately, he isn't around enough. I've been pleasantly surprised at how much he seems to care about his kids, but he can't keep himself out of prison long enough to raise them."

"It's good you're here for them. If they file on Conner, can you take him too?"

"I wouldn't have it any other way—unless he doesn't want to live with me. I don't know the kid very well, but he's been good to Morgan. He's been her protector."

"Maybe if he lives with you, he'll get a chance to be a kid for a while."

"That would be nice."

"Hey, did Sabre tell you they caught that guy on the kid-die-porn case?"

"No. I wasn't working on it. What's it about?"

"Some guy was taking nude photos of his girlfriend's children and selling them online."

"What a creep."

"For sure. But for him, it was all about the money. At least, as far as they know. It wasn't his first time, and he didn't intend it to be his last. He'd hook up with women on this online dating site, but only those with children. Then he'd weasel his way into their lives and their homes, and take photos of the kids. He's a disgusting individual."

~~~

JP flashed back to the online dating site he'd found on Sabre's computer, and the situation hit him hard. "Oh no," he said out loud, emotions flooding over him. Anger and guilt fought for dominance. He stood and started pacing.

"What?" Bob asked.

"Sabre didn't help catch the guy, did she?"

"I'm afraid so, but I've said too much. You two are having enough trouble. I don't need to add to it."

"You have to tell me. What did she do?"

When Bob didn't answer, JP said, "Okay, let me tell you. She signed up for a dating site to see if she could lure the guy in."

Bob looked wide-eyed at him.

JP went on. "She pretended to have children and made a date with the guy." He paused. "How am I doing so far?"

"How did you know?"

"How could you let her do that? She could've gotten hurt. Not to mention that she was probably interfering with a police investigation."

"You know how she is. There's no stopping her when she decides to do something. I went with her, and was there the whole time. I took the photos, and my client, the mother on the case, was able to identify him."

"Sabre just met him for coffee and that was it?"

"No," Bob said. "Wait. How did you know they met for coffee?"

JP didn't answer. "She met him more than once?"

"Yes, but the feds were involved, and they made the arrest as soon as they connected. Bob gave him a look. "How did you know they met for coffee?"

"I was there."

Chapter 60

JP knocked on Morgan's door and entered when she invited him in. When Morgan saw him, she asked, "What's wrong?"

"I really dropped my candy in the sand this time."

"I hope it wasn't chocolate, because it's really hard to get sand off of chocolate."

"Worse. I need to apologize to Sabre. Want to go? Because I'm not leaving you here by yourself, and I really need to make amends."

"What did you do, Uncle Johnny?"

"I jumped to conclusions and didn't trust her when I should have."

"I'll try to keep a better eye on you," Morgan said. "Keep you out of trouble."

"Are you ready?"

"Do you have any flowers, or perfume, or diamond jewelry?"

"No."

"A stuffed animal, maybe?"

"No."

"That's what they always do in the movies, or some other grand gesture."

"I'm not a *grand gesture* sort of guy, but I do need to tell her how sorry I am."

Morgan jumped up. "I can help you. Give me a couple of minutes. I need to do something first."

"Don't take too long."

JP went back to the patio where Bob was waiting. "You can stick around if you want, but I need to go see Sabre."

Bob stood to leave.

"Thanks for coming by, my friend. You saved my butt this time. I hope it's not too late."

"She'll be glad to see you. She hasn't been able to figure out what was wrong with you."

"I've been trying to figure that out myself for half a century. Sometimes I get a little hard-headed."

Just as Bob left, Morgan came out carrying poster boards under her arm. "Let's go."

"What's that?"

"I'll tell you on the way."

~~~

JP and Morgan pulled into Sabre's driveway.

"I hope she's home," JP muttered.

"Didn't you call her?" Morgan asked.

"No, I was afraid she wouldn't see me."

Morgan looked over and shook her head. "You really messed up, didn't you, Uncle Johnny?"

"Yup."

"You know what you have to do now, right?"

"I don't know if I can do that."

"You need to. I know these things. I watch a lot of Hallmark movies, and this always works. Besides, I want to help, and how could she resist a cute kid like me?"

"You're right, Munchkin." He tousled her hair. "I'll do it for you."

JP rang the bell. It seemed like a long time before Sabre opened the door, barefoot and wearing her favorite tattered t-shirt and sweatpants. A small smile played on her face when she saw the sign JP was holding. It read: *I'm sorry*. He moved that sign behind the others he was holding. The next one read: *I messed up big time*. He shuffled again. The next sign read. *I'm really, really sorry.* Sabre broke into a full grin. Then Morgan turned around her sign: *He really means it.* The girl displayed a second message: *Please forgive him.* The next one pleaded: *He needs you (and so do I).* Sabre was laughing by the time Morgan turned her final sign: *Even though he's a big dope.*

"Hey, you didn't show me that one." JP gave her a friendly elbow.

"Come in," Sabre said.

Morgan shrugged and looked at JP. "It worked, didn't it?"

Standing in the foyer, JP explained what he'd seen on her computer and at Starbuck's.

"I should've told you in the first place," Sabre said. "But I was afraid you'd try and talk me out of it."

"I would've, but when I realized you intended to do it anyway—as I know you would have—I could've been there to protect you."

"It was stupid, but I didn't really think there was any danger." Sabre quickly added, "And there wasn't."

"That's not the point. There could've been. I couldn't stand it if anything ever happened to you. You mean the world to me."

JP had forgotten for a second that Morgan was in the room. He glanced at her, and she gave him a thumbs up.

"Good move, Uncle Johnny."

Chapter 61

Monday morning Sabre checked the delinquency calendar for Conner's case. No one had given her any notice that there was a hearing set, but she wanted to make sure. It was not on calendar. She knew Villareal was investigating, because he'd been to see Roxy and Muriel. She didn't know what else he'd done, but she hoped he had confirmed everything Muriel had confessed.

Sabre was almost done with her dependency calendar when her phone rang.

"Hey, kid," JP said. "I just got a call from Gene. He says Muriel is gone."

"What do you mean 'gone'?"

"Gene went by the house, and Roxy told him Muriel wasn't there when she got up."

"Roxy's awake already? She doesn't usually get up until after noon."

"Apparently, she was up early today, about nine, she claims. She's called Muriel a couple of times, but it goes right to voicemail."

"If she takes off, we may never get Conner out of custody. And if they don't drop the charges, we need her to testify."

"Gene and I are out looking right now. I'll keep you posted."

~~~

JP had returned home and was working on the computer when Sabre and Morgan arrived. Morgan gave him a hug, announced she had homework, and ran to her room.

Just as Sabre sat down, the bell rang. JP got up and answered the door. His brother stood there, looking sheepish.

"What are you doing here?" JP asked.

"I came to say goodbye to Morgan," Gene said.

JP stepped outside and closed the door behind him. "You can't do that. I'm already skating on thin ice, just knowing where you are and not turning you in. And what exactly do you mean? Are you taking off?"

"I'm gonna go see my parole officer—turn myself in. I'll serve my time. The kids will be in good hands with you, and maybe next time I'm out, I can stay out."

"Dammit, Gene. I can't let you see Morgan. There's a 'no visitation' order until you appear in court. If the judge or DSS finds out I let you have visitation, they'll put her in foster care. Do you want that?"

"No, but I need to see my little girl. Each time I leave, I never know if I'll ever see her again. It drives me crazy."

"Keep your voices down," Sabre said, coming out to join them. "Morgan will hear you." She extended her hand. "You must be Gene. I'm Sabre, your son's attorney."

"Nice to meet you ma'am. Jackie says you're the best. I sure appreciate you helping him through this mess."

"Sorry, I forgot you two hadn't met," JP said. He faced Sabre. "Now please tell my idiot brother that he cannot see Morgan this way." JP turned back to Gene. "You're not going to mess this up for her. I won't let you."

"There's a better way to do this," Sabre said. Both Gene and JP stopped talking and focused on Sabre as she explained. "I should be able to set it up so you can see her at her court hearing tomorrow. You should be there anyway. If I make the arrangements ahead of time, I'm sure Morgan's attorney will not object. The social worker knows how much Morgan wants to see you. Your dependency attorney will be there, and he can help you as well. I'll let him know you plan to attend and introduce you as soon as you arrive. They'll take you into custody at court, but if everything goes right—and it should—you'll get to see Morgan. I should be able to arrange for you to see Conner as well. I know it would be good for him."

"You have a lot of 'shoulds' in there."

"It's not a perfect plan, because there are a lot of variables, but it's the best way for you to see your children."

"What could go wrong?" Gene rolled his eyes.

"Everything," Sabre said. "But I'm pretty certain the social worker and minor's attorney will work with us. And judges are usually good about allowing parental visits. The biggest problem would be law enforcement. You probably know better than I what they'll do. The best-case scenario is that we do the hearing, you have your visit, and then they arrest you."

"And the worst?"

"They arrest you when you arrive at court. But even if they do that, you'll likely get your visit with Morgan, but it'll be in a room with plexiglass between you," Sabre said. "And you wouldn't be able to see Conner."

Gene looked at JP, and nodded his head toward Sabre. "Is she a straight-shooter?"

"You can hang your hat on it."

"How is your parole officer to work with?" Sabre asked Gene.

"She's pretty reasonable."

"You may want to notify her what you're up to, but you can decide that."

Gene was quiet for a few seconds. "Let's do it."

"Can you be there at eight-thirty?"

"Yep."

"Do you need a ride?" JP asked. "I can pick you up."

"No."

"Are you sure? It's no trouble."

"I'll be there, little brother," Gene said flippantly. "Don't you worry."

"Have you found Muriel?" Sabre asked Gene.

"No, but she'll show up. I have someone on it."

"What does that mean?" JP asked.

"It means I'm not gonna leave my son languishing in the Hall. I like Muriel, but I'm mad as hell for what she's done to Conner."

After Gene left, JP asked Sabre, "Can you really pull this off?"

"I sure hope so." She picked up her phone and started making calls.

Chapter 62

JP and Sabre waited outside the courthouse for Gene to show up. Morgan was upstairs with Bob. Sabre checked her phone: *8:25. Where was he?*

Gene's attorney, Terry Chucas, a short, slender man in his fifties approached them. "Is he here?"

"Not yet," Sabre said.

"But you think he'll show?"

"He said he would."

"He says lots of things," JP interjected.

Terry turned to JP. "You don't think he'll show up?"

"I gave up trying to second guess my brother forty years ago. The one thing I've learned is that if I bet against him, I win more often than when I bet with him."

Another ten minutes passed and still no Gene. The social worker came out to where they were standing and asked about him.

"Not here yet," Sabre said.

"I'll be in the courtroom," the woman said. "Come get me if you need me."

They continued to wait. JP started to pace back and forth along the sidewalk. Sabre could see his anger building. He turned when he was ten steps away and said, "If he disappoints Morgan, he'd better not show his face to me again."

Just then a car pulled up and Gene got out. "Hey, Jackie, you got some money to pay the Taxi driver?"

JP shook his head and walked over, pulling his wallet.

"I'm just yankin' your chain," Gene said, then paid for the ride.

"You're an ass," JP said.

"I know."

Sabre and Terry walked toward the two men.

"Hi, Gene. Glad you could make it," Sabre said. "This is Terry Chucas, the attorney who was appointed to represent you."

A woman in her early sixties, with little makeup and wearing a plain dark suit, approached the group.

"Who's that?" Sabre asked.

"My parole officer."

Sabre stiffened, hoping the PO wouldn't stop everything right there.

"Good morning, Georgianne. You're looking as lovely as ever."

"Thanks, Gene," she said. "But you know that crap doesn't work with me."

"It don't hurt to speak the truth."

"Keep that in mind the next time you try to untangle a mess you've gotten yourself into."

Terry Chucas spoke up, aiming his remarks directly at Georgianne. "I'd like to speak to my client in private for a bit, if that's okay with all of you."

"I'm just here to make sure everything goes smoothly and that Gene's taken into custody before I leave." She nodded toward the courthouse. "I think we should move this party inside." She eyed her parolee. "Not that I don't trust you, Gene, but I've been down similar roads."

"But never with me," Gene said.

"You're right. Or we wouldn't be standing outside now."

They all went inside. Chucas and Gene went to the end of the hall, where they could speak privately. Georgianne stayed about thirty feet from them, positioning herself between Gene and the exit. Bob came downstairs to join them, and they all walked to Department One. JP waited outside while Sabre and Bob went in to let the bailiff know they were ready to do the case. They were greeted by the county counsel.

"I understand the parents are submitting on the report," Linda Farris said.

"That's what I've heard," Bob said. "The father will likely go back into custody for a while, and the mother hasn't been doing her programs. She signed up for parenting classes, but never went. She can't seem to make the appropriate arrangements for therapy even though the social worker gave her all the information she needed on two different occasions. She's had only two visits with Morgan but has spoken to her several times on the phone. Neither of the parents are objecting to the caretaker."

"This should go smoothly," Linda said.

Sabre hoped so, for Morgan's sake, but she knew nothing was a sure bet. They all went inside the courtroom and were soon joined by the parents and their respective attorneys.

"In re Morgan Torn," the court clerk announced.

The county counsel said, "Linda Farris for the Department of Social Services."

Bob stood. "Robert Clark for the minor, who is not present in the courtroom. However, the paternal uncle, John P. Torn, is seated in the back. He is the present caretaker."

"Richard Wagner for the mother, who is present, Your Honor."

"Terry Chucas for the father, who is also present in court."

"Thank you," Judge Hekman said. "How are we proceeding this morning?"

Linda Farris spoke first. "I believe we have an agreement, Your Honor."

"The mother is submitting on the recommendations by the Department," Attorney Wagner said.

"The father is also submitting on the revised recommendations," Attorney Chucas said. "He's in agreement with the placement of his daughter with the paternal uncle, as well as the new visitation order. Mr. Torn has agreed to facilitate visitation at the prison, as long as it is feasible and the minor wants to visit. However, Your Honor, we'd like to speak to a special visitation order today at the courthouse. Would the court like me to do that now?"

"Yes, please."

"The father has surrendered to his parole officer, who is here in the courthouse. He understands that this will likely result in his incarceration. There are no new charges against my client, but he may have a parole violation, which he is fully prepared to deal with. Arrangements have been made to have Morgan at court today so she can see her father in an appropriate setting. We ask that the court approve the visit."

The judge looked at the county counsel, who said, "We agree, Your Honor, the social worker thinks the visit would be good for the minor."

Richard Wagner said, "No objection by the mother."

Judge Hekman turned to Bob. "Does Morgan want the visit, Mr. Clark?"

"Very much so, Your Honor. She's close to her father and has asked about him every time I've seen her. She has also spoken often of him to her uncle. Just to err on the side of caution, although I'm not sure it is needed, I'll be present for the visit, as well as the paternal uncle."

"Does that work for you, Mr. Torn?" Judge Hekman asked Gene.

"Yes, Your Honor. I'm fine with that. I just want to see my daughter."

The judge ordered the mother to participate in her programs, placed Morgan with JP, and set a review hearing for six months later. Then she turned to Bob. "Mr. Clark, where is your client now?"

"She's upstairs, Your Honor."

"Would you go get her please? I'd like to talk to her."

JP whispered to Sabre, "Why does she want to see Morgan?"

"My guess is the judge will ask Morgan if she wants to see her father."

"That's a no-brainer. She loves that man."

Bob left the courtroom and returned with Morgan. When the girl walked in, she immediately spotted her father. Her eyes lit up, and a huge smile crossed her face.

"Hello, Morgan. I'm Judge Hekman. How are you this morning?"

"I'm good, ma'am." Morgan looked at the judge when she spoke, but then her gaze returned to her father.

"Have you ever been in a courtroom before?"

"No, ma'am."

"Does it make you nervous to be here?"

"No, ma'am." Morgan glanced around at her surroundings. "It's remarkable."

"That's an interesting choice of words."

"Did I use the word wrong? Doesn't it mean *outstanding* or *extraordinary*?" Morgan glanced at her father, as if asking for confirmation. He nodded at her. "Yes, ma'am," Morgan said. "It's remarkable."

"Do you know why you're here?"

"Not exactly. I know my dad goes to court a lot, and now my brother does too. I know this is where you decide if I get to keep living with Uncle Johnny. I always wondered what court was like."

"And you find it *remarkable*?"

"Yes, ma'am."

"Do you like living with your Uncle Johnny?"

"Yes, ma'am, but..." The girl hesitated.

"What is it, Morgan?"

"It would be even better if my brother could live with us too. Can you take care of that?"

"I can't do anything about that right now, Morgan."

"I was afraid of that, but I didn't think it would hurt to ask," Morgan said.

Chuckles were heard around the courtroom.

"It never hurts to ask." The judge smiled softly. "Is there anything else you'd like to ask me?"

"Yes, ma'am."

"Go ahead."

"Can I hug my daddy?"

"How about if you see him after this hearing and you can hug him then?"

Morgan's smile covered her whole face.

The judge continued. "We have a special room where you can spend time with him. Thank you for coming to court today, Morgan. You've been very enlightening."

"Enlightening." Morgan nodded her head. "That's a good word."

"As to the special visitation request by the father," the judge said, "this court finds it would be in the best interest of the minor to have that visit." Hekman turned to Gene. "And you, sir, need to get your act together. Your daughter needs you."

"Yes, Your Honor," Gene said.

"This court is adjourned."

Chapter 63

Morgan bolted toward her father when she saw him. He picked her up and hugged her tight.

"I knew you'd come to see me, Daddy."

"I had to see my favorite gal."

JP and Bob watched as Morgan interacted with her father.

"They're really close, aren't they?" Bob said.

"I'm surprised," JP said. "But he must be doing something right, because Conner loves him too. I just wish he'd straighten up and stay out of the pen long enough to raise his children."

"Sometimes they grow up in prison and finally figure it out. Maybe this'll be the time."

"Or not. The guy hasn't figured it out in fifty years. He's always on the wrong horse and sittin' backwards."

The visit lasted for almost an hour. Gene and Morgan stayed engaged, neither of them distracted from their time together. Finally, the bailiff came in. "It's time to go," he said. "Your parole officer is outside."

"How long will you be gone, Daddy?"

"Six months at the most. That's all I have left on my sentence. Jack...er Uncle Johnny said he'd bring you once in a while if you want to come."

"Really? You never let us visit before."

"I know, but it's all going to be different this time. I promise."

JP bit his lip. He hated to see his brother make a promise. Morgan had already had too many broken.

Gene hugged his daughter and she held on tight. "You be good now, little one," he said as he let go, his eyes wet.

"You be good too Daddy, so you can come home to us." Her voice cracked as she spoke, and tears streamed down her little face.

The bailiff nodded at JP. "If you'll take Morgan out, Sabre has Conner in an interview room, and I'll escort Gene to see him."

Gene forced a smile as Morgan left. And although the girl was crying, she didn't cling to him or fight to hold on. She left with poise and what appeared to be confidence. JP wondered if it was a front, or if she was just used to him leaving.

"You're a brave girl," JP said to Morgan, once they were outside.

"He'll be back. My dad always comes back."

~~~

Sabre sat in the interview room, with Conner on one side of the plexiglass and her on the other. This visit would not be as comfortable as the last. But when Gene walked in, Conner appeared pleased to see him.

"Hi, Dad."

"Hi, son."

Conner's mood suddenly changed. His chin dropped to his chest, and he seemed unable to meet Gene's eyes.

"I'm sorry, Dad. I know you never wanted to see me behind bars."

"Look at me, son." Conner lifted his head, and Gene continued. "It's not your fault that you're here. It's more mine than yours. And don't worry, you won't be here for long. Your grandma will come around, and Sabre will take care of the rest."

"I don't know."

"Trust me, it's all going to work out. I promise."

Sabre wondered how many times Conner had heard Gene utter those words, and how many times his father had failed. She'd seen it repeatedly with parents who couldn't stop using drugs or stay out of jail, constantly letting down their children. Although Gene appeared sincere, most of the others had meant it too. They just couldn't follow through. Sabre didn't expect anything different from Gene, but Conner did.

"I trust you, Dad."

"Thanks. I also promise this will be my last time in prison. Next time I come home, it'll be for good."

Gene changed the subject, and the rest of their conversation consisted of Conner explaining what it was like inside and the plans he had for when he got out. Sabre stood back and let them visit. They only had about twenty minutes before the bailiff came to get Conner.

"Son, you stay out of trouble now," Gene said, as they both stood. "It won't be long before you are out of here, and I want you to keep your grades up."

"I will, Dad."

"I know you'll be there for Morgan, but it won't be as hard now with your Uncle Johnny around. He won't let anything happen to her."

"I know."

"And one other thing. When you get out, you'll probably live with Johnny. You do what he tells you, just as if it was me telling you. He ain't had any experience being a parent, but he's pretty sharp. He'll learn quick."

"Don't worry. I won't get into any more trouble. I *never* want to come back to this place."

The bailiff took Conner back to the Hall, and Georgianne met Gene at the door and took him into custody.

Chapter 64

JP started to think that Gene hadn't taken care of getting Muriel into court. Several days had passed and, so far, there was nothing new from the DA's office. He knew they were investigating, but Sabre hadn't received any reports.

JP drove to Muriel's house. Roxy answered the door, with mussed hair and wearing a nightshirt. She looked hung-over or strung out. JP glanced at the time on his phone: *12:37 p.m.*

"Is your mother here?"

"No."

"Do you know where she is?"

"No." She made no move to let him in.

"When was the last time you saw her?"

"A few days ago. Before Gene went back to prison."

"We need to find her so we can get Conner out of custody. Do you have any idea where she might've gone?"

"I don't know. She took her suitcase. For all I know, she might've gone home."

"What do you mean?"

"England. She's always talking 'bout it, and she was pretty upset 'bout the whole Conner thing. Mom felt bad that he was locked up for what she done, but she thought she would die in prison and the most he'd get was seven years or so."

"Have you heard from her since she left?" JP detested standing in the doorway with this wreck of a woman, but he needed information.

"No. I told the cops that too. They've been here looking for her a few times. I hate having those cops hang around." Roxy scowled. "Mom ruins everything, even when she's not here."

"Yeah, it makes it tough to have your parties, right?" JP suspected she didn't notice the sarcasm.

"For sure. It's not like we're doing anything wrong or illegal, but no one wants to be here when cops are hanging around."

"I'm sure they're about as welcome as a porcupine at a nudist colony."

Roxy grimaced, then gave JP a blank look.

"Never mind," JP said. He asked a few more questions about Muriel's relatives and friends, both in England and locally, but Roxy had little information to provide. He finally gave up and left.

Before he drove away, he called Ron. "I want you to go by Soper's house and see if Muriel's car shows up. Don't stay. I don't want him spotting you. Just try different times of the day. Drive by every couple of hours. Can you do that?"

"Sure, I'll get right on it. But I'm glad you don't want me to stay there." Ron chuckled a little. "I'm still healing from the last beating."

JP's next call was to Sabre, and he told her what he was doing.

"Do you think it's safe for Ron?"

"He'll just drive by occasionally. He's far more aware now."

"I hope you're right," Sabre said. "I spoke to Larry Villareal, the investigator for the DDA."

"I know who Villareal is," JP said.

"That's right. Anyway, they've been trying to find Muriel, but I think just for more questioning. They've also been looking for Bullet's cell, but they haven't found it."

"I wonder how much manpower they put on finding the phone."

"I don't know, but we're running out of time." Sabre paused. "Remember the Copley case, where they used dogs to find that grave?"

"Yeah, why?"

"I did some research and found a local K-9 trainer here in San Diego. They're a private company that trains dogs for the police, but they also have dogs for hire. If I set it up, would you be willing to go with the handler to search?"

"Of course."

"Good. Are you available this afternoon, about one-thirty?"

"You already set it up, didn't you?"

"Tentatively. I wanted to make sure you weren't busy."

"That'll work."

"We need Muriel's scent and Bullet's too, if you can get them. The K-9 service said we could use dirty clothing or personal effects that are used daily. But they said the best thing would be shoes that had been worn a lot. They don't get washed, so the scent is usually strong. I called Roxy, and she said you could pick them up."

JP drove back to the house. Roxy looked even worse than when he'd been there an hour ago. But this time Roxy invited him inside.

"Conner's attorney said you needed Mom's shoes."

"That's right."

She led him to Muriel's bedroom. "Help yourself."

"Does everything in this closet belong to your mother?"

"What's not hers is Bullet's."

The tidy walk-in was three-quarters full with woman's clothing. The rest of the stuff appeared to be Bullet's. JP obtained an old pair of Muriel's walking shoes and placed them in a bag he'd brought with him. Then he bagged a pair of men's boots, careful not to touch them either—trying to keep his own scent off. He had never worked with canines, but he figured the less the dog had to discern the better.

When they left the bedroom, Roxy turned toward the back door. JP saw himself out. He suspected Roxy was joining whoever was in the backyard playing loud music. He shook his head. *She sure didn't wait long for Gene to be out of the picture before she started her parties again.*

Chapter 65

As per Sabre's instructions, JP met the dog handler, Chuck Booker, at the training facility. JP rode with Chuck and his dog, Whiskey, to the area where Muriel claimed she tossed the phone. They drove to the crime scene first, then started back toward San Diego. JP instructed Chuck to stop at the first speed limit-sign, which ended up being 1.3 miles from where Bullet was killed.

JP had no idea what kind of a throwing arm Muriel had, but if she got any distance at all, the phone would be down lower in the canyon. She could have thrown it straight out, or to either side, and there were lots of shrubs and trees to maneuver through. Suddenly, it looked like a vast area to cover, but at least it hadn't rained since she made the toss.

"What do you think?" JP asked Chuck.

"It's hard to say. We could get lucky, or it could take a while. The problem is that the phone was probably airborne until it hit the ground or stuck in some foliage. So there's no scent to follow until we get closer to it. Do you know if the woman is left or right handed?"

JP thought about when he had seen Muriel. He hadn't witnessed her write anything, but the first time he met her, she nervously twisted a loose thread on her blouse with her right hand. "Right, I think, but I'm not sure."

"Okay, then unless she was aiming for something specific, there's a greater chance it went north. I'll direct Whiskey to the north first, then we'll work our way south. Where are the shoes?"

JP handed him the bags. Chuck put on latex gloves, removed the shoes, and sat them down for Whiskey to smell. Whiskey went back and forth between the two pair until Chuck gave him a command to start searching.

Down the hill they all went. Whiskey sniffed at things as they searched, but gave no response indicating he had found the scent. About thirty yards out, Chuck turned the dog west; they walked about twenty yards, then headed south. They kept going for another sixty yards, covering the area that would've likely been in Muriel's throwing range. Still nothing. They walked east for another twenty yards, then turned back and covered another section. No luck.

"We're starting to run out of ground, unless this woman had an arm like Rosie Black," Chuck said.

"Who's Rosie Black?"

"She was the pitcher on the Queen and her Court, four women who competed against pros. She threw so fast that most professional players couldn't hit the ball. Johnny Carson clocked her on his show at over a hundred miles per hour. I saw her play once. My mother took me when I was ten. I was in Little League and had complained because they were talking about letting girls play. I think my mom wanted me to see that women could excel at sports, just like men."

"Did you learn the lesson?"

"I sure did."

They traipsed through the brush and started back up the canyon on the south side. "It's getting dark," Chuck said. "I think we need to call it for the day, unless you want to continue with flashlights. Whiskey is okay, but we won't be able to see very well."

"Whatever you think." JP didn't want to give up yet, but they could come back the next day if they had to. Chuck and Whiskey were available.

As they started back, Chuck asked, "Are you certain this is the right spot?"

"I think so. Muriel said she stopped about a mile or two from the crime scene, right in front of a speed-limit sign. I didn't see another sign for several miles down the road."

"We'll walk up the south side and cover the area at the top that we missed by heading north. It seems too close to the road, but maybe she can't throw very well."

They worked their way back, still within a good mile of where Bullet had been shot. This time they walked due west, then north, then east toward the highway, covering a quarter of a mile—with no luck.

"You want to keep going?" Chuck asked.

"We still have a little daylight," JP said. "I say we go until we run out."

"Same direction or do you want to go further south?"

"Let's keep working our way toward the crime scene."

They did another quarter-mile section and started the last leg up the incline. They were nearly to the top when Whiskey started digging at the ground, covering a three or four foot area. The dog stopped and sat down, looking up at his handler.

JP and Chuck quickly approached where Whiskey sat at the bottom of a tree, but they didn't see a cell phone. Dusk was making it difficult, so JP took out his flashlight to search with. He plowed through sticks and pine needles, trying to uncover the hidden cell phone. Whiskey sat still.

"It has to be here," Chuck said, helping JP look.

They continued to rummage through the area, but they kept getting further and further away from Whiskey. Still nothing.

They went back and Chuck walked the dog away, then gave him a command. Whiskey returned to the same spot and sat down under the tree. JP shined the light upward, and there it was, lodged on a branch.

"She didn't throw this from that speed-limit sign," JP said.
"Nope. Even Rosie Black couldn't have thrown it this far."
"Why would Muriel lie about that?"

Chapter 66

JP and Sabre pulled into the parking lot at her office, and a moment later Derek drove up and parked his truck. He wasn't alone.

"Look at that," JP said. "Derek found Muriel."

"I guess your brother kept his word on that one."

"Well, slap my head and call me silly. Gene came through, just when I least expected it."

Sabre and JP walked toward the truck. Muriel stepped out, looking visibly shaken. "Hello, Sabre."

Sabre greeted her, then said, "Come into the office."

JP approached the driver's side of the truck. "Are you coming in, Derek?"

"No, thanks. I'll wait out here. Just see that she doesn't slip away."

"Are you worried about that?"

"I'm not taking any chances."

"Fair enough. I'll bring her back to you myself."

Muriel followed as Sabre and JP entered the office. Sabre took a seat behind her desk, and JP pulled a chair out for Muriel directly across from Sabre. He stood about six feet back, guarding the door.

"I've made a mess of everything," Muriel said. "I shouldn't have left."

"You're here now." Sabre's tone was soothing.

JP felt less patient. "Where've you been?"

"I was at a friend's house."

"Have you spoken to the investigator?" Sabre asked.

"Not since that day with you. I understand they want to talk to me. Roxy told me several cops and investigators have been by the house."

"They've been checking out your story," JP said. "Why did you come back?"

"Derek found me and was very persuasive."

Neither JP nor Sabre asked how he had persuaded her. Sabre didn't want to know and was sure JP felt the same. Although, she assumed it hadn't been physical, because Muriel had no visible signs of injuries.

"I had to help Conner," Muriel sank into her chair as if she were trying to hide. "I thought he'd be out by now, and they'd just be looking to arrest me. But I guess it doesn't work that way."

"I'm not certain," Sabre said, "but I think they see you as his accomplice."

"But he didn't do anything."

"That's what we'll have to prove in court. Are you willing to testify?"

"Yes."

"What will you do now?" Sabre asked.

"I'm going home. I already called the investigator, and he told me to come into the office tomorrow at nine-fifteen."

JP and Sabre exchanged glances. Muriel stood to leave.

"Please, don't hide out again. Conner needs you to testify."

"I'll walk you out," JP said. He took her by the arm and escorted her to Derek's truck.

When he returned, Sabre asked, "Do you find it curious that Villareal just told her to come into the office tomorrow?"

"Yup. I don't think they're going to arrest her, or he wouldn't have trusted her to show up."

"Maybe he was afraid she'd spook and run away again," Sabre suggested. "So they plan to pick her up at her house tonight."

"I don't think that's likely. The investigator would've wanted her to come in right now—while she was willing—or he would've gone out to meet her. There's something else going on."

"Like they don't believe her story at all?" Sabre asked.

"Exactly."

"But they have the phone now with her fingerprints."

"Unless they didn't get any prints. We don't know what they found."

"That wouldn't be good. We need both the phone and her testimony to convince the judge that Conner is innocent. I don't think one without the other will be enough." Sabre picked up her cell.

"Who are you calling?" JP asked.

"DDA Benson. She needs to share the discovery she gained from the phone." The call went to voicemail, and Sabre left a message, asking for a callback. "It's late," she said to JP. "I expect she won't get back to me until tomorrow. Do you think Villareal will tell you anything?"

"Not without Benson's approval."

Chapter 67

Sabre had finished her calendar at juvenile court and was back in her office working when her cell rang. She checked the screen and saw it was Marge Benson. A heavy feeling landed in her stomach when Marge told her the news. Sabre hung up and called JP. "I just spoke with Benson. Muriel's fingerprints are not on the phone."

"Was it wiped clean?"

"No, they found Bullet's and one other set, but they don't know whose they are."

"But not Conner's?"

"No, thank God."

"We need to have another talk with Muriel," JP said. "I'm going there now."

"Where is she?"

"She had her appointment with Villareal this morning, then she went back home. I just talked to Ron. He's been watching her since about midnight when he relieved Derek. Then Ron followed her to the appointment this morning and back. But he needs to go home and get some sleep, so I'll relieve him."

"I'll meet you there," Sabre said.

~~~

"Muriel, what's going on?" Sabre asked. They all sat at the kitchen table, with JP on the end so he could watch both women.

"I don't know what you mean." Muriel twisted a button on her shirt.

"I know you want to help Conner, but you're making things worse when you don't tell us the truth." Sabre locked eyes with Muriel. "Your fingerprints were not on the phone."

Muriel was silent, so Sabre explained that the technicians found Bullet's prints and another set that wasn't hers.

Muriel's pitch rose as she asked, "Whose were they?"

"They don't know."

"So, they weren't Conner's. Doesn't that help him?"

"Not really. If they had been his, the evidence would've been very damaging, but they think he had an accomplice."

Muriel looked pensive for a moment. "Someone must have found the phone after I threw it, and they touched it." Her voice quivered. "I was there when Bullet was killed. It was me."

"That's the other thing," JP said. "You didn't throw that phone from the speed-limit sign. You had to have tossed it from much closer to the crime scene. Why did you lie about that?"

"I guess I forgot. Everything was so crazy. Or maybe it got moved. That would explain the other fingerprints."

"But not why yours weren't on it," JP said, watching her face. "Were you helping Conner?"

"No!" Muriel was adamant, "I'm the one who killed Bullet. Conner was not there. They have to believe me." She stared at Sabre. "You need to make them believe me."

JP found her last statement curious. When they left her house, Sabre turned to him "Why do you think Muriel is suddenly trying so hard to take the blame? She let Conner sit in the Hall all this time. And supposedly, she intended to let him stay in custody for seven more years. Does it seem odd to you?"

"It sure does. I have to wonder how much her confession is influenced by Gene, via Derek."

"Do you think they threatened her?"

"I don't know what to think any more." JP headed for the sidewalk. "But I know Gene was determined to get Conner out. Look what he has done so far. He violated his parole to help find the killer. He had Conner beat up in the Hall to get him tried as a minor. He had Derek find Muriel. I don't put anything past him."

"I don't think much of his tactics, but he sure seems to be protective of his son."

"I guess you gotta give him that."

"What now?" Sabre asked, as they climbed into his truck.

"There's nothing else I can do right now. So unless you think of something, I'll keep an eye on Muriel. If you come up with an idea, I'll call Ron or Derek to take over."

"That's good, because no matter what, we'll need Muriel to testify at Conner's trial."

Chapter 68

Sabre and JP spent most of Saturday reading through Conner's file and JP's reports. They took breaks only to eat and spend time with Morgan. The trial was getting close, and Sabre was concerned that she might not be able to win this one. By the afternoon, she felt trapped and frustrated. She went for a long run and tried not to think about the case, but that only worked for a few minutes. Then her mind would find its way back to Conner.

Ron and Derek had been taking turns watching Muriel, but she had stayed put. Something was keeping her from running away again. Maybe it was the fear of Derek's *persuasion.* Maybe it was Muriel's concern for her grandson. Whatever it was, Sabre was glad, because Conner didn't stand a chance without her testimony.

When Sabre returned from her run, she cleaned up while JP and Morgan cooked dinner on the grill. Sabre stood near the sliding glass door and watched the two together, impressed with how JP had adapted to his new role. *He would make a great father,* she thought. A feeling of sadness passed through her. She didn't know if she'd ever be able to give him that.

Sabre shook it off and went outside. "What can I do to help?"

"Don't worry, Aunt Sabre, we got this," Morgan said.

Sabre smiled. *Aunt.* She liked the way it sounded.

The three ate on the patio, then had a nice quiet evening as a family. After Morgan went to bed, Sabre and JP entered his office and took another look at the whiteboard. Most of the suspects had been crossed off. "Maybe we need to have another look at the original list," JP said. "We must've missed something or someone."

"Maybe." Sabre had a new worry. "What if calling Muriel to testify hurts us more than it helps? She's obviously lying about part of her story."

"Why would she lie?" JP asked.

Sabre knew he was playing devil's advocate. They had solved more than one case with that approach. "To get the suspicion off Conner."

"So, she thinks Conner killed Bullet, feels guilty for bring-ing Bullet into his life, and now wants to take the blame?"

Sabre nodded. "Maybe. I don't know. She either lied before or is lying now."

"What other reason would she have to lie?" JP prompted.

"She could be protecting someone else."

"Like Soper, you mean?" JP shook his head. "We've already danced that dance. He had an alibi, and I don't think she'd protect him over her grandson. She's not that into him."

"You're right. Unless he had something on her, she wouldn't choose him over Conner."

"That might be it. Maybe Gene has dirt on her, and he's making her take the blame."

Sabre was skeptical. "What could he possibly have on Muriel that would make her take the blame for murder? What could be worse than that?"

"You have a point. I get so irritated with my brother for putting those kids in this situation in the first place. I'd like to believe Gene. I'd like to trust him. I'd like him to be the brother I had before that whole mess with Dad when we were kids."

Sabre could see the pain in JP's face. "Who is it you're really mad at? Gene, or your father?"

JP closed his eyes and shook his head. "Both, I guess." He took a deep breath. "Enough of that. We need to figure this out."

They spent the next few hours perusing the files again. They had a new forensics report to go over. "Look at this," JP said. "There's no way Muriel killed Bullet. The person at the crime scene had a size-ten shoe and estimated weight of around a hundred forty pounds. Muriel's shoes that we used for the K-9 were more like a size six."

"And she can't weigh more than a hundred pounds at most."

"I hate to say it, Sabre, but that's more like Conner's size." JP gave her a sympathetic look. "Do you think Muriel knows Conner did it and is just trying to save him?"

Sabre shook her head. "Conner seemed genuinely surprised, and rather disappointed, when he found out his grandmother confessed. It was as if he'd lost her in that moment, like he discovered she was not the woman he knew her to be. Which makes me again think he didn't do it. But if Conner did kill Bullet, I don't think he confided in Muriel. She must be basing her concern for Conner on something else."

"Everything we discover leads back to Conner, Sabre. Maybe we're too close to see it."

Sabre grimaced. "Maybe it's just that I don't want to think Conner did it, because he's such a great kid." She paused, took a deep breath and said, "I'm still not convinced it was him. The only way he could have killed anyone was by accident. That kid just doesn't have it in him. And I've given him every opportunity to tell me that it was an accident." She sighed. "But he sticks to the same story."

JP sat silently.

"You don't agree?"

"It's not that. I know Conner is a great kid. But in the same situation, Gene never would have changed his story either. His father may have taught his son more than we realize."

"He's not Gene." Sabre closed the file she was reading. "I'm beat. Let's call it a night."

Sabre peeked in on Morgan, then joined JP in his bedroom. He was already asleep by the time she got into bed. She lay there, mulling over what she had read, when suddenly it hit her. She sat upright. "That's it," she said aloud. She shook JP's shoulder. "I know what happened."

JP mumbled.

Sabre stretched out next to him, put her arm lightly on his shoulder, then scratched JP's back.

"That's nice." He rolled over and kissed her.

"You awake?"

"I am now."

"Good." She sat up again. "I know who killed Bullet."

"You do?"

"Roxy."

"What? How did you arrive at that?"

"She's a big woman, with large feet. The weight and the shoe print would be about right."

"Okay." This time JP sat up. "What else do you have?"

"Roxy and her mother are very close. She's quite protective of her, and Roxy had access to the gun. In fact, she's the only one who really knew where Gene hid it originally."

"But how did Roxy get the gun into Conner's closet? And why would she put it there?"

"I think Muriel was telling the truth about that." Sabre worked through the scenario as she talked. "Roxy told her mother she'd killed Bullet. Then Muriel took the gun, wiped it clean, and put it into the kids' room when she tucked Morgan in that night. She probably intended to remove it, but never got the chance."

"I don't know. Morgan said her mother never left the house that day."

"That was the clincher that got me thinking. Morgan saw her mother come into the living room that afternoon."

"Which was usually when she got up."

"But she was already dressed. Have you ever seen Roxy dressed before evening?" Sabre didn't let JP answer. "She goes right from her bedroom to the kitchen in her night clothes and gets a cup of coffee. She didn't do that. She talked to Morgan for a few minutes, then went to her room. She probably waited until Muriel got home and then confided in her."

"We'll need evidence to get the DA's office to move on this," JP said.

"I know. That's a problem."

JP kissed her lightly on the forehead. "I have an idea."

"Of course you do." Sabre smiled.

"Good work, baby. I'll get you the evidence first thing in the morning. Actually, since we're working with Roxy, it may take until the afternoon." He pulled her toward him. "Now, let's finish what you started."

"You mean scratching your back?"

"Not what I had in mind, but you can start there."

Chapter 69

The next morning, Sabre took Morgan to visit Conner. JP waited until a little after noon before he drove to Roxy's. Ron was sitting out front.

"Anything going on?" JP asked.

"Not much. I've only been here an hour. Derek spent most of the night. He doesn't seem to mind putting in the hours."

"He has a close friendship with Gene." JP felt a tinge of envy as he remembered how close he and his brother were as kids.

"He must," Ron said. "It got pretty loud last night. I was here until midnight. Earlier, three guys and a woman showed up. I could hear them in the backyard getting rowdy."

"Did you look to see what they were doing back there?"

"Just once. It wasn't pretty." Ron shook his head. "What are you doing here this morning?"

"I need to see Roxy. Sabre has a new theory. I'll check in with you on my way out."

Muriel answered the door and invited JP in. He wasn't exactly sure how he would pull this off, but he had to get something with Roxy's fingerprints—without her or Muriel knowing. He was afraid he had arrived too early, but he'd wanted to get there before Roxy got up. If he timed it right, she would go straight to the kitchen and get coffee. He'd brought his own coffee thermos, intending to get her to touch it somehow. He gripped the container at the bottom, hoping he didn't look too conspicuous.

"What brings you here today?" Muriel asked.

"I have a few more questions for you and Roxy...er...Roxanne. Is she up?"

"No, but she doesn't know much about what happened."

"She might know this."

Muriel ignored his comment and asked, "What else do you need from me?"

"We're trying to nail down the timeline for the events of the morning Bullet was killed," JP said. "Do you mind if we sit in the kitchen? I might have some questions about what happened in there."

"Okay." Muriel walked into the kitchen, JP followed, and they sat down at the small table.

"This is where Bullet beat you up for the last time?" JP asked, glancing around the room. He didn't wait for an answer. "Tell me exactly what happened after he left on his bike that morning. What did you do?"

"I got dressed and left."

"Did you shower or clean up beforehand?"

"I washed my face and changed my clothes, because they were bloody."

"When did you get the gun?"

"After I got dressed, I went to Roxanne's room. She was asleep, so I quietly went to her closet and took the gun out of the box."

"Did you leave the box behind?"

"Yes, but what difference does that make?"

"I'm just trying to get the full picture," JP said. He was mostly stalling and waiting for Roxy. "What did you do with the gun?"

"I took it with me."

"I mean, did you put it in your pocket or your purse? How were you carrying it?"

"In my purse."

"Did you check to see if the gun was loaded?"

"No. I just wanted to scare him. I didn't plan to kill him."

"You told me earlier that Gene wasn't here that morning, but I know he was. Gene said he came into the kitchen while Bullet was pounding on you and threw him against the counter. Is that what happened?"

Muriel looked like she didn't want to answer, but after a moment, she nodded.

"Did Gene leave before you did that morning?"

"I don't know."

"What about Conner? Was he still here when you left?"

"I don't know when either of them left. All I know for sure is that Morgan was here and Roxanne was asleep."

"But Roxanne could've left right after you did?"

Muriel gave an uncomfortable laugh. "Roxanne doesn't get up that early. Even after she's up, it takes her an hour to get rolling. She has to have coffee before she can even function." She wrinkled her brow. "What are you implying?"

"I'm not implying anything. I'm just trying to figure out who all was where."

Muriel seemed to relax a little. JP kept asking questions, stalling as long as he could. It took another fifteen minutes before Roxy strolled into the kitchen in a skimpy t-shirt that barely covered her bottom. JP said hello, and Roxy mumbled something incoherent.

"She'll be better after her coffee," Muriel said.

JP continued to ask questions while he watched to see if Roxy touched anything that he could confiscate. She walked directly to the cupboard and removed a mug, then picked up the coffee pot and poured. She grabbed three packets of sugar, tore them open, and dumped the sweetener into her cup. She laid the empty wrappers back on the counter. Then she picked up a spoon next to the pot and stirred her coffee.

JP wanted to get his hands on both the spoon and the used sugar packets. But he wasn't confident he could pull it off.

"When did Soper and Rankin leave?" JP asked Muriel.

"They were already gone before Bullet hit me."

JP decided it was time for the backup plan. He stood and walked toward Roxy, extending the thermos. "Do you mind giving me a little coffee?" She took the thermos and held it as she poured coffee into it. "Thanks, that's plenty," he said after a few seconds. "Just set it down, and I'll add some sugar if you don't mind."

"No problem." Roxy walked to the table and took a seat, sipping on her hot drink.

JP thanked Muriel, hoping she would leave, but she remained in the room. He turned to Roxy. "I'm trying to figure out what time Gene and Conner left the house the day Bullet was shot. Do you know?"

"No idea. I was asleep."

"I was afraid of that, but I appreciate your help."

JP walked over to the counter to retrieve his mug. He had his back to both women. He acted like he was putting sugar in his coffee and purposely spilled a little on the counter. He pulled a paper towel from the spool and scooped up the spoon and packets Roxy had touched. He held the thermos by the bottom again, careful not to touch where Roxy's fingers had been.

"I think I'm done here. We're trying to help Conner, but it's not looking good." The women exchanged glances. "Thanks. I'll see myself out." JP left the room.

~~~

JP set the bagged thermos, the spoon, and the empty sugar packets on the investigator's desk and explained what he wanted.

"I can't do that for you on a hunch," Villareal said.

"It's more than a hunch. The shoe size and the weight are right. They match the evidence at the crime scene. Roxy had access to the gun. And motive. She also can't account for her whereabouts. It's all there."

"That's not enough. We need hard evidence to get a warrant or to make an arrest."

"You didn't have much when you had Conner arrested."

"We had a witness who saw the gun in his closet and another independent witness who heard him threaten to kill the victim."

JP sighed. "Conner is a really good kid. Granted, I don't know him well, because we just met. But based on what I've learned about him so far, I don't believe he could kill anyone, even in self-defense. He's kind and sweet and he's had a rough start." JP studied the investigator's face. "I know how important family is to you, Larry. I know you'd move heaven and earth to protect one of yours, especially if you believed in him. I'm just asking you to follow up on this lead."

"You know the prints won't hold up in court. We have chain-of-custody issues."

"I know, but if you check the prints on any of these items, and they match the prints on the cell phone, then you know Roxy was involved. When you get your warrant, I'll bet you'll find the shoes that match the footprints. And you can get more of Roxy's fingerprints for court. I know you'll find a way to get to the truth. That's all I'm asking for—that you find the truth." JP stared at Villareal. "Unless you've changed a lot since we worked together, I know you don't want to see an innocent kid convicted. You couldn't live with yourself."

"I'll think about it."

Chapter 70

"I just got a call that Conner's case is going on calendar this morning," Sabre said to JP.

"Do you know why?"

"No. The call came from the DA's office. I guess I'll see when I get there."

"Can I go? I want to be there for Conner."

"Of course. But let's take separate vehicles. I'll drop off Morgan at school on the way, and I'll meet you there."

"Do you have other cases on calendar?"

"Just a couple. But Bob can handle them, if I need to leave."

"That works for me," JP said. "What do you think the hearing is for?"

"I hope it's a dismissal, but I'm afraid to count on it."

"What else could it be?"

"Any number of things. Problems in the Hall, maybe another fight. There are all sorts of reasons for special hearings. Whatever the cause, it needs immediate attention or we would've gotten more notice."

~~~

When they arrived at the courthouse, Sabre went directly to the attorney's lounge to check for reports. She found a one-pager and smiled broadly as she read it.

"Are they dismissing his case?"

"Yes, they've arrested Roxy." Sabre read further, then said, "When Villareal told Muriel that Roxy's fingerprints were on the phone, she spilled."

"So, the man came through," JP said. "He must've checked the prints on my thermos."

"It doesn't say anything about a forensics test, so maybe he just bluffed."

"Either way, it worked."

Sabre summarized what she'd read so far. "Roxy apparently caved right away when they confronted her, but she gave the same story Muriel had—that it was an accident—except it was her at the crime scene. Roxy claims that she saw how badly Bullet had beaten her mother and couldn't take it anymore. She went to scare him."

"My guess is that she went because he was her supplier."

"Maybe." Sabre read further. "It says her shoes match the footprints, so they have a solid case against her." She shook her head. "Roxy was too stupid to throw away the gun or her shoes. Just the phone."

"And Muriel was covering for her daughter, so that's why she didn't know exactly where the phone was in the canyon." JP shrugged. "Or maybe she didn't really want us to find it."

"You know what's hardest to believe?" Sabre said.

"What's that?"

"That Roxy got up early enough to commit the crime."

"Her mother's beating must have been loud enough to wake her." JP tensed at the thought.

Bob walked into the lounge. "Good morning, Sobs. Nice to see you, JP. Are you here for a hearing?"

"They're dismissing Conner's case." Sabre grinned.

"That's great news." Bob walked over to the box where the petitions were housed for new cases. "And look, there's a petition on Conner." He picked it up and found the corresponding report. "They arrested his mother?"

"Sabre figured it out," JP said.

"How?" Bob asked.

Sabre let JP do the talking. He explained about Muriel covering for someone and what the evidence revealed. "Sabre remembered something Conner had said about how his grandma always did things for Roxy. Then she realized Roxy matched the approximate weight and shoe size of the killer—and she had the gun. She was the only other person Muriel would've covered for. Muriel didn't want Conner to go to prison either, so she tried to take the blame herself. She thought her daughter would fare even worse in prison than Conner, but up until the end, Muriel still thought she could sacrifice herself."

"Wow."

Mike, the bailiff, came into the attorney's lounge and told them the judge was ready. Sabre hadn't had a chance to speak to Conner before the hearing, but she didn't want to delay it. The sooner they had the hearing, the sooner Conner would be released. They followed Mike to the courtroom, and Sabre sat at the table. JP waited in the back. Within five minutes, Conner was brought into the court. The look on his face told her he didn't know why he was there.

The bailiff seated the boy next to Sabre. "It's all good," she said, as the judge took the bench. "Well, it's mostly good." She realized Conner didn't know his mother had been arrested. She wasn't sure how he would take it.

The clerk called the case, and the parties were introduced, including JP.

"Young man," Judge Feldman said. "I'm sorry you had to experience our court system and the juvenile detention facility. Sometimes it takes a while for the wheels of justice to start rolling." Conner glanced at Sabre with a creased brow, as if he understood, but was afraid to hope. The judge continued. "The case of Conner Eugene Torn is dismissed with prejudice."

Conner smiled. "It's over?" he asked Sabre.

She nodded.

"I understand there is a petition filed in the dependency court," the judge said. "Is that correct?"

"Yes, Your Honor," DDA Benson said. "In Department One."

Sabre stood. "Judge Hekman said she would hear the case immediately after this one, Your Honor. The attorneys on that case are already assembled, so if Conner could be brought to that courtroom right away, it would be appreciated."

The judge looked at the bailiff. "Can you take the minor now?"

"Yes, sir," the bailiff said.

"And please start the paperwork so the minor can be released as soon as possible," Judge Feldman said.

Sabre and JP left the courtroom.

"What happens now?" JP asked.

"It depends on what authority Chucas and Wagner have to act on their clients' behalf. It's a new case, so we're back to detention, and the parents will have the right to a jurisdictional trial, which they would lose, since they're both in custody. Then they'll have the right to a dispositional trial to determine where Conner lives. If they don't contest anything, the case will go quickly. The Department is recommending detention with you. The only other alternative would be foster care."

"Would they do that?"

"There's no reason to."

"So, Conner will be coming to live with us...er...me?"

"Is that what you want?"

"If that ain't a fact, God's a possum."

Sabre laughed. "That's a yes?"

JP gave one nod of his head. "Yes, ma'am. That's a yes."

Chapter 71

Sabre, JP, and Conner stopped at In-N-Out for lunch. JP couldn't remember ever seeing anyone enjoy a hamburger as much as Conner did. The boy thanked them both for the lunch and for helping him and his sister. Someone had taught the kids good manners. JP was pretty certain Grandma got the credit for that one. She was basically a good woman in spite of her misguided efforts.

They all were quiet as they finished their lunch, then Sabre's phone rang. She answered and had a brief conversation. "That was Lori, the social worker. She said they arrested Soper and Rankin on drug charges, both manufacturing and distribution. Apparently, they were partnered with Bullet."

Conner shrugged, but didn't comment.

"Did you know they were selling drugs?" JP asked.

"I know they used something, but I didn't know what. I figured they were selling it, because my mom was getting it somewhere."

"And your dad? Did he use drugs?" JP spoke before he thought. He wished he hadn't put Conner on the spot. He didn't really want to know the answer anyway.

"Are you kidding?" Conner shook his head and wrinkled his nose in disgust. "Dad hated drugs. He not only gave us regular lectures on the evils of drugs, but he set an example. He said he used some when he was young, but he wished he hadn't. He didn't even drink that much around us. He'd have a beer or two, but he never got drunk." Conner took a sip of soda. "He does smoke though, but he's trying to quit."

~~~

After lunch, they parted ways. Sabre stopped to pick up Morgan, while JP drove Conner to see his new home.

On the way, JP called Ron to let him know what had happened and to tell him he was done at Muriel's.

"Hallelujah!"

"I knew you'd be happy, but I didn't expect you to be this excited about finishing the job."

"Don't get me wrong. I'm happy about the kid getting released, but this also means I can finally have my date with Addie."

Conner didn't say much on the way, except for repeatedly thanking them for getting him out of the Hall. JP wondered how he was processing the news of his mother's involvement and arrest. It had to be hard—for many reasons. He didn't want to make Conner uncomfortable, but he had to let him know he was there for him.

"Knowing what your mother did must be hard for you." JP glanced at Conner, who was staring straight ahead. "I'm not asking you to talk about it now, but just know that if at any time you want to talk, I'm here for you. If you have questions, or need to vent, or whatever. Okay?"

"Okay."

When they got to the house, JP took him straight to the spare bedroom.

"This will be your space," JP said. "I've been using it as an office, but I'll move my stuff to the living room."

"You don't have to do that, John...Jack...Unc...What should I call you?"

"Anything you want. My friends call me JP. Your dad calls me Jackie. Morgan calls me Uncle Johnny. Sabre calls me all sorts of cute names. Whatever makes you comfortable." JP paused. "Preferably not the cute names Sabre uses."

"I think I'll go with Uncle Johnny. That's the way Dad always refers to you."

"I like that."

"You can still use this as an office," Conner offered. "I just need a place to sleep."

"No, you need your privacy, and I already have my computer at the desk in the living room. That's where I work most of the time anyway. The sofa opens up into a bed for now, but this weekend we'll get you a real bed."

"You don't need to go to that trouble."

"It's no trouble, and I expect you'll be here for a while." JP studied Conner's face. "If that's what you want."

Just then Morgan burst into the room and threw herself at Conner. He picked her up and swung her around. "You're getting too big, Morgonster."

A smile filled Morgan's face, and for the first time, she made no objection to his nickname.

From the Author

Dear Reader,

Thank you for reading my book. I hope you enjoyed reading it as much as I did writing it. Would you like a FREE copy of a novella about JP when he was young? If so, scan the QR code below and it will take you where you want to go. Or, if you prefer, please go to www.teresaburrell.com and sign up for my mailing list. You'll automatically receive a code to retrieve the story.

SCAN ME

Teresa

Made in the USA
Middletown, DE
05 July 2024